LUCY KNOTT is a former profe̶s̶s̶i̶o̶n̶a̶l̶ ̶wrestler with a passion for storytelling. Now, instead of telling her stories in the ring, she's putting pen to paper, fulfilling another lifelong dream in becoming an author.

Lucy is a self-professed hopeless romantic, her husband being the reason behind her desire to write.

Inspired by her Italian grandparents, when she is not writing you will most likely find her cooking, baking and devouring Italian food, in addition to learning Italian and daydreaming of trips to Italy.

Along with her twin sister, Kelly, Lucy runs TheBlossomTwins.com, where she enthusiastically shares her love for books, baking and Italy, with daily posts, reviews and recipes.

You can find Lucy on Twitter @TheBlossomTwins or @LucyOsterfeld

How to Bake a New Beginning

LUCY KNOTT

ONE PLACE. MANY STORIES

HQ
An imprint of HarperCollins*Publishers* Ltd
1 London Bridge Street
London SE1 9GF

This paperback edition 2018

1

First published in Great Britain by
HQ, an imprint of HarperCollins*Publishers* Ltd 2018

ISBN: 9780008310103

MIX
Paper from
responsible sources
FSC C007454

This book is produced from independently certified FSC™ paper to ensure responsible forest management.

For more information visit: www.harpercollins.co.uk/green

"Typeset by Palimpsest Book Production Ltd, Falkirk, Stirlingshire
Printed and bound in Great Britain by
CPI Group (UK) Ltd, Melksham, SN12 6TR"

For Chris.

Chapter 1

Beans on Toast

Ingredients:

Bread
Butter
Heinz baked beans (Always stock up when you go to Target)

What to do:

Toast bread and heat up beans in a saucepan or microwave. (Never tell Amanda you use the microwave.)

Butter toast and drizzle beans over the top. (Doesn't taste quite like home, but it will do, I suppose. Don't get sad, you're living your dream and don't be ungrateful, the boys are awesome, and you've worked so hard to get to this point. Mmm beans, I wonder what Levi is up to? Why does England have to be six hours ahead when you're spending another night alone and could do with a sister chat? Just eat your beans.)

Sabrina realized that she had been mindlessly shuffling paper for the past fifteen minutes. It was gone five in the afternoon and she needed to go home and pack. Yet, she was sitting at her desk, eyes wide, staring at the mini chandelier that hung from the ceiling. The crystals bounced light off the walls and led to the dreamy state Sabrina found herself in as she daydreamed about the day that Levi first burst into her office.

Why did she always do this to herself? Every Christmas for the past two years she couldn't get him out of her head. Was she really that lonely? Couldn't she fantasize about men who weren't off limits? Better yet, couldn't she stop fantasizing altogether and venture into the real world and meet a non-rock-star man who wasn't way out of her league? She huffed to herself as her phone rang, startling her. Seeing that it was her baby sister, Louisa, she put on an enthusiastic smile and answered with the cheeriest hello she could muster.

'Are you all packed? Do you have everything ready for tomorrow?' her not-quite-as-cheerful-sounding sister asked abruptly.

Sabrina blinked away the dancing crystals of the chandelier that were starting to give her a headache and went back to shuffling papers as she answered her sister's questions. 'Yes, yes, of course, Lou. I have everything organized – you know me, what am I if not organized?' She felt a twinge of guilt for her white lie, but she didn't want her sister to worry. Normally, she was the queen of packing, but with the band's new release approaching and her brain often getting distracted by a certain drummer, she hadn't quite been herself lately.

'OK, so you *will* be on that flight tomorrow?' Louisa asked, her voice a little imperious.

All Sabrina's attempts at bubbliness evaporated. She snatched the band's schedule from the desk and made her way to the door to head to the photocopier room. She was too tired to deal with Louisa's sceptical, patronizing tone.

'Lou, please. It's Grandpa's ninety-sixth birthday; of course I will be on that flight tomorrow. I *am* going to be there,' she said with force. Her heels echoed along the deserted corridor. The cool office interior, bland cream walls and stark white furniture personified elegance and a modern flair in Lydia's eyes, but at this time in the evening when most of the staff had gone home, it screamed cold to Sabrina. It lacked vibrancy in her mind and could do with some fresh flowers and a pop of colour.

'Well, I'm just checking. It's not going to be some glam, flashy party,' Louisa added, a hardness to her voice that stung Sabrina and caused anger to bubble in her stomach.

'I know it's not going to be a bloody glamorous affair and I don't bloody care. You know how much Nanna and Grandpa mean to me. I wouldn't miss this for the world. I miss them, and I miss you all and I will be on that plane tomorrow, so please, give it a rest.' She practically punched the copier to life and let out a frustrated sigh. She was growing tired of her sister's guilt trips over missing family affairs, especially when Louisa knew how hard she worked, and especially as Louisa knew she was busting her butt for their big sister Amanda's best friend and not just some random pop act.

Sabrina made a mental note to start adding pictures of the piles of paperwork and late-night sessions to her Instagram, to break up the once in a blue moon flashy press events – maybe this would appease Louisa.

'We all miss you too and can't wait to see you,' Louisa whispered after a minute or two.

Sabrina collected the photocopies and decided to call it a day. She picked up her pace, wanting to get back to her office and get home to pack. It had been months since she had been home and though she felt nervous about leaving her boys, she could do with the break.

'Look, I'm sorry for getting snappy with you but I'll be there, and it would be nice if you believed me, for once,' she said, softer

3

now. As she walked past Lydia's office she noticed the light was on. It hadn't been on earlier. She had thought Lydia had gone home for the day. Squinting her eyes and sending a quizzical look through the glass, she noticed Lydia was not alone and her breath caught.

'Is everything OK, Brina? I'm going to head to bed now – it's pretty late here,' Louisa said.

Sabrina tiptoed into her office as quickly and quietly as she could and gently closed the door behind her. She steadied her breath to answer Louisa: 'Erm, sorry, yes, Lou. I'm fine and gosh, yes, please get some sleep. It's already morning there. I love you and I'll text you tomorrow.'

'OK, love you, Brina,' Louisa said before putting the phone down.

Sabrina placed her phone in her bag and shook her head. She needed to pull herself together; she was being ridiculous. Tears pricked her eyes as she gathered her belongings and dashed out of her office. Without glancing back at Lydia's window, she took the lift to the ground floor. When the doors opened she marched to the huge glass doors and swung them open with force, letting the cool LA breeze graze her warm cheeks.

She felt ashamed for her dramatic performance and scolded herself for allowing Lydia to get to her so much, but this had been the final straw. Lydia could boss her around, criticize every move she made and talk down to her all she wanted – it was business; it was work – but to mess with her heart in this way was beyond ruthless.

How could she work for such a horrible woman? It was Lydia who had warned Sabrina to stay clear of dating clients. The company didn't tolerate it and Sabrina was asked to promise that she would not date any member of San Francisco Beat. This rule, however, had only come into play after Lydia had heard that Levi and Sabrina had got rather close at the band's album launch party two years ago. Sabrina had never heard of it prior to the event.

And Sabrina hadn't intended to be unprofessional, but it just sort of happened.

Naturally, she had pulled away from Levi, worried about being taken seriously, scared that she would get in trouble, that she was breaking rules. How silly had she been to throw away what she and Levi had – and for what? There hadn't been any rules then, but now Lydia had gone and created and enforced those stupid rules. And she'd made it abundantly clear that when one of the boys dated it should be with a fellow star – a model, an actress, someone who could raise their profile, someone who was definitely not Sabrina.

She dragged her feet along the sidewalk towards her apartment. How could she have been so naive? Of course, Lydia had only been jealous – she had wanted Levi for herself. Sabrina realized this, but it was too late. The image from moments ago now burned in her brain: Lydia with her arms wrapped around Levi's neck, falling with him onto the couch in her office.

Sabrina shuddered. She didn't know what hurt more: the fact that this woman hated her so much or that she had thought Levi had felt the same way she had that night they kissed. Who was she kidding? What guy waited two years for someone? She didn't live in a fairy tale; this was real life and in real life she had chosen work. She had stomped on the book of love without turning another page, and in doing so had well and truly placed Levi in the friend zone.

She didn't have a right to be sad. It had worked out well for everyone. The band were doing fantastic and she had progressed tenfold with her job in spite of Lydia. Yet here she was, with another Christmas upon her, daydreaming of Levi. Whether she had the right to or not, she did indeed feel sad. She needed her grandpa's pizza and she needed it now.

Chapter 2

Grandpa's Pizza

Ingredients (I'm sure this makes a lot of mini pizzas; need to check on pizza for one?):

10oz yeast
1lb flour
Olive oil
1oz butter
Mug of water
Cheese and sauce

What to do:

Once yeast dough is formed (thank you, Grandpa), roll it out to fit the trays/baking sheets.

Place trays in clear bags (not Tesco bags like Grandpa did once; they will melt) and leave in warm oven until risen.

Once the base has risen, take the trays out of the bags.

Turn the oven on and when ready, cook one side of the base until golden brown.

Flip over and add sauce and cheese like Grandpa does.

Place back in the oven and allow cheese to melt and edges to turn golden.

With a tear in his eye Grandpa reached out and touched Amanda's arm. He pulled her towards him and gave her a kiss on the cheek.

'Thank you,' he said with so much sincerity that Amanda couldn't stop her eyes from welling up too. She paused for a moment to take in his features. His bright blue eyes glistened, the wrinkles on his round face crinkled up and a small smile developed at the corners of his mouth as he looked at her. If hearts could leap from one's chest, smile and do happy dances, Amanda was certain that's what hers would be doing right now. Her chest felt fit to burst, she loved this man so much.

'Grandpa, *grazie*. I'm so excited. I think I finally have it all up here now,' she said, knocking her knuckles against her forehead. She then wrapped her arms around his waist and squeezed him tight. 'Come on, let's go and sit in the living room and have a break.'

Before they could leave the kitchen, Grandpa did his usual check. Deep down, Amanda knew he didn't doubt her knowledge in the kitchen, but at the same time she was aware that Grandpa liked being thorough. He loved teaching her and repeating the steps to every recipe numerous times and she loved learning from him and could listen to those steps every time he repeated them.

'It will take about …' Grandpa started.

'… an hour,' Amanda finished. Both were looking at the oven door.

'Ah, you know.' Grandpa's face lit up as he said this. He nodded and walked in the direction of the front room to join the others. He had his arms outstretched, touching the walls as he walked. They were his guide now; he didn't quite trust his failing eyesight. His shoulders were hunched from years bent over the kitchen counters and his legs wobbled delicately with each step he took.

Amanda puffed out her chest. She loved the feeling of making her grandpa proud. Then she subtly walked behind him, his shaking legs making her anxious that he would fall. They had been in the kitchen for the better part of an hour, making pizza dough. At ninety-five years old that was no mean feat. You still couldn't get him out of the kitchen when he had his heart set on cooking. These days, however, he knew when to stop and rest, when his legs couldn't take his weight much longer and no amount of his determination and strong will could hold off the aches and pains.

Grandpa went to sit down beside his youngest granddaughter – Amanda's baby sister, Louisa – on the soft grey couch. Louisa placed a hand on the small of Grandpa's back, guiding him down, aiding him with his balance as his old knees did their best to bend. Then she scooted up to give him some space and make sure he was comfy.

Amanda made for the little blue chair in front of the fireplace. This had been the girls' favourite spot to perch when they were kids. In the cold months, they would run in from school, drop their schoolbags at the foot of the stairs and race to the living room, ready to fight for the chair. With their arms outstretched over the flames they would try to capture the heat, as Grandpa shouted, 'Careful not to roast,' with a chuckle. They would tell their *nonni* about their day and what they had been up to while taking it in turns to sit on the chair, indulging in soft, buttery Bauli cakes as crumbs sprinkled the carpet.

Things hadn't changed much, except these days Amanda had to position herself more carefully in the chair. When she looked up she caught sight of Louisa who was grinning, her brown eyes looking from the chair to Amanda. They weren't kids any more. The precise movement – a twist of the hips and a gentle shuffle to avoid getting stuck between the armrests – was certainly a sight to behold. She couldn't help but reciprocate Louisa's grin. She would not get stuck today; she'd mastered this by now.

'Grandpa, would you like a biscuit?' Louisa asked, picking up the tin and offering it to him.

'Just one?' he questioned, making both girls laugh. Amanda watched him tuck into his chocolate biscotti. Tears threatened her eyes again as she replayed his 'thank you' in her mind. Though Grandpa could be impatient at the best of times, his passion for cooking knew no bounds and it was getting harder for Nanna to help him in the kitchen.

The girls' mum would often tell him that he couldn't start whipping up things left and right and then leaving it for Nanna to finish and clean up. Mum would have to explain to him that Nanna was getting old too. This frustrated Grandpa. He would get bossy and occasionally snap when the girls tried to help him.

Today, hearing him say 'thank you' after Amanda had helped him mix up the pizza dough and prep it to rise in the oven had melted her heart. Not only because in that moment he seemed to acknowledge his sometimes-bad moods and apologize for them, but also because she couldn't imagine not being able to cook whenever she wanted. She understood his need to be in the kitchen; after all, he had passed on that same passion to her. She knew how important cooking was to him. His 'thank you' had been filled with gratitude – all because of the simple act of being there for him, allowing him to do what he loved.

'One for Amanda too,' Nanna said to Louisa, pointing at the gold tin of biscuits on the coffee table. Tins of biscuits were a permanent fixture in the living room. '*Mangia, mangia,*' Nanna continued, as she turned to look at Amanda.

'I am, Nanna, I am, look,' Amanda replied, her nanna's voice snapping her out of her thoughts. She stood up out of the chair, with a ninja-like swivel of her hips, so they wouldn't get caught under the tiny armrests, and took a biscuit from the tin. She smiled at her nanna and stuffed the whole thing in her mouth.

'You're a cheeky girl,' Nanna said, with a tut and a shake of her head.

Amanda took another biscuit and bent down to kiss her nanna on the forehead. 'I love you,' she said, with a mouthful of amaretti.

'God bless you,' Nanna replied, her voice wobbling slightly. '*Grazie, grazie* for helping Grandpa.'

Amanda leant down and kissed the top of her forehead once more, her nanna's rose scent filling her heart with contentment.

'What time is it?' Grandpa asked, squinting through his round glasses, to see the clock above the fireplace better.

'Nearly time, Grandpa,' Louisa answered. Both sisters knew all too well why he was asking. Amanda and Louisa's sister, Sabrina, was due any minute and Grandpa had spent the better part of the morning looking at the clock. It had been a while since he'd had all three of his granddaughters together. His excitement was clear from the sparkle in his eyes.

'Ahh, I ask you too many times,' Grandpa said, shrugging his shoulders and placing his hand on top of Louisa's biscuit-free hand.

'No, no, it's OK, Grandpa – we're excited too. We understand,' Louisa replied, chewing a crunchy Pirouette thoughtfully.

'But what more is there for me to think about?' he continued, turning to face Louisa.

Amanda smiled, knowing this action meant Grandpa was about to impart some wisdom.

'At my age, what is more important than family? What do I have to think about? To make sure they are fed, me and Nanna have food for them. I must think about you girls being safe. Your mamma, yes, she looks after you and well, yes, your daddy can provide for you, but me and Nanna, we can only do so much.

We can help too. We are always thinking like you are our own daughters.'

Her grandpa's broken English made Amanda's heart soar. The girls were fluent in Italian, but they often alternated between the two languages when speaking with their *nonni*. It helped them all: the girls to keep their Italian fresh and their *nonni* to understand English better for when they needed to speak with English family and friends.

At that moment, the doorbell rang. Both girls looked at each other with Cheshire-cat-like grins. Louisa sprang up from her seat. Amanda stood up, less frantic. Both Nanna and Grandpa sat upright, their eyes shining like they had just won the lottery.

'She's here,' squealed Louisa, gently shoving Amanda out of the way and racing to the door. 'I'll get it.'

Amanda merely chuckled and walked behind, allowing her little sister to take the lead. Louisa often got angry with Sabrina for moving away to LA and leaving everyone behind, but it never changed how excited she got when Sabrina came home. Amanda, on the other hand, was a little more reserved. She was pleased her sister had followed her dreams and over the moon that Dan and his band were in good hands, but there remained a part of her that stubbornly missed Sabrina and was mad with her for being so far away too.

'The eagle has landed,' Mum reported as she came through the front door first, arms loaded with birthday balloons and cards, having just picked up 'the eagle' from the airport. 'Safe and sound – she's home,' Mum said. Her eyes shone as she kissed Amanda and Louisa, as they passed each other in the corridor. Mum continued to the living room to say hello to her parents, as Amanda walked leisurely outside, and Louisa practically flew.

Like a local celebrity, Sabrina, the middle child, was standing in the middle of the path, between the cherry trees and the fence. Her sandy blonde hair was blowing in the breeze and she had clearly picked up an LA tan. Amanda noticed her bronzed skin glowing under the soft British sun, as Sabrina waved and said hi to the neighbours.

'All right, Jennifer Lawrence, it's only been an entire year – we all haven't missed you that much,' Amanda shouted into the street, from her position leaning casually against the doorframe.

Sabrina turned to face them at the same time Louisa leapt outside and nearly bowled her sister over with a hug.

'I've missed you, Brina,' Louisa said, sweetly, as Sabrina gasped for air, Louisa's hug choking her. Amanda looked on in amusement.

'I've missed you too, Lou. It's good to see you. It feels good to breathe in this British air.' Sabrina took a big breath in, as Louisa let her go, and then she let out a deep sigh. Amanda knew she loved parts of her life in LA, but it comforted her to know that it hadn't stolen her sister just yet. Watching her hazel eyes soften as she took in the surroundings, she could tell Sabrina was happy to be back and that nothing compared to home.

'You look exhausted. So, what presents did you bring back?' Amanda asked, leaving her position by the front door and wandering over to join the party.

'Always so kind with the compliments, aren't we? I might have gifts for you, but I'll be needing a hug first,' Sabrina said, and waved her arms in the air, dramatically motioning for a hug, while giving her big sister her best puppy dog impression.

'That we are, and it better be an awesome gift. I can't just be giving away free hugs,' Amanda said, rolling her eyes and stepping forward to hug her sister.

'Come on, Brina, Nanna and Grandpa are so excited to see you. You know what Grandpa's like – he hasn't stopped asking about you all day. Plus, we've held off with the birthday celebrations till you got here,' Louisa said, grabbing her sister by the arm and pulling her towards the house. Amanda strolled calmly behind them. Though she didn't quite display her emotions on her sleeve like Louisa did, there was no hiding the bright smile that was now etched on Amanda's face.

***

The dining room was full of colour. Red, green and white balloons were bunched up – dangling from the doorframes and curtains – and wrapping paper had been strewn across the table, as had bags of pasta and vibrant Italian cake boxes.

Sabrina's eyes drifted round the table. She took in everyone's features, everyone's movements: her mother's chocolate eyes sparkled with pure delight; Dad had his hands resting on his stomach as he leant back in his chair, stuffed and happy from all the food; Grandpa's eyes twinkled; Nanna's smile reached all the way to her ears, making her look twenty-one and carefree again; Amanda's green eyes focused intently on the food in front of her and Louisa simply watched her grandpa, making sure he had everything he needed.

Everyone talked over one another, laughing uncontrollably in between devouring each piece of pizza quicker than the speed of light. In that moment, she felt content, like there truly was no place on earth she would rather be. All the stress and drama of work melted away like the mouth-watering mozzarella she was chewing; it was heaven on earth.

'Grandpa, I sure have missed this,' she said, holding her piece of pizza in the air, like it was a trophy.

'You can get pizza in America, no?' Grandpa replied with a cheeky grin.

'Ha, you know as well as I do, Grandpa, that no pizza on the planet tastes as good as this. No one will ever be able to make it taste as amazing as you do,' Amanda said.

Sabrina loved the passion her sister had for their grandpa's food. It made her laugh hearing Amanda's voice rise with pride when talking about his pizza.

'It's crisp, yet chewy, with the perfect amount of crunch, and it's as light as air,' her big sister continued.

Sabrina watched as Grandpa's gaze met Amanda's and he gave her a small wink. They were like two peas in a pod.

'Hear, hear,' Sabrina chanted, raising her wineglass now that her pizza had been demolished. She felt dizzy on love and Lambrusco, but her eyes threatened to roll back in her head. Amanda had been right: she not only looked exhausted, she absolutely felt it too. Her bones were heavy, her neck tight. She rolled her head from side to side, hoping it would loosen up.

'It's good to have you home, sweetheart,' Dad said, raising his glass and clinking it against hers.

'It feels great to be home, Dad.' Sabrina smiled softly. It really did feel wonderful to be home. Her shoulders relaxed at the thought of not having to deal with her wouldn't go amiss in a Disney villain line-up, Cruella de Vil of a boss, Lydia, for the next few days.

The warmth of the room and the bubbles from the Lambrusco made her feel a world away from LA. Tonight she was surrounded by the people she loved more than she could say, and who genuinely loved and cared for her. '*Buon compleanno*, Grandpa,' she shouted, raising her glass to the room once more. Seeing her grandpa's face light up would keep jet lag at bay for a while longer.

'*Mamma mia, grazie, grazie*. How many girls have I got here now?' Grandpa said. His voice filled the small dining room, his happiness radiating to each of them.

'*Buon compleanno*,' Nanna shouted, clapping her hands together. 'Louisa, get the *pandoro*. Come on, come on.' Nanna too was thrilled to have all her girls round the table together. Any time this happened was cause for cake and celebrations, but when it came to birthdays and special times like Christmas, Nanna looked like a child, her face etched with glee. She looked to her husband and whispered, '*Buon compleanno*, my dear,' before cutting a huge slice of *pandoro* and placing it in front of him.

She then went back to cutting more big chunks of cake and passed everyone a piece. 'Be happy, happy,' Nanna continued. 'Ahh *grazie*, God.'

Sabrina wasn't sure her stomach could handle the mountain of *pandoro* in front of her, after eating so much pizza and drinking a fair bit of wine, in addition to jet lag that had now kicked in, but it smelt so buttery and delicious and Nanna was staring at her expectantly. Not eating it was not an option – it was never an option. Plus, she was only in town for a week. She had to eat all her favourites while she could get them, and it was Grandpa's ninety-sixth birthday after all.

With these thoughts sloshing round her brain, she laughed to herself and took a huge bite. No sooner had the vanilla flavour hit her taste buds than her slice had gone. So much for not having any room left.

'*Grazie*, Nanna,' she whispered, with a chuckle.

Chapter 3

Grandpa's Pancakes

Ingredients:

Flour
Sugar
Egg
Milk
Butter
Nutella

What to do:

Mix around 4 tablespoons of flour with 2 teaspoons of sugar, an egg and a cup of milk, until smooth.

Heat up a saucepan and add a dab of butter.

Pour in a ladle full of pancake batter and swirl round like Grandpa does.

Smother in Nutella.

The birds were chirping in the garden. The whistles of the wintry winds could be heard through the glass. There was a peacefulness to a Sunday morning that Amanda couldn't get enough of. It was her one full day away from work and that meant she was up at the crack of dawn ready for a day of spending time with family, catching up on reading, cleaning and actually getting to experiment in her own kitchen. Though she had taken yesterday off too – for the first time in a very long time – Sundays always felt special and she liked to make the most of them.

'Rise and shine, sleeping beauties,' Amanda said walking into her guest bedroom and opening the silk pink curtains wide, to let the morning sunshine boldly fill up the room.

'Oh gosh, what time is it?' Louisa whined, pulling her pillow over her face. She was lying next to Sabrina in the double bed.

Sabrina threw her arms up to shield against the imposing light. 'Jet lag is a thing, Amanda – look it up. I need rest,' she said, her eyes still firmly shut.

'There's no time for rest. You're only here for a week. I told Grandpa we would pop over for leftover cake before we hit the shops. And I don't get much time away from the kitchen, which means we won't get much time this week to do said shopping, so, we are going to make the most of today,' Amanda told them, cracking open a window to wake them up with fresh air, which received further moans.

'Chop, chop. You too, Lou. With our work schedules we rarely see each other and you live fifteen minutes away from me – and that's a bit pathetic,' she added, with an edge to her voice that made Louisa sit up straight. Amanda wasn't exactly blaming

Louisa, she was mad at herself too. The schedule of a chef wasn't for the faint-hearted.

Amanda busied herself with her routine Sunday morning cleaning while waiting for her sisters to get ready. She was halfway through dusting the window ledges when they appeared before her, surprisingly fully dressed and ready for the day. Amanda was the early bird out of the three of them. She did enjoy a lie-in every couple of months, but just like her grandpa, she always had something to bake. Cooking in the morning while still in her pyjamas had become a little piece of bliss for her.

Sundays were usually Sabrina's only day off in LA. Amanda was aware of this fact, and knew Sabrina liked to sleep in, but she would have plenty of time for that on her vacation in the coming weekdays when everyone else was working. As for Louisa, an extra hour and grumpy would be kept at bay, but once they were at Nanna and Grandpa's, Amanda knew her baby sister would be anything but grumpy. *Nonni* were special like that. Amanda just had to get her up and moving.

The clock had just moved past eight-thirty as Amanda, casually glam and put together in her black pinstriped trousers and oversized rose embroidered grey jumper; Sabrina in her usual floaty dress and tights ensemble, minimal make-up yet as gorgeous as ever; and Louisa with her sleek black blazer, skinny blue jeans and white Converse pumps, stepped out into the crisp December air, giant teddy bear coats covering their individual fashion tastes.

Growing up, the three of them were chained together at the hip and that's how they thought it would forever be, but dreams and jobs had led them in different directions. Amanda and Louisa hadn't been too fond of Sabrina leaving them and jetting off to LA. They had disapproved at first and it had taken a lot of convincing on Sabrina's part that it wouldn't be for too long and that she still honoured their pact – this pact being that by the time they all reached thirty they would have houses on the same street, a five-minute walk from their mum and dad.

Slowly the girls began to understand Sabrina's dream and had come around to being supportive. Amanda of all people knew the importance of travelling, having spent so much time away herself. It was always temporary though, and her heart always led her back home.

The girls made time to visit each other as often as work would allow. This week it was Amanda's turn to play host and she couldn't have been more thrilled. The strain of jobs, and the fact it had been a year since Sabrina's last visit, had been causing an unwelcome tension over the past few months. Amanda didn't care for being snappy, but at times she was aware that she could be. It wasn't a trait she wanted to exude. She hoped today she and her sisters could get some much-needed girl time for the sake of their sanity.

Amanda, the oldest of the girls, was baking and cooking up a storm by the age of eight. Though all the girls enjoyed cooking with their *nonni*, Amanda had taken to it like a duck to water, and it was very rare to see her out of her 'I can't keep calm, I'm Italian' apron. The days spent in the kitchen studying their nanna and grandpa were priceless and her passion never faltered when she left their house.

At twenty-seven, Amanda was now a fully certified chef. She had qualifications, certificates and diplomas in professional patisserie, culinary arts – you name it. She had travelled the world taking numerous courses and immersing herself in different cultures and their cuisines. That was until three years ago. After a month exploring San Francisco, she had come back feeling inspired and full of vigour and decided to put her travel plans on hold. She wanted to focus on learning all there was to know about running a restaurant. She found herself a cosy spot in Manchester Piccadilly, at the popular Rusk, where she served British food with an elegant twist.

Amanda had been there two and a half years now and besides having to deal with a rather sleazy sous chef, she was happy, or more accurately, she was comfortable. It suited her. After her years spent travelling, she liked being close to her mum and dad, Louisa and home comforts.

When it was Amanda's turn to have the girls over, they knew they were in for a few tasty treats. All Sabrina ever wanted when she came home from LA was Grandpa's pizza. She requested it every night, and as for Louisa, she could never say no to pizza. After a brief stint away in London for university, her baby sister appreciated Amanda's home cooking that much more.

Amanda had doubled over laughing when Louisa had expressed sheer horror at the foods she saw her fellow students eat. It seemed their *nonni* and Amanda had created a little bit of a food snob in Louisa – no microwave meals or Pot Noodles for her.

***

Grandpa was waiting in the garden perched on an old brown garden bench, in his heavy black padded coat, when the girls pulled up.

'Grandpa,' Louisa shouted, un-clicking her seatbelt and opening the car door before Amanda even had the car in park.

'Lou,' Sabrina yelled. But Louisa was blissfully unaware of giving her sisters a mild panic attack as she wrapped her arms around their grandpa. Amanda turned off the engine. Seeing the joy on her grandpa's face, now that all three of his granddaughters were with him, melted away any twinge of annoyance at her little sister.

She walked over to Grandpa and kissed his forehead. 'I love you,' she whispered.

'*Anche io,*' he replied, kissing her cheek.

Sabrina opened the front door, calling to Nanna to inform her of their arrival as Amanda and Louisa helped Grandpa up.

'Now, let's get inside for some coffee and cake and to warm you up,' Amanda suggested.

***

The afternoon brought with it an icy nip. Amanda rubbed at the sleeves of her grey jumper. Shopping with a puffy jacket on was never a good idea. Being hot and stuffy while trying to weave in and out of bustling crowds and undressing in a tiny changing room with a million layers on never produced a successful shop and so she had left her teddy coat in the car. However, the jumper she was currently sporting was not ideal when the breeze picked up, causing Amanda to shiver. The only thing keeping her from aborting the shopping mission was a happy stomach full to the brim with Cantuccini and birthday trifle.

Amanda let out a deep sigh as Louisa linked an arm through hers, warming her up slightly. She felt a little lighter, and colder, than she had done in days; no doubt the pure happiness she felt spending the weekend with her family, and Sabrina being home, had everything to do with that. She navigated the crowds with Sabrina to her left and Louisa clutching on to her right.

Manchester was jam-packed, the Christmas Markets in full swing. The giant Santa proudly sat on display front and centre. Amanda was taking it in, enjoying the freedom of having a weekend off. She had no Jeff to contend with and no hot and tense kitchen to see to. As much as she loved her job, a weekend off every so often was rather wonderful. If she just had Dan here with her too, it would be perfect.

***

Dan carefully placed a cup in Amanda's hands, his own hands then wrapping around hers, so she didn't drop it. She had her eyes closed and a bright smile on her face. The tip of her nose was red from the frosty night air.

'OK, take a sip, but be careful – it will be hot,' Dan said, his warm hands guiding the cup to her lips.

Amanda felt something cold touch her lips first. She licked them, and the delicious taste of vanilla whipped cream danced on her taste buds. She knew it was a hot chocolate of some kind, but she didn't want to spoil the fun just yet, and Dan was smarter than that – he knew not to make it that easy.

She blew in the direction of the cold whipped cream and slurped to get past it. She could taste a rich coffee, with a smooth blend of chocolate and something she couldn't put her finger on. Damn it, she thought, her pride not wanting to let Dan win.

'Any guesses?' Dan asked. He still hadn't removed his hands from on top of hers. Though Amanda kept her eyes closed, she knew he was smirking. Her brain tried to come up with the right answer. She took another sip, stalling for more time, but she could not place the mystery ingredient.

'Ooh should we have Nutella crepes next?' she said, to change the subject.

'You have no idea what it is, do you?' Dan questioned as she opened her eyes and looked down at the cup. 'You are a cheat,' he added, removing his hands from around hers and placing them in his coat pockets.

Amanda blinked a few times to ease the glare of the lights. 'No, I'm just hungry for crepes,' she teased, shaking her head at Dan's mock disappointed look.

'You call yourself my best friend and you can't even recognize eggnog,' Dan scoffed, a playful grin playing at his lips. Dan liked his eggnog because he loved all things Christmas. Amanda knew this, but still, she never would have guessed eggnog.

'I said eggnog,' she noted, batting her eyelashes and taking another sip. Dan laughed and put an arm around her shoulders and started walking in the direction of the crepes.

The Manchester Christmas Markets felt magical this year, having Dan by her side. He loved the food huts the best, just like Amanda *did, but he also enjoyed the details and craftsmanship of the many homemade gift stands. He was an artist through and through.*

Amanda's toes were numb by the time they headed for home. She hadn't been able to get Dan away. They had to see every stall, drink another chocolate eggnog – the man was obsessed – and explore every nook and cranny of Manchester city centre before he agreed that the toastiness of Amanda's house was calling his name too. It was safe to say Dan liked the place, Amanda thought to herself as they walked arm in arm, and for some reason that made her feel good.

***

Amanda cleared her throat and shook her head, angry with herself for letting Dan seep into her thoughts. She had been doing so well to keep phone calls and texts to just once or twice a week over the past few months. She wasn't about to let the romance of Christmas ruin her efforts of keeping thoughts of her best friend just that, simply thoughts of a best friend and nothing more.

'Ooh, that's gorgeous,' Louisa said, pointing at a piece of clothing that looked more suitable to adorn an art gallery wall than an actual person.

'If you say so,' Amanda said, sarcasm dripping from her tongue. She laughed, glad of the distraction when Louisa hit her with her handbag.

'Can we go in?' Sabrina asked, eyeing the sales sign. 'I bet they've got tons of dresses on sale now that summer is over,' she added, excitement in her voice.

Amanda was about to tell her that she needed to stock up on warmer clothes now she was in England, then it hit her that it wouldn't be long and Sabrina would be back in LA, no doubt needing a floaty dress for every day of the week. 'Lead the way,' she said instead, with a forced smile.

23

Amanda absent-mindedly flicked through the dress racks. It wasn't that she disliked shopping, she quite enjoyed it. Though she didn't have Louisa's flair or guts for exquisite pieces or Sabrina's penchant for floaty ensembles, she knew a knockout dress when she saw one. Her work outfits weren't much to be desired, so she enjoyed making an effort when she was out of the kitchen, but effort for her still had to be comfy. She was a boots and pants kind of girl and couldn't say no to an oversized slouchy jumper.

No, it wasn't that she disliked shopping, it was more that she kept getting the itch to pick up her phone. As they weaved in and out of the racks, it was like a battle was going on in her brain. She was starting to get on her own nerves, with this whole inability to live without Dan. When had she become so dependent? She needed to get lost in a book or some music or something because shopping clearly wasn't doing the trick. Then again books and music would be pointless too, she realized. Why did he have to like all the same books she did? And why did Dan have to be a bloody rock star?

'Are you OK over there?' Sabrina asked, peeking at Amanda from over a rail. 'You look like you're trying to solve an algebra equation in that brain of yours and we know maths isn't your strong suit,' Sabrina added with a laugh.

Amanda hastily looked down and focused on the dresses before her, spotting one she knew Sabrina would adore. She grabbed it and held it up, which immediately changed the subject.

'Oh, that's beautiful,' Sabrina gushed, moving in to claim it.

'Wow, that's perfect for you,' Louisa said, surveying the peach floral number and giving it her approval. 'Good job, Amanda.'

***

A few hours later, weighed down with bags of clothing, they walked through Amanda's front door. They deposited their bags

24

in their bedrooms and made quick work of getting into their comfiest PJs. Then Amanda set about making snacks as Sabrina and Louisa got the DVDs ready in the living room. Within the hour they were settled quite comfortably in their favourite spots.

Amanda lay sprawled out across the single couch, her legs stretched out over the armrest. Louisa made herself cosy on the three-seater couch and Sabrina had taken blankets and cushions to the floor of the white, blush and gold washed living room. It was warm and snug and much to Sabrina's delight there was pizza and an array of Italian cakes at arm's reach and *What's Your Number?* was playing on the TV. This had been their go-to movie for the past five years and these moments were what the girls lived for. Family was everything to them.

'Could you get any dreamier than Chris Evans?' Louisa sighed. Her eyes were glazing over with every word Chris Evans spoke.

'Hmm, I'm more a Harry Styles circa 2015 girl myself,' Amanda replied matter-of-fact, pulling her legs back over the armrest and tucking them under the blanket she had draped over her middle.

'Ooh, tattoos and a man bun,' Sabrina teased, grabbing another slice of pizza.

'He kind of looks like Dan,' Louisa piped up, causing Amanda to shove the whole slice of pizza into her mouth.

Sabrina noticed Amanda's jaw tense. Something was up because Dan was usually more of a happy topic of conversation, apart from when Sabrina and Louisa pestered Amanda about her feelings for him and whether she liked him more than just as a friendly companion. Louisa hadn't suggested anything of the sort tonight, just that Dan resembled Harry Styles, albeit a slightly more broad and bearded version of Harry Styles, but tattooed and luscious hair all the same, with a chiselled jaw and piercing eyes. But at that suggestion Amanda's whole body had closed off.

For a while a calm silence enveloped the living room as the girls dug in to pizza and helpings of *sfogliatelle*, while gazing at the TV screen, as though it had them hypnotized. Chris Evans could have that effect on a person.

Amanda broke the silence. With her eyes firmly fixed on Chris Evans, she asked the question that Sabrina knew was burning on her lips. Amanda asked her every time she saw her, but this time it had taken her two whole days to bring it up and Sabrina wasn't sure why.

'Speaking of Dan, how's he doing these days? And can we invite Chris Evans round for tea? Have you not bumped into him yet, Brina? Really you need to get on that. You can't be all high-profile LA, getting into all these hip places and not have arranged some sort of meet-up for your dear, sweet sisters with all these gorgeous men.' Her voice came out in a rush as she tried not to linger on the Dan question, clearly wanting to keep it more as a flyaway query.

Sabrina knew her sister too well. Something was definitely going on in that head of hers.

Sabrina fell about laughing. 'I wish I could snap my fingers and make that happen. Jeez, Amanda, if I could do that, do you not think I would have done it already? And your darling Dan is doing fine – his usual focused self,' Sabrina said, her voice softening. She kept her gaze on Amanda, but Amanda chose not to meet it and kept her own firmly on the TV.

Dan was Amanda's best friend and lead singer of San Francisco Beat – music's hottest act – and, thanks to Amanda, Sabrina was their manager. Sabrina hadn't been able to believe her luck when Amanda had sent them her way two and a half years ago. In addition to Dan, there was bassist Dylan, who was the shy type with a sweet nature; guitarist James, who had a penchant for telling jokes and never took anything too seriously; and finally you had Levi, exceptional drummer and heartthrob to many across the world.

Levi was one to keep an eye on; though an absolute sweetheart, his charm, undeniable good looks and five-star flirting abilities could often lead to trouble. Sabrina had assured Amanda that she would be professional and always do right by the boys. Sabrina had been their big break, but they had also been her saving grace and she wasn't about to screw it up. But there were times when keeping things professional was exhausting.

She enjoyed the banter between her and Levi and his playful nature so much. She found that with him she gave as good as she got. Sabrina hadn't told her sisters about the night she and Levi had kissed. She had worried that it would further cement Louisa's theory that her life was perfect. Though she ultimately knew her baby sister would be happy for her, she hadn't wanted to add to her ammo for teasing her.

Furthermore, after Amanda's last break-up Sabrina was all about encouraging Amanda to face her fears and not be afraid of love. Sabrina hadn't wanted to confide in her big sister that she had run from Levi and her own feelings like a coward. It would set a bad example.

'You do realize I have been in the country for over twenty-four hours and you are just asking me that question now. Is everything OK?' Sabrina asked, Amanda's fast-talking and intense gaze not going unnoticed.

'Oh no, you haven't broken up, have you?' Louisa chimed in, picking at a piece of *sfogliatelle* they had brought back from the Christmas Markets. Sabrina cringed, wishing Louisa could read Amanda's body language as well as she could. There were times to approach this subject with Amanda and tonight was not one of those times.

Amanda's eyes grew narrow. 'How many times do I have to tell you, Lou? You can't break up with someone you're *not* dating!' Amanda said, her tone unfriendly. She rested her head back on her cushion and closed her eyes tight for a few moments.

'Well how many times do we have to tell *you*, Amanda? You can't just be *friends* with your soulmate,' Louisa replied copying Amanda's sarcastic and mean tone while using air quotes at the mention of 'friends'.

'Whatever, Lou. Everything's fine – just wondered that's all. The question slipped my mind for a few days, no big deal. You actually get to see him every day, so I just thought I'd check in as per usual, make sure he's not giving you a hard time,' Amanda said, absent-mindedly picking at a piece of basil on the top of her fifth pizza slice.

'You know as well as I do that Dan couldn't give anyone a hard time. He's awesome, Amanda. I love working with them. The past two and a half years have been incredible,' Sabrina said, eyeing up her sister, deciding whether she could push this topic further tonight and figure out what was bothering her.

Louisa had no filter when it came to pushing Amanda's buttons about Dan, whereas Sabrina tried to be more tactful. Over the years, both she and Louisa had asked on many occasions why Amanda and Dan weren't a couple. Neither the naive nor tactful approach had been very successful. The first year or two Amanda seemed perplexed by this question, genuinely confused as to how they could ask such a thing, so they had backed off. Amanda was happy, focused and more herself than they had ever seen her, and Sabrina and Louisa had concluded that whatever their relationship status was, they should just let it be – if it isn't broke, don't fix it.

Gradually, though, Sabrina could see a flicker of sadness in Amanda's eyes when she talked about Dan. After hours on the phone you could sense that she missed him and longed for more. Dan always asked about Amanda; in fact it had become routine. Whenever he entered Sabrina's office he greeted her with a cheery hello and 'How's Amanda?' before settling in to talk about work. Of course, Amanda did the very same with every Skype call or visit, always asking about Dan. It was frustrating and rather baffling to Sabrina that they couldn't see what was in front of them, but she had faith that it would work out if it was meant to be.

'Good to know,' came Amanda's response before she dug her spoon into the Nutella jar and took a huge scoop. Putting it to her mouth, she grinned at her sisters, clearly indicating she didn't want to continue talking about Dan and most definitely looking like some sort of crazy chocolate fiend. Sabrina got the message and settled back against her pillow and blanket fort.

'Speaking of working, do you actually get much work done when Levi's around?' Louisa asked Sabrina, her face creasing into a coy grin.

'You sure are on a roll tonight with these questions, aren't you?' Sabrina said, grabbing a pillow and launching it at her little sister. 'Right, no more boy talk unless we are talking about the American dream; plus, I don't think I'm Levi's type.' She shrugged.

'Aha, so you admit to liking him?' Louisa said bouncing up off the couch.

Sabrina couldn't help smiling at her. Louisa wanted everyone to be happy. She loved love and believed in it with all her heart. It was incredibly endearing, if not a little annoying at times like this. Sabrina knew she should tell her sisters about her and Levi, but there was that niggling fear in the back of her mind. She didn't want to be a hypocrite where Amanda was concerned, and she didn't want Louisa to slip up and expose her feelings to Levi. Her baby sister could be sneaky like that; love was simple in Louisa's eyes.

'I didn't say that – I just said that I don't think I'm his type anyway,' Sabrina replied, reaching for the Nutella jar before flashbacks of Levi and Lydia appeared in her mind from the night before she left LA.

'You two are unbelievable,' Louisa shouted as she made a huge deal of standing up on the couch. 'You know I'm not so sure either of you would remember to invite me to the meet and greet should you ever stumble upon Captain America himself.' Louisa was staring off into the distance, waving her arms around, bouncing from one sofa cushion to the next. She was now practically performing some sort of lonely, depressing monologue as though she had just taken centre stage.

'I think you may have even secretly already met him and failed to mention it to me, because you both love secrets and don't like telling me anything. If I had boys like Dan and Levi in my midst I sure wouldn't play all these games,' she said, exasperated and now staring her sisters down. 'Sabrina, you have an amazing job, where you get to go to all these fancy parties and rub elbows with celebrities galore. You're kicking arse with the world's hottest rock band and you are beautiful. If you like Levi, go for it and tell him. Then, not only will you have a glamorous, perfect job, but you will also get to go home to a rock god who's good with his hands. What more could you possibly want?'

'Louisa!!!!' Sabrina shouted, gobsmacked and embarrassed by her little sister's choice of words, but Louisa wasn't done yet.

'And, you.' Louisa pointed at Amanda, whose eyes were slightly narrowed, with a hint of a smirk playing at her lips, her head tilted to one side, gently warning Louisa to tread carefully, but Louisa wasn't fazed. 'Dan isn't like your ex – aliens in outer space can see that – and if you are speaking the honest to goodness truth when you tell us that you don't see him as anything more than a friend, then you need to start dating again … properly – no one-night stands, no too busy with work, no excuses, because what, or more importantly, who are you waiting for?'

Louisa finished and sat back down on the couch. Sabrina looked at her not quite knowing what to say. Amanda brushed a hand through her long wavy brown mane. Her eyes were still squinted, like she was thinking. There was a tension in the room that hadn't been there mere minutes ago. The girls were typical siblings and rows and arguments broke out occasionally.

Sabrina could feel the heat from Louisa. It seemed something had irked her, maybe something at work, maybe a boy, or maybe she really was on to something. It made Sabrina feel silly. She was supposed to be the older sister offering advice to Louisa, but she didn't have a clue what she was doing with Levi; furthermore, she felt slightly irritated that Louisa always thought it so simple.

And, had Louisa not piped up again about how glamorous Sabrina's life was, maybe Sabrina would have chosen to do what she always did and keep the conversation light and playful, but she was getting a bit fed up.

The tension lingered over the room for a few moments before Sabrina spoke up. 'My life is far from glamorous, Lou. I wish you would stop saying that.' Sabrina played with a tassel on the corner of the cushion she was holding. 'I worked bloody hard to get where I am now, and even that took luck and a whole lot of help from Amanda. I deal with criticism and a fire-breathing dragon of a boss every day. The parties are rare and even they come with a barrel of paperwork and stress. I know I'm lucky, but it's not for lack of work.' Sabrina didn't want to sound harsh, but she needed her baby sister to lay off on the comments about her unbelievably flawless lifestyle.

Louisa tilted her head back against the couch cushion and took a deep breath. 'It must be pretty close to perfection if it keeps you away from us eleven months out of the year,' she muttered.

'It's work, Lou, and it's my dream. I don't like being away, but if I remember correctly at one point in time we were all pretty supportive of each other following our dreams. Just because you couldn't handle London, where might I add, I think you would have done amazingly had you persisted, doesn't mean I should give up on LA.'

The words sounded harsher than Sabrina had intended, but it was all coming out now. Though she knew all too well the pain of missing home, Sabrina was also aware of how talented her younger sister was, and she had hated hearing that she had left university after only a few months. However, she had kept her thoughts to herself.

Now that they were getting into the nitty-gritty of their arguing, the words burst out before she could stop them. 'You could, and should, be doing so much with your designs, instead of working a nine to five reception job you hate. Yes, I live far away, but I don't believe I've been a bad sister. I keep up with you all the time and I think you could have done that too. I think you gave up too easily.' Sabrina was looking at Louisa now, feeling more determined, like she had wisdom to impart and her baby sister wasn't the only one who could fire on all cylinders. Amanda remained silent.

'I didn't give up, I prioritized what was more important,' Louisa said firmly, her head still tilted to the ceiling. Her words were now coming out calmly but remained unkind, like she still couldn't accept Sabrina being away, yet Sabrina knew it was justified. She knew her sister was torn. No matter what Louisa said, Sabrina would still be going back to LA in a few days and there was nothing she could do about it. Sabrina felt a sharp stab of sadness in her gut. She understood that her sister simply missed her, but she didn't think it fair of her to be so unsupportive and mean.

'My family is important to me too,' Sabrina said, faintly. It hurt her that Louisa could think otherwise.

At their final exchange Amanda cleared her throat. 'As entertaining as you two are, I'm missing all the good bits in this movie that I've only seen twenty times, and if you don't start watching it I might have to play it again from the beginning, so I can better understand how Chris Evans just got naked.' Amanda looked at them both and threw them each a Baci, before pointing to the screen with a raise of her eyebrows.

Both Sabrina and Louisa caught the chocolate treats with twinning smiles and rolls of the eyes at their big sister, yet they didn't care to look at each other.

***

'This pizza is out of this world, Amanda,' Sabrina said, breaking the silence and taking another slice, now craving savoury after the sweetness of the Baci. 'Do you have the recipe written somewhere? I can't think of where I put mine.'

'It's over there,' Amanda replied pointing lazily in the direction of the bookshelf and to the book on the right of the top shelf. Sabrina followed her finger and nodded.

'I need to learn how to make it,' Louisa piped up. The tension from before had begun to ease, as the sisters brushed the conflict under the rug. It would pop up again and they would address it when the time was right.

'I chatted to Grandpa today about making some stuff while he had us all together. He wanted to make you lasagna while you're home, and I'm pretty sure he had more yeast prepping in the kitchen when we were there this morning.'

'When does he not have yeast prepping?' Louisa said, and all the girls let out a chuckle. There was always something being prepped in their grandpa's kitchen.

'We can go tomorrow morning and make it with him and you can practise,' Amanda continued, sitting up a little straighter on the couch and grabbing her glass of water.

'Found it,' Sabrina shouted, flicking through Amanda's recipe book on her way back to the couch. Louisa scooted up and Sabrina sat down next to her, as though no argument had ever occurred.

'This is awesome, Amanda. I have recipes and notes here and there but never thought to do this.' Louisa turned each page of the book in awe. Sabrina knew that over the years, Amanda had been writing down and trying to collect every recipe she had ever eaten or made at their grandparents' house, but she didn't know she had been placing them safely in a book. The recipes meant a lot to all the girls, but they were incredibly special to Amanda. Each recipe told a story, shared a memory from the girls' childhood, and any spare moment her sister could grab she spent in her kitchen trying to perfect them.

It was one thing to just follow a recipe, but it was a completely different thing making something from the heart and truly capturing the tastes and smells that Nanna and Grandpa were famous for. Sabrina knew that much – she had tried many herself, but she was no cook. Amanda could capture their creations to a T.

Sabrina and Louisa sat in silence, mesmerized, simply reading. Amanda had included notes and quotes from their *nonni* and written down certain childhood memories that the recipes brought back, some Sabrina had forgotten. Sabrina couldn't believe it; the book was phenomenal.

'Aha, "Grandpa's Pizza",' Louisa said, reading the title aloud, pointing at the words on the page and tapping her forefinger against it.

'Erm, I might need a touch more detail – you know if you want the pizza to be cooked and edible.' Sabrina looked over at Amanda. 'Ahem, *add sauce and cheese like Grandpa does …*' she read aloud. 'You always had a way with words.'

Amanda turned to face them, moving her blanket with her. Sabrina watched her with a new sense of pride. At that moment, Sabrina felt incredibly grateful for her sister's passion. This book represented their family. It was their childhood, their lives; it embodied amazing food and a love for those you were making it for.

Louisa was still going through each page carefully. 'The thing is,' Amanda said, speaking softly now, meeting Sabrina's gaze, 'you have to make it with him. Then you don't really need notes, you just watch what he does, and you do it. You've done it before, Brina, you have it in you, you just need to practise,' she finished with a smile.

'This book is beautiful, Amanda, it really is,' Sabrina said, trying not to get soppy on her big sister. 'You know, this is the kind of thing you need to be putting on your blog, including stories with your recipes.'

Sabrina watched her big sister shrug and shift uncomfortably in her chair. 'I don't think I'll be keeping my blog. I don't think it's really for me,' Amanda replied.

Sabrina couldn't help but tut. Amanda had only started her blog 'Mangia' a couple of months ago, if that. It was beautifully designed, elegant meets rustic, homey and perfectly Italian. The posts Amanda had shared thus far had been great, but where her big sister aced nearly everything she set her mind to, the wonderful world of social media seemed to have her beat.

'What did I tell you last week?' Sabrina said, with a shake of her head. 'It's going to take time.' She looked at Amanda and smirked. 'And patience. Try acquiring some if you want it to succeed. It takes people months and years to build up blogs and social media; it doesn't just happen overnight.' Sabrina put extra emphasis on her last words.

It had taken her a good year to build her followers and show Lydia she had what it took to get likes and create a buzz. She didn't care too much for this new popularity contest, but she also couldn't argue with it either. Social media accounted for so much in her line of work and these days it could open doors of endless opportunity for people. 'Keep working on it and putting yourself out there and it will happen.'

'I am working on it, but it takes up so much time and sometimes I cook and forget to take pictures, or I've already taken a bite and ruin the shot. And I don't understand all these SEOs and why people haven't been commenting. I know the recipes are good, so why don't people like them?' Amanda moaned, took a sip of water and shrugged again.

Though listening to Amanda was frustrating, Sabrina could understand that it seemed the blog was messing with her sister's confidence.

'First off, stop whining. I just told you it will all take time and secondly, I understand you are busy and you like to eat what you bake, but you will figure it out if you want it to work,' Sabrina said, trying to have an air of sympathy in her voice but failing.

Her eyes stung from the jet lag now and she didn't want to keep discussing the perils of social media. It could be rather draining trying to comprehend it all and she knew once Amanda figured it out, people would adore her blog. Amanda just had that charm about her.

'I have to agree with Brina on that one. If you love what you are putting out into the world, which we know you do, and you want to share your recipes with everyone, just have fun with them. Don't worry about those comments, Amanda – just do it for you. Don't sit there thinking it's going to happen over night, Ms Perfect,' Louisa chimed in, chancing a sideways glance at Sabrina.

Sabrina offered a small smile, not wanting to stay mad at her baby sister for long. Louisa enjoyed social media and often shared her unique fashion sense with the world. Her pictures were creative, full of colour, and Sabrina hoped that the more her little sister's followers grew, the more confidence it would give her to pursue her fashion dreams once more.

'All right, all right, you two, no need to be so harsh. I get it,' Amanda said, with just a small hint of irritation in her tone. 'I'll make you both a copy of the book if you'd like?' she added, changing the subject and turning back around to face the TV. 'Now, please, you are distracting me from Chris Evans.'

Louisa who had continued looking through the book, while imparting her sparing words of wisdom, placed the book carefully on the coffee table. Sabrina threw a pillow at Amanda's head before she passed around the bowl of Cantuccini as they settled back down to finish the movie.

Just as Chris Evans and Anna Faris stripped off and jumped into the harbour, the phone rang with a shrill noise and Amanda reached out to grab it from the coffee table.

'Hello, hey, Mum. How are you?' she said cheerfully through snorts, putting the phone on speaker so they could all hear.

'Are you girls free to come over?' Her voice was low and shaky.

Amanda shot up to her feet, her sisters following suit. This was far from their mum's usual cheery hello. She always sounded so full of life, checking in on them when they were together. It made her happy knowing her girls were safe under one roof. She loved hearing them laughing with each other. But something was off and it unnerved Sabrina. The wave of anxiety that washed over her meant there was no time for questions.

'We'll be there as soon as we can, Mum,' said Amanda.

'Love you,' they said in unison.

Chapter 4

Grandpa's Pastina

Ingredients:

Orzo pasta, or any baby pasta
(Judge amount based on how many people you are
cooking for)
Celery
Onions
Peeled fresh tomatoes
Dialbrodo (Or any vegetable stock/broth, though this is the best)
Pepper
Olive oil

What to do:

Bring water to boil in pan. Add a drop of olive oil.

Add the celery, onion, tomato and stock. Let them boil together before
adding the pasta.

Cook the pasta as packet suggests and add pepper to taste.

Louisa often saw the world through a rainbow of colour, always seeing the light in each day. Now as she raced through the front door of their grandparents' house, a coldness coursed through her bones causing all colours to vanish. Her world appeared dark and fear overcame her. It was as though everything had come to a crashing halt.

'Mum, what's wrong?' Louisa said. Fear made her breathing ragged and she was gasping from sprinting.

'It's Grandpa,' Mum said, so faintly Louisa felt as though her heart stopped beating for a second. She buried her head in her hands. She willed her mum to say he was poorly, to tell her that the doctors were on their way and that Grandpa was just having a rough night, but her stomach twisted, and she immediately felt faint. The piercing pain in her chest already told her the words that were coming next, the magnitude of the impact they would have on her life causing her knees to go weak.

She felt her mum's arms wrap round her, followed by her dad and her sisters, who had rushed in behind her. 'He's gone,' Mum continued.

Louisa felt her body go limp, her legs unable to stay strong. She collapsed in a heap on the floor. 'No, no, please, no, Mamma. He's OK, I'll go wake him up – he'll be fine.' Her body shook violently; tears gushed down her cheeks. She was screaming, and she didn't know how to stop. 'He can't be gone, I need to speak to him.' She felt her mum kneel beside her but couldn't bring herself to uncurl from the fetal position in which she lay to look at her. She couldn't control her tears; her jumper sleeves were wet through. 'I'm sorry, Mum, I'm so sorry.'

Silence engulfed the room. Nothing could be heard except harsh intakes of breath and the muffled crying as tears flooded each face.

'What are you saying sorry for, sweetheart? It's OK,' Mum whispered after a few minutes or more.

Her kind voice caused Louisa to inhale a painful breath. 'I'm sorry for not being strong for you. I'm sorry.' She buried her head in her mum's shoulder.

'Oh, sweetheart, it's OK, it's OK, it's hard for us all,' Mum replied, tears escaping her brave brown eyes. Louisa hugged her tight before opening her eyes to see Amanda and Sabrina with their heads tucked in against their dad's shoulders. She loved her family – how they understood each other and how close they were.

'We just saw him this morning, Dad. He was doing fine, he was happy and laughing,' Sabrina stammered, barely audible. Louisa could hear her cries too.

'I know, sweetheart, I know,' Dad replied, sniffling. He gave Sabrina a kiss on the top of her head and wrapped his arms around her.

***

Amanda wanted to make a joke. She wanted to make everyone smile, to make everyone giggle the way Grandpa always did if someone was sad. But as she stood with her head on her dad's shoulder, no jokes or funny comments were coming to her, just an overwhelming sense of grief. Her head was thumping, and her fists were clenched.

She wasn't ready for this. She was ready to prepare the house for Christmas festivities, to make sure the kitchen was fully stocked with all the ingredients she and her grandpa would need for the chestnut pastries. She needed her grandpa to help her, to show her how it was done. She couldn't make them as well as he did yet. She needed to watch him one more time, maybe even two or three to be the master chef that he was.

This wasn't fair. It wasn't time. She let out a cry and ran to the living room. Punching the cushion, she wanted to throw it across the room. She felt her blood pressure rising as her sobs got louder and her fists grew white from clenching them so tight. She looked around the room, the living room she had spent her entire life feeling content and safe in. The cosy room that had hosted afternoons of coffee and biscuits, while listening to Grandpa's anecdotes.

She didn't feel like herself. She wanted to run. She needed to escape from this bad dream. Twisting her head around manically, she searched for Grandpa's smiling face. He would come in any minute and greet her, give her one of his big, comforting hugs and tell her everything was going to be OK. She stood staring at the door, panting, praying.

A few minutes passed before her sisters and Mum and Dad walked in. Her knees buckled, and she fell onto the couch, burying her head in a cushion. She could feel her chest rattling, her heart twisting and turning painfully, like it was trying to escape too, trying to get rid of the hurt that was just too much. Usually Amanda was the strong one – always there with a quick joke or sarcastic comment to keep things light and playful. Now that energy had vanished as tears stung her face.

Minutes passed by as her brain tried to compute all the words that her mum was saying to Sabrina, but her heart was having none of it. She felt utterly hopeless.

'Girls, he was happy. He wasn't in pain,' Mum was saying. Amanda scrunched up her nose, closing her eyes tight. She couldn't stand to hear her mum sobbing. 'My wish was that he would go peacefully in his sleep when the time was right, and I got my wish. He went to lie in bed this evening and when Nanna went up she found him.' The tears tumbled down her mum's soft cheeks and Amanda's heart wished it could take away her mum's pain more than anything in the world.

'That's good, Mamma – you always looked after him so well. I'm glad he didn't suffer,' Amanda heard Louisa say. She could hear the pain in her baby sister's voice and it killed her. Her mum

41

had lost her father, Dad had lost his dear father-in-law, Nanna had lost her soulmate, and she and her sisters had lost one of the best friends they'd ever had. She cried into her cushion as Dad sat down next to her and rubbed her back.

***

'Where's Nanna?' Sabrina asked, looking towards her dad, her face red and blotchy. She wanted to form a plan. She wanted to fix this, make it better. That's how her brain worked. She couldn't stand there and feel hopeless; she had to make sure everyone was OK. Yet, she felt glued to the spot. No plans were forming; no solution came to mind. What could she possibly do to fix this?

Her grandpa was gone, and she couldn't bring him back. The whirlwind of emotions swirling around in her brain had destroyed her organized mind. Logistics had been thrown out the window. How could she bring him back? That's the only plan she wanted to figure out.

'She is sitting upstairs with him now. We wanted to give her a minute to pray by his side. And ...' Dad paused. 'We wanted to tell you first and ask you if you wanted to see him. I'm sorry it's not nice to have walked in here and found out like this but there didn't exactly seem like a perfect moment or time. We wanted to give you the option before he was taken away.'

Sabrina didn't want her grandpa to be taken away. Her breath caught at the thought. She wanted to see his smiling face and hear him talk about what he had learnt from the TV that day. 'I don't want him to go anywhere,' she said, collapsing to the floor, her shoulders bouncing up and down as she sobbed uncontrollably. Mum reached over to her and embraced her, trying to ease the pain.

'I know, honey, I know – you don't have to see him if it's too much. You keep hold of the memory of his smiling, cheeky face,' Mum said, smoothing a hand over Sabrina's hair.

'I'd like to see him, if that's OK?' Louisa said. 'But in a minute.'

Sabrina watched Louisa wrap her arms around herself, not knowing quite what to do or where to look. Her baby sister was brave. She wanted to see her grandpa herself, but she didn't think she had it in her to see him in his current state.

'Whenever you're ready,' Dad replied, taking her in his arms, unable to bear seeing his children look so distraught. 'If you all decide you'd like to, we can go up together.'

***

Amanda couldn't move. Even though she wanted to see her grandpa, she wasn't sure she physically could. Her body felt weak; she felt sick to her stomach. What felt like hours passed by before, one by one, everyone stood up. Amanda watched them. No one was rushing her or forcing her to go, but in her heart she knew she wanted to see him and say goodbye.

It took all that she had within her to pull herself together and stand up. Her legs felt like lead. They were heavy and painful, causing her feet to shuffle across the carpet as she grabbed hold of Louisa's hand. Silent tears were rolling down everyone's cheeks as, hand in hand, they made their way to the stairs.

As the top of the landing came into sight, fear enveloped Amanda. Louisa gripped her hand tighter as they stepped back to let Mum and Dad go first. Amanda entered her grandparents' room. Her eyes grew cloudy as tears prickled her eyelashes when she caught sight of Grandpa lying in his bed. He looked peaceful, like he was sleeping, all wrapped up in his blanket.

Sabrina sat on the edge of the bed next to their nanna, who was sat in her chair by Grandpa's side. Mum and Dad stood each with a hand on Sabrina's shoulders. Amanda couldn't let go of Louisa's hand. Her mind raced with images of Grandpa sitting up, turning to them all and saying hello. She might have been an adult, but in that moment she didn't understand anything. She felt powerless. Why couldn't she wake him?

43

With all the strength she could muster Amanda walked over to Nanna and hugged her tight before walking over to the bed to kiss Grandpa gently on his cold head. She whispered the words: 'Thank you for everything,' while her heart shattered into a million pieces. Her body began trembling as tears erupted from her, loud and aggressively. The pain was too much.

Mum grasped her tightly as Sabrina and Louisa followed suit, kissing Grandpa and stroking his forehead. When they were done, the three girls turned and fled from the room. It was too much seeing their dearest grandpa like this and they wanted to allow for Nanna and Mum to have some time with him too.

Amanda re-entered the cold living room and sat huddled up on the corner of the couch closest to the fireplace. She loved sitting by the fire. It brought with it so much warmth and comfort and memories of Grandpa telling stories as she and her sisters nibbled on Italy's finest cakes. She let the memories play out in her mind, like a highlight reel, for a while.

***

The club was quaint, dark and dingy. Amanda felt it wouldn't go amiss along the colourful San Francisco streets. Her black and gold buckled boots stuck to the floor with every odd step she took. She made her way to the front row and rested her elbows on the stage. When she saw the microphone stand a flurry of butterflies let loose in her stomach.

She looked to the clock. In ten minutes' time her very best friend, whom she hadn't seen in eight months, would be gracing the stage. She couldn't help the smile that spread across her face, making her ears blush. Suddenly feeling hot in her giant teddy bear coat, she unzipped herself and placed her coat between her and the stage edge.

She looked around noticing the small room was now packed and as people edged up closer to her, the hotter it got. Dan would have to forgive her sweaty state when she squeezed him to death after the show. Excitement bubbled in her. She couldn't wait to see him – the man who had shown her around San Francisco and who was now on her home turf. Sabrina had set them up with a few gigs in Europe to test the markets and Amanda thought her sister a genius.

***

'Oh my God, you guys were amazing,' Amanda gushed at Levi, thumping him in the arm as he reached the spot where she was standing, in the now empty hall. He shoved her back softly before pulling her into a bear hug.

'Look at you – you look gorgeous, as always. I'm so glad you could make it,' he said, just about cracking one of her ribs in the process. James and Dylan had appeared next to him by the time he put her down.

'Thanks, Levi. You guys look incredible too. It's so good to see you,' she said, hugging James and Dylan. 'What do you think of home sweet home?' she asked baring her pearly whites and waving her arms around the dimly lit room that housed a bar on one side. The barman had set up drinks for the boys and waved them over.

'Well, we haven't seen too much yet and we're only here for a few days, but it looks pretty good so far,' James replied, leading the way to the bar and the drinks. He picked up the one tall glass of red wine and handed it to Amanda before passing out the beers to the boys. She took her glass gratefully, smiling that the guys had thought to inform the barman of her drink.

'We'd best make the most of the next few days then,' she said. 'I don't care that you are big fancy rock stars now, I'm going to need you all to myself,' she added with a playful grin.

'Sounds good to me,' came a warm raspy voice from behind her. Her grin grew wider and Amanda winked at Levi before turning to face Dan.

'Ooh, aren't the lead singers supposed to be the worst of the pack?

So much ego with being front and centre all the time. Not all places in Manchester are built for such royalty, and boys ...' Amanda cocked her head back to glance at the rest of the band before locking eyes with Dan once more '... do you really think I can take this wild and crazy rock star home to meet my parents?'

She heard Levi, James and Dylan crack up behind her. Dan's eyes twinkled under the low lights. She watched as his lips turned up into a cheeky smirk. He walked towards her with ease and calm, took the wineglass out of her hand and placed it back on the bar. Amanda stood watching his movements, chewing her bottom lip. She was trying not to crack up with laughter like the others, but she felt deliriously happy.

Just as she was about to open her mouth and tease Dan some more, he grabbed her around the waist, wrapping her up in his Versace scent, wet hair and solid frame. Amanda breathed him in. She couldn't put a finger on what it was about this man, but he made her feel safe and like she could be her true self with him. Though she had been speaking to him via social networks since she left San Francisco, being in his presence again felt terribly good.

'All right, all right,' Amanda started, trying to push herself out of Dan's strong grip, 'always trying to be centre of attention.' She smirked, then turned to pick up her wineglass and take a sip. 'It's nice to see you.' She looked at Dan, who hadn't taken his eyes off her.

'Baby girl, it's a lot more than "nice" to see you,' he said, giving her his slow smile and collecting his own beer from the bar.

Dylan and James were now chatting amongst themselves. Levi, Amanda noticed, still had an eye trained on Dan, while also keeping up with what the others were discussing. She chuckled to herself how these boys knew each other like the backs of their hands. Dan was always watching over Levi, Levi always watching over Dan. They had that protective bond that came with being best friends since the age of three. They knew what was going on in each other's lives, always. Levi had let Amanda in, but she was conscious of not *stepping on his toes when it came to Dan. He was Levi's best friend first and foremost.*

'You are right – it's pretty fantastic to see you,' she said, taking another sip of her wine and falling into conversation with Dan seamlessly, chatting about everything and nothing.

***

Amanda didn't know why she felt nervous, but the palms of her hands were sweaty, and she had to blink back the dizziness as she looked at Dan and then turned the handle on her nanna and grandpa's front door. Her family knew all about Dan. She had told them about him when she returned from San Francisco and they had occasionally popped on to Skype and waved a cheery hello to him, so it wasn't like they were all complete strangers.

And really, it wasn't a huge deal for them to like him. He was simply a friend, and with him living halfway across the world, it wasn't like they had to see him all the time or put up with him and Amanda's wild and crazy antics. She wasn't a teenager any more either. Yet, her pulse was thumping rather loudly at being mere moments away from Grandpa meeting Dan in person.

The chatter in the living room drew closer but once Dan and Amanda came into view, the voices hushed. Louisa's jaw dropped at the sight of him, which caused Amanda to laugh and her shoulders to drop slightly. Mum jumped up to greet him and instantly enveloped Dan in a hug. Dad stood tall, reaching out a hand in a very British hello.

Watching Nanna struggle to get up as fast as everyone else, Dan stepped over to her chair, leant down to her and gave a her a big hug and a kiss on the forehead while uttering the words 'Ciao, bella.' By this time Grandpa was standing and as Dan straightened up, both men came face to face. Grandpa's eyes sparkled bright blue and his cheeks dimpled with a smile. They both stuck out a hand before stepping forward and embracing each other in a hug.

Amanda watched in awe before scooping up a biscotti from the table and plonking herself down on Nanna's armrest, as she allowed complete happiness to wash over her.

Three hours later, she was walking with Dan back to her house. It was a fair walk from her grandparents' house to her own but certainly doable. And this evening the fresh air was welcome. As Amanda breathed it in, she felt the pain of previous heartbreak lifting. There had been no tension and no awkwardness in Dan visiting her family. There had been no uneasy silences, no uninterested pauses, no yawning as Grandpa asked question after question or rattled off joke after joke. There had been none of that. In its place had been a natural stream of conversation, merry laughter and Amanda wasn't entirely sure who had asked more questions: Grandpa or Dan.

'Well, you've ruined me,' she said to Dan, as they walked side by side down the cobbled street.

'How so?' Dan questioned, giving her a sideways glance. Amanda could see a hint of a smile playing at his lips, as they passed under a streetlamp.

'Well, my next boyfriend is going to have to be Superman, like actually Superman,' she said then paused, looking back up to Dan, who she noticed was now full-on smiling. 'Why are you smiling? Are you about to tell me you are in fact Superman? Great, there's no hope for me now then. I mean, Batman is no match for Superman. I guess I would be fine with Captain America. You couldn't tell Sabrina and Louisa though – they have dibs on Chris Evans.'

She was aware she had started to ramble, but it felt good to be able to talk with no filter. In fact, it felt amazing. Tonight, had been a dream. After her last boyfriend, and his not so embracing attitude towards her family, tonight had felt truly special. Granted Dan was not her boyfriend but watching him with her family made her realize what she wanted, and she suddenly felt more confident in not settling for less.

'I'm pretty sure Superman can't just go around telling people

he's Superman, baby girl,' Dan said, winking at her as they made their way to her front door.

Amanda searched his eyes before rummaging around her bag in search of her keys. 'Oh, my goodness, you are Superman – I knew it,' she muttered under her breath, making Dan laugh. They stepped inside, and Amanda immediately busied herself in the kitchen turning on the kettle, as Dan took off his shoes and wandered over to the CD player. 'Well, Superman, if you could be so kind, next time you bump into Thor or Captain America can you put in a good word for me? I know you're all on opposite teams but Batman does nothing for me and God of Thunder sounds incredibly manly,' she shouted from the kitchen.

'I'll see what I can do,' Dan said, as she joined him in the living room with a tray of tea and more biscuits, this time a classic British selection. There was no beating Italian cookies and cakes, but Amanda felt Dan needed the full British experience while he was in England too. He couldn't possibly leave without having tried a custard cream or jammie dodger. 'Grandpa is rather brilliant,' Dan said, as he reached for a blanket and draped it over Amanda's feet that were curled up close to his thighs.

Amanda took a sip of tea and wriggled her toes in thank you. 'I think so too,' she replied, 'and I think Levi might have to be careful. It looked like Grandpa might want to steal his best friend.' She laughed.

'I don't think Levi would mind – he could probably do with a break from me every once in a while.' Dan shrugged, picking up his own cup of tea. Amanda watched him closely, taking in his floppy hair and broad chest. He definitely fit the Superman build.

'Is that another one of Superman's magical powers? That he can impress and fit in with any family seamlessly?' Amanda asked, her tone a little less playful now and more serious.

'I don't think Superman would need to rely on magic when the family is so warm and inviting and feels like his own. There's no need to put on airs and try to impress when everyone is able to

49

relax and be themselves,' Dan said, his voice soothing and now, too, more serious, having noted Amanda's need to talk and get her thoughts out.

'See, I want that, Dan. I want a boyfriend who can do all that you just did. Why is that so difficult to come by? It was like pulling teeth with Jason. He barely said a word to Grandpa, couldn't eat a biscotti if his life depended on it, just to see Nanna happy – no, he couldn't do any of it, couldn't deal with the language barrier. It bored him.' She was fiddling with the blanket now, flicking dustings of crumbs onto the carpet.

'Hey, baby girl, it's OK. Some men don't realize a good thing when it's in front of them. They're too wrapped up in themselves to see what's before their eyes. Your grandpa is a wealth of knowledge. Talking to him is fascinating. Your dad is a role model for any man and your nanna and mum are angels. Louisa too, she's beautiful,' Dan said, leaning forward and tousling her hair. 'And Jason was a jerk – it's not your fault. These are simply things we experience in order to understand ourselves better, to know what we want and what we don't want. They help build our character. Look at how much you have grown since you broke up.'

Amanda finished her last sip of tea, allowing herself time to accept Dan's words. 'You're right, as always,' she said, snuggling further down into the blanket and resting her legs across Dan's. 'It's just sometimes so hard to fathom that people can be so thoughtless and rude, but that's my mistake and I've moved on.'

'It's not necessarily a mistake. We need those moments where our passions lead us down uncharted paths. It's good for the soul to follow our wild side every now and again. Sometimes it can lead to beautiful things; other times not so much. You should not be scared to do so,' Dan said. Amanda noticed he was uncharacteristically staring into his mug and not at her when he spoke.

'I take it someone's followed their wild side on more than one occasion?' she asked with a hint of playfulness back in her tone, yet Dan didn't look up. Amanda's brow furrowed. 'Or, someone has been too scared to follow his passion?' she questioned, a little unsure of herself. It wasn't like Dan to be scared. She watched as he quietly placed his mug on the table and picked up a jammie dodger.

'Bit of an odd name for a biscuit huh?' he replied, with a wink, before taking a bite. 'It's pretty good though,' he added. Amanda felt a little taken aback by Dan's lack of communication. They didn't keep secrets; they told each other everything, or at least that's what she thought, but Dan feared something, and he clearly didn't want to open up about what it was.

However, Amanda knew all too well that asking questions wouldn't help. He would come to her when he wanted, and she would be there for him, like he always was for her. Wrapped up in her cosy blanket and the tea having made her body nice and warm, she decided to change the subject, knowing Dan would appreciate it.

'So, what did you and Grandpa get to talking about?' Amanda queried, unable to stop herself. 'Don't think I didn't notice you disappear off into the garden for a good thirty minutes.' She nudged Dan's thigh with her toes.

'Ah, I see, you can't bear to be without me for more than ten minutes, can you?' Dan said, as he casually brushed a hand through his hair and leant back into the settee. Amanda simply stuck her tongue out in jest, coming up with nothing to argue the fact. 'That's for me to know and for you to find out,' Dan finished, as he surveyed the plate of biscuits. This time he chose a chocolate bourbon, which made Amanda smile – that was her favourite.

'What are we? Five?' She chuckled, helping herself to another chocolate bourbon. As she took a bite, Dan tickled her feet, causing her to shoot up on the settee, waving her hands frantically to get him to stop. Her bourbon biscuit was sent flying across the room. 'Dan,' she yelled, 'don't do that,' but Dan didn't seem to hear her. Her usually sophisticated friend had turned into a five-year-old in a matter of minutes and she was no match for his thick legs and strong arms.

51

Amanda's mind had drifted back to the day Dan had met Grandpa. It had been perfect. Seeing Dan and her grandpa get on and have their own little bromance had melted her heart. She hadn't been able to put a finger on it at the time but looking back she understood that those small moments with Dan, those faint signs of butterflies in her stomach, they had led to the unusual feelings she was currently having for Dan. But she buried them deep as the cold made her shiver. The fireplace was void of any roaring fire. No one had put it on this evening: that was Grandpa's job. In its place was just a miserable pile of black and dusty coal.

Her lips wobbled as her ears pricked up to the noises around her. She wasn't quite certain how long she had been staring into the cold empty coals, but the stories it evoked were getting too much. Dan was supposed to see Grandpa again. Amanda took in a ragged breath.

She had heard Mum and Louisa go out for a walk a little while ago. Mum had said she needed the fresh air and Louisa couldn't stand being in the house without Grandpa. Dad, Nanna and Sabrina were in the kitchen. She could hear them faintly, chatting over cups of coffee. With wobbling legs, she stood up taking the couch throw with her, in search of the phone. She didn't have to search long as she found it on the table in the hallway, where Mum had been when she broke the news.

Picking it up she sat at the bottom of the stairs and wrapped the blanket round her legs while she leant against the wall. She glared at the phone for a second, her fingers trembling. The thought of breaking Dan's heart with this news made her feel queasy, but he needed to know, and she needed him. She needed her best friend, her best friend who would know exactly what to say and do to make the world complete again. Though it was that needing him that over the past few months had started to scare her silly, she dialled Dan's number.

After four rings, he answered, drums crashing in the background.

'What's up, baby girl? It's been a while.' The all too familiar raspy voice enveloped Amanda with warmth – a warmth that made the tears fall hard and heavy once again.

'Amanda, Amanda, what's wrong?' Dan's usually calm voice was now filled with concern. It pained Amanda, as she encouraged the words to come out of her mouth. She didn't want him to worry about her. 'You have to tell me what's wrong. Are you OK?' She heard him turn to the others and yell at them to stop all the noise. Dan didn't yell.

'Dan, Dan, he's gone,' she whispered into the phone, the tears still streaming, making her cough with their salty taste. She tugged at the blanket. The drums went quiet. She knew Dan must be busy with rehearsal, but he stayed with her. Amanda clutched the phone tight to her ear. Neither of them spoke for a few minutes, but they didn't need to. Dan let her grieve, not rushing her to speak or answer questions. He simply waited. He would always wait.

'It doesn't seem real,' Amanda said, her words cracking as she finally spoke.

'Oh sweetheart, I'm sorry. I'm so sorry,' Dan said. He was sniffling; he was crying too but trying to be strong for her. He was doing a better job of it than she had done for her mum and sisters. 'I will be there in two days, OK?'

Amanda was quiet, trying her best to calm her breathing and listen to Dan's words. Once they registered, she surprised herself by laughing through her sobs. She sat up, uncurling her back. 'Don't be daft – you're busy. Sabrina was telling me you guys have so much to do before the album releases.'

'You're the one being daft if you think I'm going to stay away,' Dan said, a little of his calmness back in check.

'Dan, it's OK. Really. I imagine it will only be a couple of days before we head to Italy, so it's OK, really it is.' Mum and the girls had talked about what would happen when either *nonni* passed, just to be prepared. Right now, Amanda felt as though she was far from prepared. Their *nonni* wanted to go back to Italy and they had all agreed. It would be a busy few days, but Amanda would see the plan through and make sure her grandpa got his wish.

Though hearing Dan's voice had lightened her heavy heart somewhat, him being next to her was what she needed most, but she couldn't allow that. He was busy. She couldn't cry on his shoulder day after day when he had a band to worry about and his own family to think about. It wasn't fair.

'Hey,' Dan whispered softly, 'be with your family now, baby girl. Go and sit with Nanna and laugh, just laugh and fill that house with memories of your grandpa. I know it will be hard but his memory lives through you now. He's still there – you know he's still there. You know how stubborn he is. He won't ever leave you and I will be with you soon.' Dan's words caused Amanda to chuckle again. He was right, of course. Dan was always right. 'And if you need me you call me, day or night; you just call me, OK?'

'How are you always right?' Amanda replied. Her heart rate quickened as Dan's gentle laugh filled the line. She didn't want him to go but she needed to be with her family; she needed to be strong for them. 'I'll talk to you soon, OK? And thank you, Dan, thank you.'

'Love you, baby girl.'

***

The heavens had opened as Louisa frantically grabbed at her portfolio of designs, trying to keep it under the umbrella that was doing its utmost to escape her firm grip. A car whizzed past grazing the puddles that lined the pavement. She let out a sigh of relief. She needed to make the next bus before the weather grew worse. She quickened her pace as a strong gust of wind sent her umbrella twirling through the air. In the very same moment, a car flew past with no concern for pedestrians and sent a wave of water over her, soaking her and her precious portfolio through. It was just her luck today.

By the time she walked through the door of her student accommodation, Louisa was drenched, her work ruined and her heart heavy. Throwing her dripping shoes and sodden bags to the side she went in search of food. She was starved. The fridge bore nothing, and her stomach grumbled with disapproval. Grabbing the only thing she could find, a banana, she made her way to the couch and sunk into it, just as her phone beeped with a text.

'Grandpa just wanted to say hello and see how your exam went today? Love Mum.' Louisa read the text and promptly burst into tears. How could she let Grandpa down? The exam had been awful. She had messed everything up. She was behind on coursework and was coming up empty on inspiration. This wasn't the life she had envisioned when she thought about moving to London.

When starting up her course in fashion at London College of Fashion at King's Cross, she had dreamed big. She had chosen London because she wanted to immerse herself in the fashion industry and London offered it all. Not only was the course fantastic but the fashion scene in London was incredible as well. From bloggers, to agencies, to fashion week, the opportunities were endless.

But here she was six months later, struggling to meet the demands of the course and missing home terribly. She placed the banana on the coffee table, suddenly not feeling very hungry. Glancing at her phone, she noticed she had a bunch of notifications. Scrolling through absent-mindedly she paused on her sister Sabrina's latest Instagram photo. She wore a gorgeous sleek black skater dress and her barely there make-up made her look like an immaculate doll.

Louisa hated the tug of jealousy that she felt. Sabrina had it all and she hadn't even been able to score one fashion event or get one A since she'd been in London. Furthermore, she had failed miserably in keeping to her word and visiting home, and it was only two hours *away. Fiddling with her wet hair with one hand and giving her sister's picture a like with the other, she took a deep breath in and went in search of her suitcases.*

***

Louisa had been there with Grandpa when the coroner came to take him away. She had stood motionless, unable to speak, unable to move. Her mind was grateful that he hadn't suffered and that he had been able to go the way he did. At ninety-six she couldn't be selfish and complain that she hadn't had enough time with him. Yet her heart argued that she could complain. It wanted to scream to the heavens; it wanted to bring her grandpa back. Her heart wasn't as selfless as her brain. She wanted more time. Though she saw her grandpa every day, it still hadn't been enough.

After she collapsed for the second time against the wall, Mum suggested that they get some air. They were now both wrapped up in Grandpa's heavy outdoor coats, the ones he sometimes used to do the gardening in when it was icy out. They were taking a walk around the block.

The sky was a rich, inky black, the air causing her warm skin to cool at its icy touch. As the wind whipped around her face, Louisa began to feel her mind ease. She could see the stars twinkling above and naturally looked out for the brightest one.

'He's not gone far.' Mum spoke softly, her gaze too on the brightest gold star above. 'Not really. We can talk to him every day.'

'You know I will, Mum,' Louisa said, with pause. 'Mum? Do you think he was proud of me? I mean, I didn't finish uni and he didn't get to see me have a proper job like Amanda and Sabrina. Do you think he was disappointed in me?' Small sobs seeped out as Louisa spoke.

Mum stopped walking and turned to face her youngest daughter. 'Oh, sweetheart, of course he was proud of you. Don't you ever think otherwise. He adored you and loved that you gave London a go. He was proud of you for trying it and for taking a chance. And, honey, you know he was elated when you came back. My goodness, he wouldn't have said it for fear of stopping you going after your dreams, but having you back at home made him happier than any degree you could have gotten. Selfish or not, sweetheart, he loved getting to spend time with you each day. He couldn't have been prouder of the women you all grew to be. The love you have for him and the family – oh he never stopped talking about you.'

Louisa's eyes were blurry, tears filling up at an alarming speed, a mixture of happy tears flowing with the sad ones. She reached her arms around her mum's neck and hugged her tight, words having escaped her. She thought about all the designs she and her grandpa had come up with and all his favourites and wondered what on earth she was supposed to do without her biggest muse. The tears wouldn't stop.

Mum rubbed her back before stepping back and looking Louisa straight in the eyes. 'Sweetheart, he treasured every moment you spent together and loved being a part of your life. Every day I'd hear about a sketch you had drawn and even when you weren't there he was making notes of some design or clothing someone wore on TV that he thought you might like. Honey, you are amazing, and he knew that and believed it with all he had.' She paused, rubbing Louisa's arms. 'Come on, let's get back inside – it's getting a bit nippy,' Mum added, giving Louisa a tight squeeze. She stayed like that for a few moments before leading the way back to the house.

Louisa rested her head on her mum's shoulder as they walked back towards the house. The roads were peaceful now. Only a few cars raced by while they walked. The fresh air was bringing back feeling to Louisa's numb bones. With every step came a stab of pain. Tears came and went as she thought happy thoughts in between the sad ones. She thought about how she needed to get her designs out into the world and make her grandpa proud and she thought about his voice, his smile and his hugs and how much she needed them. The mixture of emotions was torture. They walked back into the house and found Amanda sitting on the stairs.

'Hey,' Amanda said, standing to greet them. Louisa noticed she looked a little pale and her smile was forced. 'Fancy helping me in the kitchen?' she asked Louisa.

Louisa appreciated her sister's efforts and smiled broadly, knowing what her sister was thinking. 'Sure, I think it's what everyone needs right now,' Louisa replied, taking off Grandpa's jacket and abandoning her thoughts for a little while. She needed the break.

Sabrina and Nanna were huddled around the kitchen table, staring into their coffee mugs, while their dad was keeping busy refilling the kettle. Louisa walked over to their dad and took over making coffee.

'Dad, do you want to take Mum and Nanna into the living room and get the fire on?' she asked, gently taking the kettle from his shaking hands.

'Course I can, sweetheart, thank you,' he replied, kissing her forehead.

Louisa was used to her grandparents' house being full of warmth, love and laughter, as it had been just yesterday. She took a deep breath, with no energy left for any more tears, and knew what Grandpa would do in this situation to make everything a little better. She had to keep him with her and she knew exactly what that meant. It seemed so did Amanda.

Louisa grabbed Sabrina by the hand and pulled her to her feet. She passed her the chopping board and a tomato and hugged her tight. Giving Sabrina a task would help distract her and keep her busy. She then set about collecting a pan and joining Amanda in getting together all the other ingredients they needed to make her favourite *pastina*. Grandpa had fed this to her way before she ever got her first tooth. It was comfort food at its finest.

Side by side the girls chopped tomatoes and celery, boiled the water and added the seasonings, before sprinkling in handfuls of the tiny pasta to the water to let it cook. In no time, the simple dish was ready. Louisa gathered up bowls, while Amanda added a plate of toast to the tray and Sabrina carried the coffee into the living room.

Louisa sat cross-legged by the coffee table, placing her bowl of steaming hot *pastina* in front of her. For a few moments, no one spoke. She stared into the steam, willing her moments of strength she had had in the kitchen to continue. She looked around the room and as the aroma of fresh celery, cherry tomatoes and Dialbrodo filled the room, Louisa could see grateful smiles form on everyone's faces.

It was too much. Her strength vanished as pools of tears gathered in her eyes. His face was missing – his kind, soft, always grateful face was missing from the bunch. She curled her toes underneath her and with shaking hands picked up her spoon. She didn't want her nanna to see her tears. She wanted to be strong for everyone.

She closed her eyes, sniffed and placed a spoonful of the baby pasta in her mouth. The buttery flavour and slight crunch of the celery satisfied her taste buds. A small smile appeared on her face as she recalled how her grandpa had made her *pastina* a million times, probably, over the years. It was still her favourite.

She looked up to see colour was rising back into her nanna's cheeks and Dad was filling up Mum's bowl with some more soup. The fireplace now boasted golden flames that were keeping them all nice and toasty, but not too toasty, of course; heeding Grandpa's words, they were careful not to roast.

Chapter 5

Nanna's Cocoa Biscuits

Ingredients (Really need to make note of measurements, but Nanna makes it look so easy):

Flour (A few tablespoons?)
Cocoa powder (Depends how chocolatey you want them?)
Caster sugar
Ground almonds (A whole bag?)
Cinnamon
Bicarbonate of soda
Egg
Honey
Water

What to do:

Pre-heat the oven to 170.

Combine all dry ingredients in a bowl or on a tray like Grandpa does.

Make a well in the middle and add the egg, honey and a few spoons of water.

Knead until a soft dough forms. Add more flour if needed.

Roll out and cut into circle shapes.

Bake for 15 minutes. Check them. You will know when they are done.

Naples International Airport hadn't changed a bit from how Amanda remembered it, though compared to Manchester Airport at five-thirty this morning and Italy during the summer season, today it was quaint and peaceful. There wasn't a flurry of people around, just two families of four and a few women who looked as though they had come straight from a festival. Amanda envied their studded boots and sultry nude lipstick. She adored Italian fashion, though she was not as trendy, up to date or as bold as Louisa, even on an off-day Amanda would be able to rival the stunning bohemian outfits these women wore; chequered trousers, teamed with a loose-fitting flowing blouse or oversized knit, it was very simple and very her.

Her current state, however, was extremely unlike her and on a par with her sister's favourite pyjama outfits. She had not been able to muster the effort to put together her usual chic ensemble since Grandpa passed and so she wore an oversized tracksuit jacket with a pair of baggy grey pants that she had tucked into shoes that looked like UGGs but were definitely not UGGS – not at that price tag. She smiled at the gorgeous Italian women and felt a tiny spark ignite inside her. She took this to mean that her grandpa was gently reminding her to be the feisty, confident Amanda he so loved. 'In due time, Grandpa,' she whispered to herself.

The noisy car horns were a sharp contrast to the tranquillity inside the airport, but as they stepped outside the soft scented breeze of Italy instantly engulfed Amanda with a sense of home. By the toothy grins appearing on both her sisters' faces, she knew they felt it too. They spotted their taxi driver and headed in his direction, smoothly, no rolling over people's toes with suitcases or being bumped into by rushing travellers.

Amanda helped her nanna into the black seven-seater SUV and pulled the strap gently, making sure it was nestled comfortably across her chest, before jumping in next to her. She placed her handbag at her feet and watched out the back window to see if her dad and Louisa needed any more help with the bags. It looked like they were doing a fine job aiding the taxi driver with the game of Tetris their suitcases had come to be. Satisfied that they could handle it, she turned back around and wriggled to make herself comfortable in her seat.

Mum passed around the travel sickness tablets and a bottle of water and Amanda gratefully accepted. It had been a while since they had done this drive, but they remembered it all too well.

'Keep those out for your sister,' Mum said, as she passed two more tablets to Sabrina.

Amanda washed down her own with a big gulp of water, before passing the bottle to her nanna and encouraging her to take some. The car boot slammed shut and Louisa and Dad took their seats in the taxi. Amanda looked around to see everyone focused on the road ahead, their brows crinkled. Simultaneously they all took a deep breath as the car pulled away from the kerb. Closing her own eyes, she prayed for a safe journey and for no one to get sick, before distracting herself by asking her nanna a question.

'Nanna, what was your favourite childhood Christmas dish?' she asked, placing a hand on her nanna's.

'Eh, Amanda, people say Italy is magic but the Amalfi Coast, Orzoro, my home, it is like a paradise. At Christmas the food is even better, out of this world.' A dreamy look appeared on Nanna's face and a smile grew as memories filled her head. 'Two days before Christmas, we begin making the cakes. *Zeppole*, *panzerotti*, the chestnut pastries Grandpa made, all kinds, all beautiful.' She kissed her fingers, like you see the Italians do in the movies. Grandpa and Nanna did this all the time when expressing the quality and unparalleled richness of Italian food.

'The mamma and papa and the *bambini* put out the nativity – oooh, my girls, the nativity is like nothing you've ever seen before. Eh, it's magnificent. Of course the *alberi* you see everywhere, you'll see.' Amanda felt the butterflies in her stomach as the car rolled down the hills. In an hour or so they would be in a place that filled their hearts with so much joy. A place that made her feel so lucky to have a connection to. She wanted to hear every story, every memory that Nanna could share and had to remember to stay strong for her. 'The laughter around Christmas time can be heard across the village, ooh yes. Everyone is happy, happy,' Nanna continued.

'It sure does sound like paradise, Nanna,' Amanda said, resting her head on her nanna's shoulder. 'I'm so excited we get to see it at this time of year. I want to see and do all the things Grandpa would have been doing,' Amanda noted. Listening to her nanna's words, she couldn't help but think of how the Christmas foods her nanna spoke of would be perfect for her blog. Re-creating such special stories and sharing such precious memories was where her passion lay, but for now, her blog would have to wait. She was here in Italy for her family and her grandpa and social media was not important. Raising her head from her nanna's shoulder, Amanda looked out the window and got lost in the views that crept up on them.

***

The streets of Napoli were less manic this morning compared to the summer season. During the height of the holidays there would be bumper-to-bumper traffic, Vespas weaving in and out between cars and people honking their horns at every turn. Now though, in early December, a few cars dotted the roads.

Amanda thought about informing the taxi driver of this change. He was still driving as though a victory at Silverstone depended on it. There were simply no rules in Italy when it came to driving. If this man wanted to drive in the middle of two lanes, then it seemed no one could stop him. Amanda resigned herself to putting her trust in the driver, telling herself that he knew the roads better than she did and that he would get them to their destination safely. She instead chose to focus on the views that lay before her and the stories her nanna told.

It was hard to decide which window to look out of. To the left, a vast plane of land with nothing but worn apartment blocks and rusty metal railings that popped up in between a mixture of low and high stone walls and remnants of shops and olive trees went as far as the eye could see. Among the run-down landscape, amidst the fog that rested on the skyline where the sky and sea met, lay Mount Vesuvius. An intimidating gloomy formation that threatened all who were brave enough to inhabit its surroundings.

To the right, looking past her nanna and Sabrina, the window played host to billboards and trees upon trees upon trees. Off in the distance, if Amanda squinted, she could make out Capri, nestled in the middle of the shimmering sea.

Amanda closed her eyes and let out a light breath. In the pit of her stomach she was getting that familiar fuzzy feeling, that sense of home she always got when she came to Italy. Now, though, it was mixed with a heavy thudding in her heart. She rested her elbow on the shallow window ledge on the door of the car and laid her head in her hand. Being in Italy was going to be hard without her grandpa. It felt wrong being here without him. Every memory she had of enjoying this magical place included him. She missed him.

The roads were beginning to narrow now. The distance

between the car, the low branches and the brick walls were getting terrifyingly thinner and people were popping up under canopies and in doorways, braving the cold for a cigarette. The car climbed higher up the mountain and as far as the eye could see olive trees filled every garden. The mountainside was littered with them.

As they drove through the town of Agerola, colourful cars lined the streets. Amanda loved these tiny towns. They displayed so much character, each unique and a world unto themselves. They had a mystery about them now, at this time of year when they were still and peaceful, devoid of bustling tourists. The shops were dormant, all the lights were off and darkness engulfed the windows.

Amanda could make out the shadows of buckets and spades in one tiny window, hanging on pegs waiting for the enthusiastic children in the New Year. She looked to her sister, Sabrina, and offered a smile. Her sister smiled back. Their nanna glanced at each of them with a smile of her own. Amanda then turned to the back seat to look at her dad and Louisa and noticed her dad was paler than usual. British folk weren't known for their glorious tans, but he was currently passing for Casper's twin.

'Are you all right back there, Dad?' Amanda asked.

'Keep looking forward, dear,' Mum shouted from the front.

'Here,' Amanda said, passing over a bottle of water. 'Try closing your eyes, Dad, and keep your head straight,' she added, as Louisa took his hand in hers. The girls all felt sympathy for Dad. Some of their early trips to Orzoro as children had not been pretty and after one or two messy accidents Mum had learnt to stock up on Wet-Naps and plastic bags whenever they made this trip.

The roads began to descend, winding down into the depths of the mountain. Amanda gasped noticing a speckle of Christmas trees twinkling from a few of the tiny windows and hotel lobbies. The most dazzling decorations appeared hanging from the street-lights and the views of the sea became crystal clear as the roads dropped and staggered.

'Arrrgh,' Mum moaned expressively, tucking her knees to her chest and closing her eyes. Amanda looked up and spotted the reason for her sudden outburst. A bus was coming at them in the opposite direction. Everyone let out a collective gasp. Amanda wondered how on earth both the bus and their taxi were supposed to fit side by side on the cliff-top. Apparently that thought hadn't crossed the taxi driver's mind as he just kept gunning along.

As the bus got closer, Amanda pictured the Knight Bus in *Harry Potter* and prayed it were a real thing, as right now the edge of the cliff was looming, and she was certain the little taxi didn't stand a chance going up against the larger bus.

'Arrgh, oh God,' Sabrina shouted, as the taxi whizzed past the bus, the driver not breaking a sweat. 'Are we OK? Did we make it?' she asked panting ever so slightly.

Amanda untucked her head from between her knees, opening her eyes slowly. 'I think so, yes,' she stammered. 'Yes, I think we did.' She could have sworn she saw the taxi driver smirk.

***

'We're here,' Mum announced. Amanda had been lost in a trance watching the tiny specks that faintly resembled fishing boats, from this high up, bobbing in the water. She had been completely taken in by the splendid view and hadn't felt the car come to a stop.

'I forgot how terrifying that car journey is,' Sabrina said stepping out of the SUV and looking over at her mum, eyebrows raised. Amanda noticed her shivering slightly, unlike herself. Sabrina was wearing one of her trademark floaty dresses. Even with a teddy coat over the top it was not appropriate for the weather conditions in Italy, in early December.

Before Amanda could say anything, Mum laughed and nodded. 'It's not for the faint-hearted.'

'Oh, my gosh, I thought we were going to drive off the edge

of the cliff back there. You'd think they would have made these roads wider by now. Nanna, *mamma mia*.' Louisa jumped out of the taxi with boundless energy, making her way over to help Dad with the bags. Everyone looked at her and laughed. Even Nanna couldn't hold back a grin. The Italian air seemed to be just what the doctor ordered.

'You're way too sprightly for someone who's just experienced the road of one thousand turns,' Dad said with a chuckle and one hand cradling his queasy stomach. 'Right, do we have everything?' he asked, patting down his jacket and checking the boot one last time, to a chorus of yeses. He thanked the taxi driver and joined the others.

Amanda threw her backpack onto her back and pulled her fluffy hoodie tighter around her neck before taking hold of Nanna's arm and guiding her away from the taxi. Mum walked behind with the rough noise of rolling suitcases beginning to fill the once peaceful town, as Mum, Dad and the other girls dragged the heavy bags along the cobbly path.

'You hold on to Amanda, Mamma. OK? I'll be right behind you,' Mum told Nanna as they reached the staircase of a hundred or so jagged, concrete steps that would take them up to Nanna's home. The steps were mildly steep, sprouts of weeds peeking out of the creases where one step met the other. Every ten steps or so they were met with a white or brown door to the left of them, that led to other people's homes, some of whom had been friends of Nanna's since she was a *bambina*.

'We got this – you ready?' Amanda said, noticing Nanna's eyes were starting to water. It was rather windy and cold out, but her heart tugged. She knew the tears forming in her nanna's crystal blue eyes were from sadness and not the cold. 'It's OK, Nanna, you take your time. I'm here,' Amanda added.

She could recall countless stories Nanna had told her growing up. As a child, Nanna and her sisters and brothers would race up and down these stairs playing games. Other times they would be so eager to see their papa when he came home from work, they would race to the bottom to welcome him. Or every other day when her mamma went shopping and needed help with the bags, they would rush to help her, giddy about the treats that awaited them.

Amanda herself remembered the summers she would jog up and down them, counting as she went. Over a hundred steps to get to the top. It was perfect for a morning workout or stroll to clear your head. But it had been twenty years since Nanna had been home, twenty years since she had climbed these steps. Amanda wanted her to take her time and savour the moment and the memories.

She watched her nanna closely as they began climbing. Amanda felt so much love in her heart, it almost hurt. She was grateful beyond belief that she was getting to experience this with her nanna and couldn't wait for her to be reunited with her sisters. On the other hand, her ears kept pricking up waiting to hear her grandpa shout out from behind her to pick up the pace. He wasn't one for getting old; he was a big kid at heart and would never have let these steps defeat him.

She tried to push those sad thoughts to the very back of her mind. It would do her no good to have a breakdown in the middle of these steps. Her thighs were already seizing up. She hated to think of what pain her elderly nanna must be in. Bar the watery eyes, Nanna was putting on a brave face. She had to push forward for her family and be strong.

'Eh, Valentina, what's taking you so long?' Speaking of sisters: as they reached halfway, Amanda and the rest of the family looked up following the beautiful Italian accent that sang out from the mountains. Three heads were peering over the balcony, three women waving frantically and yelling. Amanda looked from their faces to her nanna's. Nanna's whole being lit up, her face beaming as the tears fell freely and the roars of laughter most definitely could be heard all across the village.

'I'm not young any more,' Nanna shouted back, throwing her head back with a howl, before continuing to press on with a whole lot more bounce in her step.

'You haven't changed – still beautiful, our sister,' Zia Sofia bellowed. They neared the top of the stairs and the laughter turned to wails and '*mamma mias*' as Nanna's sisters reached out to envelop her in a warm hug the minute her toes touched the pavement. They pinched her face and kissed her cheeks and there wasn't a dry eye to be seen. Amanda turned to help the rest of the family heave the bags up the last few steps and placed them next to the large dirty-white iron front door.

'Valentina, Valentina, you're here,' cried Zia Sofia, Nanna's youngest sister. She was glued to Nanna's side, with her arms wrapped around her, her grip snug.

'We've missed you so much,' Zia Rosa cried. Nanna's eldest sister was shaking a tissue in the air, her watery blue eyes, which matched her younger sister's, were looking Nanna up and down.

Amanda stood back with Sabrina, their arms around their mum. Louisa stood with their dad. Amidst the heartbreaking events of the past week, it felt like a new bud had bloomed: a fresh life and a sign of hope. In the middle of an old balcony, on the moutainside of the Amalfi Coast, this moment was taking place. A reunion of sisters, a celebration of family. It was one of the most beautiful yet heart-wrenching scenes Amanda had ever witnessed. The love and admiration she had for the women before her was incomparable.

To reduce the chance of the floodgates opening Amanda went to busy herself with the bags, playing with the ribbon on one of the carry-ons. She was studying her address label when Nanna waved her arms in their direction, welcoming the family to say their hellos. The crying and '*mamma mias*' started all over again the minute her aunties laid eyes on Mum. Well, really they were Mum's aunties but ever since they were little the girls had always referred to their mum's aunties as their own. It had been more than ten years since Mum, Dad and the girls had visited, so of course they had to be given the once-over to make sure they were eating right and had enough meat on their bones.

'Valentina, she's all grown up,' Zia Emilia, the second eldest sister shouted through tears, gaping at Mum. '*Il mia bambina.*'

Mum was smothered in kisses, checked up and down and squeezed so tight, Amanda couldn't help but chuckle. Her aunties were strong for such small women. Amanda joined in with the welcoming party, cuddling and squeezing her aunties back before Dad ushered them all in out of the cold.

The house smelt exactly like Amanda remembered it: a mix of florals. Her nanna and aunties had always loved flowers and given the occasion there were flowers everywhere and many pictures of Grandpa next to his favourite Saint: Padre Pio. A cool freshness blew through each room. There was no carpet, just tiled floors with giant patterned rugs, yet there was warmth. An elegant old-fashioned perfume tickled Amanda's nostrils and made her feel instantly high and joyful with its powerful scent.

She wandered around looking at all the pictures of her grandpa. He had been a tall and handsome man when he was younger. He had a look of Frank Sinatra or James Dean about him, a look that wouldn't go amiss beaming from your TV screen. Grandpa himself used to say: 'I was a very busy young man,' which would have the girls in hysterics. Amanda didn't doubt him. They would simply laugh and tell him he was cheeky.

The black-and-white photos were truly precious. His smile shone bright from each one and clearly showed his zest for life. You couldn't help but feel inspired when you were around him. Amanda's favourite photos were those of him and Nanna getting married. Right here in their home of Orzoro, down by the water, in front of the famous orange beach hut. They had a square coffee table on the cobbles and a top of it was a small round wedding cake decorated with a smattering of pink flowers of all kinds – nothing fancy, a simple thin sponge sat on a cake stand – as all the family gathered around, mouths open wide, all caught in the middle of laughing.

Amanda loved looking at pictures of her *nonni*. She could get lost in imagining what life was like back then. From what her *nonni* told her, they didn't have it easy. Growing up was an adventure in the mountains.

'That's my favourite too,' Louisa said, appearing at Amanda's side and pointing at their grandparents' wedding picture.

Sabrina joined them too. 'I keep expecting him to walk through the door with a goofy look on his face, like it's all been one big joke,' Sabrina said.

Amanda sighed heavily. 'It wouldn't exactly be the funniest of jokes, but I'd take it over this.' She glanced around the flower-filled room once more, feeling like her bravado could only last so much longer. Italy certainly had an aura about it that made her feel close to her grandpa, but at the same time the ache of his absence weighed on her heart.

'Everyone's making coffee in the kitchen. Would you like some? Ooh and I'm pretty sure I can smell those biscuits we used to have as kids – you know the cocoa ones with the little white stars?' Louisa said, with a tight smile that didn't quite match the false excitement in her voice. Amanda appreciated her attempt at trying to cheer up her big sisters and in turn wanted to be there for Louisa.

'Sounds great, Lou,' she responded, allowing her sisters to lead the way. She struggled to steer her eyes away from the photos, but thinking of Louisa's torn face from moments ago, she took a deep breath and followed after them.

Chapter 6

Italian Coffee (The best coffee)

What to do:

Fill up the filter funnel of the Bialetti with Lavazza.
(Store Lavazza in fridge.)

Add the water to the bottom of the Bialetti, assemble and place on stovetop.

Allow to boil until coffee appears and fills the top.
(It's like magic every time.)

Enjoy in espresso cups (not giant mugs — how much coffee is too much coffee?) with an amaretti or two.

For the past twenty minutes Sabrina had been staring at the door. Her heart was pounding in her chest and she had used about six tissues already to wipe the sweat from her brow. To say she was nervous would have been an understatement. Normally she could keep her cool meeting musicians and acts, as usually she wasn't allowed to say much – she simply did whatever Lydia asked of her.

However, today would be anything but normal. Today was the day that her big sister Amanda's friends were visiting from San Francisco to discuss their demo and possible representation. According to Amanda, Lydia would be stupid not to sign them. San Francisco Beat were four incredibly talented musicians, good-looking to boot, with an undeniable energy and charisma.

But that wasn't what was making Sabrina sweat out of excitement – no, it was the fact that they wanted her. Due to Amanda's influence, and her and lead singer Dan being such close friends, it was Sabrina they wished to be assigned to. When Amanda first mentioned this to Sabrina, Sabrina had laughed. There would be no way in hell Lydia would be enthusiastic about that. Amanda had assured Sabrina to trust her, Lydia would want this band under her label and therefore she believed there was an incredibly high probability that Lydia would meet their request.

The clock ticked annoyingly loudly. Sabrina rose from her chair with thoughts of throwing it out the window, when she heard voices down the corridor. This was it, the moment of truth. She had seen Dan on Skype a few times and had caught a glimpse of the others in photos Amanda had shared from her holiday, but she had yet to speak to them face to face.

Her stomach bubbled in anticipation. Where should she stand? Should she sit back down? No, she was up now, and she would have to stand to greet them anyway. She resigned to half sitting, half leaning on the front of her desk, when the room grew a touch icier. She took a steadying breath in as Lydia sauntered into her office first, making the place feel cramped and cold. It was a sharp contrast to the warmth that came next as Dan entered her tiny quarters.

As Lydia made herself comfortable in Sabrina's chair, Sabrina shook hands with Dan, James and Dylan. They each introduced themselves before the last member entered the room, showing her his back as he closed the door behind him. Sabrina watched the others take a seat on her small couch. Dan chose to rest on the arm, then she averted her eyes, looking back to the door while simultaneously taking a step forward to greet the final piece of the act: drummer Levi. As she did so, Levi turned in to the room, taking a giant stride forward to do the same and meet her. Sabrina stumbled back into her desk as she collided with his large frame, knocking her coffee mug all over her baby pink skater dress and the floor.

Both she and Levi immediately reached for the tissues, muttering under their breaths countless apologies. James and Dylan looked highly amused. Dan was eyeing up Levi in a way Sabrina could not yet read and Lydia looked as though mud had been splattered on her most expensive Dior heels. She had a face like thunder.

'That was my fault, please let me get your dress cleaned for you,' Levi said. His voice was soft and silvery, with a confident and rich tone that made the hairs on the back of Sabrina's neck prickle.

'No, no, please, it was all my fault,' she fussed, automatically placing a hand on Levi's forearm to control the situation and usher him to leave the mess and sit down. 'Please, you sit down – this is no trouble, I'll clean it later,' she added, finally looking up to meet his burning gaze. Heat flooded her cheeks the moment their eyes met. His eyes were like pools of melted chocolate; they had her hypnotized.

'I hope that doesn't stain the carpet or it will have to come out of your next paycheque.' Lydia's shrill laugh was like a pin, piercing Sabrina and Levi's bubble, which they seemed to have created in the middle of the room. She hurriedly looked away from Levi and made to stand by the door. He looked momentarily frozen as he watched her, a soft smile appearing on his face.

He walked over to her and placed a hand on her elbow and pointed towards that last spot on the couch. Sabrina could feel her soul icing over and didn't dare look Lydia's way – she could feel the daggers she was getting. She also didn't want to make any more of a scene than she already had, and so obliged Levi's gentlemanly request.

After the disastrous introduction the meeting had gone as well *as expected. Lydia had taken every possible opportunity to put Sabrina down and she hadn't been subtle about it either.*

'I would like to give you this opportunity to rethink your decision regarding management. As you can see, we have a team of fully qualified staff. I alone have been in this business over twenty years. Should you wish to work with someone more experienced, do not hesitate to speak up. Don't be distracted by young blondes in floaty dresses when you need a woman in a killer suit who knows how to take charge and get you what you want.'

And so forth. The boys had sat and listened politely for a good thirty minutes. Sabrina wasn't quite sure if the wicked witch had put a spell on them and turned them to the dark side. Then ten minutes later, after Sabrina had given them each a printed proposal of what she believed she could do for them and what she thought best for their band, based on the music she had heard, Dan had stood up, thanked Lydia and informed her that they would be delighted if the company would have them, but they were more than confident in their choice of management and that if there was a problem with that they would look elsewhere.

Sabrina had received another dirty look from Lydia before Lydia had succumbed to Dan's knee-buckling raspy voice and intent stare and handed them over to her. Career wise, that had been the best day of Sabrina's life.

***

Jet lag was fighting hard with Sabrina. Throw in the nightmares she had been having since Grandpa had passed and sleep had been next to impossible. Outside on the balcony, the birds were singing their last songs as the sun began to set. The orange hue of the sky cast golden shadows upon the kitchen as Sabrina busied herself with her aunties' espresso pot.

Sabrina adored her aunties' treasures. Just looking at the worn espresso machine lightened her mood. She thought about the millions of coffees this little pot had produced over the years, the conversations that were held while enjoying its contents, the biscotti consumed in perfect accompaniment. Italians sure knew how to take pleasure in the simplest of things. Coffee might not have been the best choice considering her current sleep deprivation, but she needed it to face the task at hand.

Focusing on pouring the rich black liquid into the cute flower-print espresso cup, she willed her worries to leave her be for a few days. The bags under her hazel eyes were more noticeable than ever. Work was draining every bit of energy she had left, and there wasn't much in reserve after recent events. After getting reacquainted with the family and enjoying a fresh bowl of home-made pasta and homemade tomato sauce that afternoon, the whole family had stepped out for a stroll around the village.

Sabrina had kept her eye on the time and with the time difference between Italy and LA had stayed behind to make a phone call. With her coffee in hand she paced the living room for a good fifteen minutes trying to pick up the courage to ring Lydia, her horrible boss.

Unlike her big sister, confidence hadn't always come so naturally to Sabrina. Sure, she was the most laid-back out of the three sisters and rarely cared what people thought, but she had to admit, it mattered what her boss thought of her. Whereas Amanda had a quick wit and could stand up to anyone, Sabrina happened to hate confrontation and tried to avoid it at all costs. Like her signature floaty dresses and pastel colours conveyed, keeping things light and peaceful was what she was all about.

Thinking back to the day that San Francisco Beat had walked into her office and changed her life, she couldn't help laughing, which eased the nerves ever so slightly. She had been a flustered mess back then, but oh how their relationship had progressed. They had helped her build her confidence up around Lydia so much, so she strongly disliked that today's task was proving so difficult.

Amid being there for her family, she had put work thoughts

on the back burner. Normally she had everything under control, planned ahead of time and with time to make a to-do list, but in this circumstance, though she was still efficient, routine had been thrown out the window. She had cancelled her flight back to the States and jumped on the plane to Italy without much thought.

Yes, she had thought of her boys, but she knew they would be more than fine without her. She had already set up a schedule for them for the week she was with her sisters and she had sent over a few new appointments that she had pencilled in the diary for them to attend this week, so they had plenty to keep them occupied. It was her boss who struck the fear of God into her. The phone call had been inevitable and, of course, the professional thing to do, but the thought of speaking to Lydia when her brain was already fried had meant that she had put it off for as long as she deemed only a tad unprofessional.

She had walked past the fireplace some zillion times already in the last five minutes. Her palms were sweaty, her legs like jelly and her only thoughts were of impending doom – not helpful. She repeatedly reassured herself that the wicked witch of LA would understand. Surely anyone would understand that at a time like this one would not be returning to work for a few days, and in Sabrina's case, in another two weeks, since she was now in Italy.

But that hadn't stopped her mind from racing. Work had been beyond hectic over the last few months. San Francisco Beat were about to drop their second album and Sabrina was the one in charge. She had been working tirelessly to get the boys set up with the best gigs in town and to ensure that it was all done the way they wanted it. She had a lot to prove to her boss and the company that this was a band that did not need perfumes or high-end underwear commercials to sell their music. All they needed was some hip bars, a stage and a good crowd and Dan, Levi, James and Dylan would do the rest.

***

Sabrina felt like she had hit the jackpot. Many a night she had walked into her tiny apartment and raised her arms above her head in a sort of victory celebratory dance. She owed Amanda a fabulous Christmas present this year. It had only been a week that she and San Francisco Beat had been working together and already she knew they were the perfect fit. The boys were everything she ever wanted as clients.

They were the epitome of real musicians, real artists, whose passion for what they did ran through their veins. Dan, Levi and Dylan had all known each other since kindergarten, where their love of drawing and music first connected them. Levi had related their initial meeting to Sabrina fondly, explaining that Dan had been impressed by a lion that Dylan had drawn one day during free play and struck up a conversation – nothing too deep, they were only three years old after all and Levi had overheard them talking and had to see the lion for himself.

Dan had been right, as would become a common occurrence – the lion was awesome and from that day on they were inseparable. Music classes saw them sitting next to each other, often going off track and ignoring the teacher's instructions, as they played to the beat of their own drum. A beat that, even at only three going on four, always sounded great and managed to be in sync with each other every single time. Levi swore he saw the teacher look astounded on more than one occasion, even when trying to tell them off.

James joined the creative bunch later in high school and it had felt like they had found their missing piece. They became quite the handful for their teachers, not in a malicious way, more in that they weren't interested in what was going on, albeit except for Dan. Levi had expressed that in hindsight Dan probably would have gotten better grades and become a genius professor or literature legend, like his idol, Jack Kerouac, had the boys not distracted him and practically given him no choice about starting a band and being their lead singer.

But Sabrina was certain Dan had made his choice with one

hundred per cent clarity and loved the band with everything he had, whether Levi knew this or not. It also explained why the band's lyrics were raw, powerful and mesmerizing. Dan definitely had a way with words and there was still time for him to reach literary legend status – not that Sabrina could see Dan vying for a title or label, though she did think it sweet of Levi to think so highly of his best friend.

San Francisco Beat played their first gig a few months after finishing high school. They had written tons of music and a novel's worth of songs, but Levi, Dylan and James hadn't been able to get Dan on a stage. There had been no school parties or basement gigs. Sabrina had found it hard to believe; in fact, her jaw had hit the floor at this piece of information.

Watching Dan perform now was something of a holy experience. Whether he was stood on the spot gripping the mic, giving nothing but his raspy voice, raw and soulful, or walking round the stage engaging with audience members and going off on long monologues about the world and the latest book he had read, he was a born leader. Sabrina just couldn't picture him nervously singing with his eyes closed or turning away from the crowds. It had taken a few years, but Dan had caught on.

Before Amanda entered their lives, they had been playing all over San Francisco. They had been given some offers and opportunities along the way, but nothing fit with what they were after: celebrity status not being on the list. They knew it sounded cliché, but they weren't in it for the money, they simply wanted to write and play and connect with people.

Levi admitted to liking the attention, as did Dylan and James, but as long as that attention came from people digging their sound, they were happy. However, the boys weren't stupid; getting older meant bills and being able to look after your family and they wanted that too. And if they could have all that from playing, they needed to get serious. Enter Amanda. Amanda was like an angel sent from above – Levi's words, not Sabrina's, though she guessed Levi was right. The boys had been a gift from above for her too, so that did kind of make Amanda a sort of guardian angel.

And here she was a week in with a full schedule lined up for the boys and a record studio booked for next week. Sabrina felt like she was on fire, like she was finally doing what she was meant to do, and she couldn't be prouder of who she was working alongside.

***

It was thinking about her boys that gave Sabrina the surge of determination she needed, albeit with shaky hands, to finally press the green call button.

'Lydia speaking.' At the sound of her boss's voice it felt like the Dementors had captured Sabrina and were trying to suck out her soul. The iciness hit her right in the chest and made her shudder. Just like that the sky morphed from an exotic blend of blood orange and deep mango to fifty shades of miserable grey.

'Hi Lydia, it's Sabrina. As you know I am currently back home in England, well, I was in England, and erm … well I'm now in Italy.' A lump caught in her throat at the mere thought of mentioning her grandpa passing. 'Well … erm, I have a family matter that I am attending to. My, my grandpa died a few days ago.' Sabrina swallowed the lump down hard. 'And well … that would explain Italy. I have family here, so I won't be able to get back to LA for another two weeks.

'With it being Christmas I just thought I could take this as vacation now, as you know I have never requested this much time off all at once before, but this was an unexpected matter and there was no way around it really. I know it will eat into next year's vacation time, but I am fine with that. I will even work longer hours when I get back if you need me to; that will be no problem, I can do that.' Her brain pleaded with her to stop rambling and stand tall but good God she was terrified. She hated that Lydia made her feel so weak. So she continued babbling.

When Lydia spoke next, after an uncomfortable pause that Sabrina knew was perfectly placed to make Sabrina sweat, her voice was low and dripping with lust, causing Sabrina to wince. 'Email me their schedule and I will see to it that everything goes according to plan. I look forward to getting to know your boys more intimately. Anything else?' Sabrina's stomach twisted into knots.

'No, that's all.' Her knuckles turned white as she held the phone with a death grip to her ear, not wanting to miss a thing Lydia said.

'OK then. Have a great day.' With that Lydia hung up and left Sabrina wondering if it had gone well or if her gut was right and something was off. Lydia had sounded way too happy to be taking on Sabrina's clients and it unnerved her to think of her ulterior motive. Her pulse quickened and a vein in her forehead throbbed as she placed the phone back on the wall. Lydia hadn't even uttered the words sorry or showed any sympathy towards her and her family. It made Sabrina feel sick and not for the first time it made her wonder why she was working for this woman.

Suddenly she heard footsteps on the balcony that brought her back to the present. She tried to shake off her anger, not wanting it to fester inside her at what was already an emotional time. She tried too, to dispel the image of Levi's face that had appeared at the forefront of her mind. Lydia was always very touchy-feely whenever she was in the vicinity of Levi and now, after having seen them together back in the offices, Sabrina knew why. Sabrina still couldn't understand them being together. Despite what she saw, she truly did not want to believe it.

And she knew it would not do well for her to let these images or feelings run wild in her thoughts. She would only cause herself more harm and stress. Letting out a heavy-hearted breath she finished her coffee and went in search of biscotti.

Chapter 7

Grandpa's Olive Bread

Ingredients:

Yeast

Tipo OO flour (Italy's finest)

Olives

Egg

Butter

A little salt, pepper and olive oil

What to do:

Prepare dough like Grandpa prepares pizza dough.

Add olives — you can chop them if you'd like.

Place in dish to cook. (Ask Grandpa for temp of oven.)

Brush the top with beaten egg.

The small village of Orzoro lay still and the sun peeked through the cloudy sky on Thursday morning. Louisa felt it symbolic to her mood. Waking up this morning she had been fighting the strong urge to hide under her flower-printed blankets and lie in the darkness forever, but a little voice in her head told her to seize the day: a voice that had sounded a lot like her grandpa's.

Her grandpa had adored the place he was born and raised. He had instilled in his girls the same strong devotion to Italian culture and they were proud of their Italian heritage. Louisa knew she couldn't waste a day in bed when the whole of Italy was at her feet.

After a simple breakfast of coffee and a chocolate *cornetto*, she dressed in her favourite graffiti-print Converse, black slimline pants and an embellished roll-neck jumper and then spent an hour or so trying to convince Sabrina to come with her on her morning outing.

Sabrina had seemed distracted after speaking with her boss the night before, so Louisa didn't want to push too much and though she knew it would probably do her sister good to get some fresh air and not spend time overthinking about work when she was so far away, she left Sabrina to enjoy her own morning at the house and stepped into the cool but pleasant outdoors.

She vaguely remembered where she was going. It had been many years since she had walked these pathways, but she decided she was happy to let her feet wander and figure it out like it was the first time she was experiencing it all. Breathing in the salty air, she allowed her jaw to loosen and her brows to unfurrow, wanting to see Italy the way her grandpa did, with a smile on his face.

Louisa walked for a while taking in every nook and cranny of each uniquely shaped building. The history burst from the stones and drew you in, making you lust for Italy even more. There was a regal feel to Italy. The grand entranceways, iron gates and ceramic pillars, though often a tad worn and rusty, still stood tall and proud. They oozed a richness that Louisa felt was rare to find anywhere else.

A few more steps past creamy tile walls and a mosaic art piece of the Virgin Mary, and the air filled with the most heaven-sent, sweet aroma Louisa had ever had the pleasure of smelling. That was saying something when her *nonni* and big sister were renowned chefs. She checked her watch and realized that it was lunchtime. Orzoro came alive during lunch and the cold weather wasn't fazing the people bustling in and out of the delicatessen that Louisa quickly realized was the culprit behind that mouth-watering smell. Her nose, and stomach, were currently directing her feet. She could barely squeeze her tiny frame inside the packed hot spot.

Her stomach rumbled at the sight of each delectable pastry. The food appeared to be absolute perfection. Just looking at the crisp layers of *sfogliatelle*, the choux pastry bursting with fluffy vanilla custard and the warm focaccia filled with plump, juicy olives, transported her back to being a little girl running around on the balcony at her aunties' house, with freshly baked treats in her hand as she looked out across the sea at the Amalfi Coast, crystal blue water as far as her little eyes could see.

A single tear rolled down her cheek at the memory. How was she supposed to go on without her grandpa? How did people do it? Suddenly, she felt weak and claustrophobic. Her heartbeat quickened, and her legs shook. She wasn't strong; she wasn't capable of moving on. Her heart felt torn, trodden on, completely crushed to pieces. Everything reminded her of him. How was she supposed to go to Italy and celebrate him, without him? The place that had his heart that he missed so much – it didn't seem fair that he was now home under this circumstance.

'*Ciao, bella.*' The silvery voice broke her out of her trance.

She looked up quickly, wiping the stray tear away from her cheek. '*Ciao,*' she replied shaking off her thoughts. '*Mi spiacente,* I didn't mean to hold up the line, erm, I'll just take one of everything?' She was playing with her wavy brown hair, tucking it behind her ear then untucking it again. As she looked up, her eyes met the most gorgeous man she had ever seen. She felt like a fool, crying while she was out in public. 'I was away with the fairies. I am sorry – you must think I'm a crazy woman.'

Her eyes connected with his. They were warm and friendly and made her insides flutter. A gentle smile spread across his handsome face.

'Crazy is not the word I would use. Beautiful yes, crazy no.' His Italian accent was thick and just as mesmerizing as his beautiful face. She just wanted him to keep talking but knew if he did she would most likely turn to mush. She needed air. Louisa could feel the heat rising in her cheeks. Her face must be beet red by now, she thought.

She couldn't do this. She was not built to talk to such striking men, who were way out of her league. She thought of her sisters, how Amanda would be confident and charming without so much as a second thought, while Sabrina would be flirty, her natural sweetness pouring out, and here she was a vulnerable, stuttering mess. She let out a shaky laugh. Oh crap, it was her turn to talk.

'I'm sorry, erm, *grazie*. You're rather beautiful yourself.' What the …? Did she just say that? Grandpa, Grandpa, Grandpa. She looked up praying he was watching over her. Help me, she whispered. It was his turn to blush – wait, he was blushing? Surely people called him beautiful all the time? He must have girls swooning over him every day, but … but he was blushing. She beamed. His eyes, she noticed, had not wandered from her face.

'Would you like to sit for coffee?' he asked, gesturing towards a small table hidden in the corner. She'd been standing there so long getting in the way and holding up the queue, 'Erm … yes, sorry, I'm staying in, thank you.' She nodded awkwardly and retreated to the corner table.

Taking off her blazer she made herself comfortable, placing her bag on the opposite empty chair, so no one would bother

her, and pulled out her drawings. She wiped her red eyes with a napkin to soak up the stubborn tears and made to focus on creating a new piece when the handsome stranger walked over and placed her coffee and a box of pastries in front of her. He looked at her bag and then to her. He smiled sweetly before turning as though to walk away, but instead he turned back to face her, placing a hand on her bag chair.

'Would you mind if I sat with you?' he asked, glancing at her work, with an apologetic look in his eyes, as if the decision to disturb her or not had been a difficult one.

'Sure,' Louisa said, after a moment's hesitation. She reached over the table to move her bag, her curiosity about this man getting the better of her.

'My name is Luca,' the gorgeous man said, sticking out his hand.

Louisa shook it. 'I'm Louisa, sorry about before. I had a few things on my mind and it all got a bit too much,' she finished, picking up a pencil and rotating it between her fingers.

'There's no need to be sorry ...' Luca started.

'What might be the problem?' Luca asked at the same time Louisa queried, 'Do you work here?' They both looked down at the table, blushing. Louisa placed the pen down and picked up her coffee, taking a sip. As soon as the hot liquid touched her lips she choked on a sudden burst of laughter. Luca's face was kind as he simply watched her.

'What a silly question,' Louisa said. 'You just served me, and I asked if you worked here.' With a mixture of nerves in her stomach and a giddiness that Luca provoked, laughter seemed to engulf her. It became a release. She laughed some more, and it wasn't long before Luca joined her. As his face creased into a smile, dimples appeared at his cheeks and he placed one hand on his belly, making him even more attractive.

Luca shuffled in his seat, pulling himself together first and then giving Louisa his full attention. He answered her question like it wasn't silly at all. 'Yes, I work here. It has been in my family for generations. My dad, he is the owner now and I will take over from him one day.'

'It's a beautiful *pasticceria*. My sister, Amanda, would love it,' Louisa said, calming herself and taking in the cosy environment. The stunning portraits of Italy on the walls were captivating.

'Your family is here, no?' Luca asked, his kind eyes making Louisa feel as though she could tell him everything. She looked at Luca and then to the box he had placed on the table. Opening the lid, she picked out a sugary biscuit and took a bite, then washed it down with a sip of coffee. Once the sugar was in her system her words tumbled out with ease.

***

An hour later Louisa walked out of Alfonso's, eyes puffy, sparkling smile spread wide across her face and feeling a mix of elation and a ball of nerves. She'd spent the entire time chatting away to Luca about every little thing. He'd listened to every word that came out of her mouth. His gaze never faltered from hers, except when she noticed he seemed to get a little nervous too. He would look to her lips, his own curling into a shy smile.

This had made her shoulders relax and she had felt at ease telling him about her grandpa. Her eyes were red from the tears she hadn't been able to control. Instead of being put off by the emotional girl in front of him, his blazing blue eyes had shown a deep sorrow and sympathy for her. He spoke of his family and how close they were and how her grandpa sounded like a great man.

Here was this undeniably sexy man who was paying her attention in the kindest way. She found herself staring at him, just wanting to take in his beauty and kindness. He seemed unaware of the attention from girls that passed by, girls whose eyes couldn't help noticing his chiselled jaw, floppy brown hair and stunning smile. Not to mention the biceps straining against his white shirt. Though Louisa had of course noticed all of this too, it was his words that had her smiling as though she had just heard the ice-cream man on a sunny afternoon in Manchester.

The wispy December air hit her as she stepped outside. Her graffitied Converse tapped a happy beat on the cobbled path that would lead her home. She took in a deep breath and looking to the sky. She whispered: '*Grazie*, Grandpa.' Suddenly she felt a tap on her shoulder. Startled she spun round nearly tripping over her own two feet. Luca was quick to catch her with his free hand. A few passers-by gasped at the scene.

'I'm so sorry,' Louisa panted. 'You scared me.'

'I meant not to frighten you.' His worried face turned into a small smile. 'You are incredibly cute, Louisa.' He looked to her lips again, a slight flush in his cheeks. 'You forgot your cakes for your nanna, and my *nonno* wanted to send these to your nanna too. Do you mind not to taking them?' While one hand was still resting warm on her waist, the other held the box of pastries as well as the most stunning pink roses she had ever seen. She felt yet another tear roll down her face. Nanna's favourite – how did he know?

***

'How long have you been sitting there, Brina?' Louisa said, looking at her sister, her face creased with concern. Sabrina was sat on the stone balcony staring at the flowerpots, her eyes glassed over.

'What? Sorry,' Sabrina whispered. Louisa watched as Sabrina rubbed her eyes and then turned to face her, her hazel eyes misty. Louisa placed the flowers and the boxes on the small garden table beside her and reached inside the box for a piece of focaccia. She tore it in two and handed a piece to Sabrina.

Sure enough, the moment the smell of warm bread filled her sister's nostrils, Louisa noticed Sabrina's spirits lift ever so slightly, as she licked her lips and her eyes became clearer. 'Hey, where've you been?' Sabrina asked, as though noticing Louisa for the first time and sounding more like herself than a second ago.

Louisa felt her cheeks flush and hoped Sabrina wouldn't notice her turning a bright shade of pink. 'I just went for a walk and thought I would pick up some stuff for dinner tonight so Amanda and everyone didn't have to cook too much. I know everyone is still a bit dazed, but Grandpa would be the first to tell us to eat.' She spoke as casually as she could manage with Sabrina eyeing her up and down.

'Aww, thanks, Lou, it smells amazing. Everyone will appreciate that. This is delicious,' Sabrina said, taking another bite of focaccia.

'Why, don't we go inside, Brina? You're going to catch a chill sitting on this tile so long,' Louisa said, noticing her sister's lips were a little blue. Sabrina was wearing a light cardigan, flip-flops and her pyjama shorts. An unusual combination to choose for an Italian winter, Louisa thought. 'Come on, I can show you what else I got. If you like that bread, you're going to love the pastries.' She stood up and led the way into the kitchen. Once inside she pushed some plates and leftovers from breakfast aside and placed the boxes down on the counter.

'It really doesn't seem real, does it?' Sabrina questioned, as she munched on the warm bread and took a seat at the kitchen table. Louisa stopped trimming the flowers she had started to place into a vase and pulled up a chair opposite her sister. She could hear Rai Uno playing in the living room and made out the murmurs of the rest of the family as they answered along to their favourite quiz show.

She sighed, the question snapping her back into the reality of their trip, the reason behind them being here. It wasn't all about eating her weight in focaccia and looking forward to the Christmas parade of the Saint here in Orzoro. It took a moment for her to form words. 'No, it really doesn't. I keep wanting to go over and say hi to him, tell him about my day and then suddenly it crushes me.'

She paused. 'You know what though?' Louisa bit her tongue in thought before pushing herself to continue. 'I don't want to believe he's gone. It doesn't feel like he's gone, you know? I don't know if I'm still in shock and I will be in for a rude awakening soon, but I just feel like we have so much love around us. He left so many happy memories and gosh, just walking around Orzoro today, all the food, the people, it made me smile. It's like Grandpa's guiding us; it's like he's reminding me he's still here.'

She looked up and found Sabrina looking right at her, slowly chewing her last piece of focaccia. Her face was soft, and dark bags had settled under her hazel eyes, bags that Louisa hadn't noticed before. LA was keeping Sabrina on her toes and it hit Louisa with force right in her chest, that she hadn't been supportive or kind to her sister in recent months. She felt ashamed.

'I'm sorry,' Louisa muttered. 'I'm sorry for being so cruel, acting as though you don't care about your family when I know that's the farthest thing from the truth. I'm sorry for not being there for you and understanding all the hard work you put in. It was wrong of me to speak to you that way when I know all you've done to get where you are. We just miss you, that's all,' she finished. Louisa looked up, hoping her sister would know she meant every word. Sabrina watched her for a moment before sharing an appreciative smile.

'Thank you for that. I'm sorry too, for being so harsh about London. I just want you to get your designs out there and get out of that awful office culture. Your talent is being wasted and you are so young. You have so much to offer – you just can't give up so easily,' Sabrina replied.

In that moment, the girls felt that connection, that deep understanding that only sisters feel. They were all trying to figure out life's journey while staying true to themselves and each other and right now they were all in pain yet all doing their best for one another. Family went through its ups and downs, but they shouldn't waste time arguing or resenting each other. Sabrina reached out and placed a cold hand on Louisa's arm. They exchanged knowing grins.

'So, are you going to tell me what's got you all flushed pink and those pretty caramel eyes of yours sparkling, or are you going to make me guess?' Sabrina added, wiggling her eyebrows. 'Spill?'

Louisa felt the heat rise in her cheeks once more and knew she was most likely a bright shade of rose right now, but she wasn't one to keep things from her sisters. For starters she was always the one harping on about singing from the rooftops when it came to love, and she still felt a hint of irritation whenever she thought about her sisters being scared to broach such a topic with Dan and Levi.

But now her mind was playing hypocrite. She had only known Luca for an hour. This couldn't be love. She was just emotional, and this giddy feeling would pass. She was a grown-up. She couldn't go around acting like a schoolgirl with a teenage crush. She suddenly realized that the love game wasn't quite as simple as she once thought, but she wasn't about to admit that to her sister just yet. She continued playing with a piece of the bread that Sabrina hadn't devoured yet.

'My cheeks are not pink, and my eyes are always this pretty – they naturally sparkle,' she replied sarcastically with a nervous giggle, trying to put off the inevitable and avoid giving the game away completely.

'You have been twiddling that piece of bread in your fingertips for an age while I've scoffed half the loaf, then you put it down, and didn't even eat it and now you are playing with it again. You buried your head in those gorgeous roses as soon as you entered the kitchen, so spill the beans, missy,' Sabrina pushed.

Louisa was not going to be able to make a lucky escape.

'Your dear sister could do with some of that radiant glow

you've got going on, so details please,' Sabrina continued, clapping her hands together, ready for juicy gossip. Louisa popped the bread into her mouth. It truly was spectacular, and she debated whether to admit that a veritable stranger had evoked such strong feelings of happiness in just over an hour, and just a few days after her grandpa had passed.

Should she feel ashamed? Would her sister think badly of her? But looking at Sabrina, Louisa saw no judgement in her eyes; instead they were warm and encouraging, hopeful of some good news, and twinkling with a hint of mischief, which made Louisa confess. She swallowed the delicious bread and bared her soul, choosing to remain true to herself and embracing the feeling of love. Who knew, maybe it would inspire Sabrina to do the same with Levi.

'Brina, I swear it was like something out of a fairy tale just like Nanna and Grandpa. I walked into this tiny delicatessen. My feet just led me there because the smell was to die for. I have to take you. Amanda would die – sorry bad choice of words.' She cringed; Sabrina chuckled. 'I saw the food and I lost it. I just thought of Grandpa and all that he had baked for us and it was terrible. I cried right in the middle of the place for goodness' sake.'

Louisa took a breath and another bite of the focaccia she suddenly had an appetite for, before continuing, 'Then I looked up. This smile greeted me, these warm eyes. I swear he could be Giulio Berruti's twin, but that's beside the point. He was lovely. Yes, gorgeous too, but just lovely. We spent an hour talking. I had three espressos – three. The sweet lady just kept bringing them over and Luca, that's his name, he listened to me, like really listened. And his eyes are as blue as the ocean. He wants to cook for me, Brina, cook for me. Do you think that's a date?'

Louisa devoured the bread in front of her, nervously anticipating her sister's response. Would it be bad? She couldn't go on a date with a stranger. Would it be good? That's how people met though, wasn't it? That's how Nanna and Grandpa met, she thought, chewing at a rapid pace.

'Firstly, let's limit espressos to maybe one a day and secondly, let's chew our food before we choke,' her big sister said, taking Louisa's hands in hers. Louisa swallowed the focaccia and smiled, as Sabrina continued.

'Thirdly, yes, baby sister, I'd say you have a date and fourthly, he sounds like an absolute dream. I can't wait to meet him.'

Louisa felt her cheeks flush for the millionth time today as Sabrina's eyes sparkled, clearly very happy for her.

'Ooh and fifthly, is that even a word? Hmm well, number five. If Giulio Berruti does happen to be his twin brother, you come to me first and not Amanda,' she added with a laugh and a playful wink. 'Ahh, that's Grandpa's doing that is – making sure you find a good Italian man. Yep, you're right, Lou, he is still with us.' Louisa noticed Sabrina's mood was suddenly a lot brighter and felt happy that she had played a part in that.

Smiling at Sabrina, Louisa got up to see to the rest of the flowers, carefully placing them in the vase that she had found. She looked up to the sky. '*Grazie*,' she whispered, for the second time that day, hoping Grandpa could hear her.

Chapter 8

Grandpa's Cream Caramels

Ingredients:

For the cream caramels:
2 pints of milk
4 tbsps of sugar
6 eggs
2 tsps vanilla
For the sugar:
8 tbsps of sugar
1–2 tbsps of water

What to do:

For the caramelized sugar:

Put the sugar and water into a small pan. Leave it on a medium/high heat and let it bubble. Don't stir it. The sugar will start to melt.

Once it's melted completely take it off the heat. Be careful not to let it burn. Trust your instincts — well, Grandpa's. (Learn to trust yours.)

For the cream caramels:

Pre-heat the fan oven to 150 degrees.

In a large pan on a medium heat, stir the sugar into the milk.

In a separate bowl, whisk the 6 eggs with the vanilla.

Once the milk and sugar mixture has come to a boil. Remove from the heat.

Take the caramelized sugar and pour a little bit into 12 pots — enough to cover the bottom.

While the sugar is setting, mix the milk mixture with the eggs.

Using a ladle, spoon the mixture into the pots — about ¾ full.

Place all 12 pots into a shallow dish and add cold water to the bottom.

Put on the bottom of the oven for 1 hour, covering with foil, so they don't burn.

The kitchen island was lined with plates of Zia Sofia's famous torte. There were five of them and now Amanda had her head buried in a kitchen cupboard in search of ingredients to make Grandpa's cream caramels. Once she found what she needed, she threw a light cardigan over the top of her apron. With night-time descending around her the house had started to get chilly.

She scrunched up her face in pure concentration. She had seen Grandpa do this a million times but had yet to get it just right on her own. The heat from the stove was creating tiny beads of sweat on her forehead, which she carefully wiped away with a damp cloth without taking her eyes off the steaming pan in front of her. The scent of vanilla made her taste buds tingle. She thought about how excited Grandpa used to get when cooking and how he never looked flustered.

She rolled her shoulders gently, encouraging her mind and body to relax. He would always tell her: 'It's easy when you know how.' And she knew how, she just had to believe in herself. As the mixture started to bubble gently she removed it from the flames, not wanting it to boil. She carried it from the stovetop and over to the worktop.

Beating in the eggs, milk and sugar, a trace of a smile formed at her lips as she thought about how much Dan would love Grandpa's cream caramels. He loved food, nearly as much as she did. Once she had poured the smooth creamy liquid into the dishes and put them in the oven, she set about organizing her ingredients to whip up another batch.

Amanda lifted her head to reach for the eggs when she caught sight of Sabrina entering the kitchen. 'Look what the cat dragged in,' she mused. 'Oh wow, I think the cat may have shaken you a bit first, roughed you up and then dragged you in.' Amanda's eyes grew wide as she looked her sister up and down, getting distracted from her task for a minute. 'What on earth are you wearing? I'm certain that's not the latest from the Chiara Ferragni collection.'

'Ha-ha, you really should be a stand-up comic or something,' Sabrina said, sounding mock offended. Amanda knew that her sister was used to her sarcastic ways by now, so much so that it rarely bothered her, but she still had fun teasing her on occasion. She watched as Sabrina pulled up her very worn-in oversized travel leggings and wrapped what could only be one of their auntie's knitted Christmas jumpers tighter round herself. 'I failed to pack enough warm clothes. I live in LA remember,' she said to Amanda.

'Well I mean, it could catch on. I can see it now ... "confused fashion".' Amanda gave a small wink in her sister's direction and then set about placing another bunch of cream caramel pots into a shallow dish. 'You didn't realize you were coming home in December and would need warm clothes? I think all that California sunshine is getting to your head,' she said, pouring the caramelized sugar into each pot.

'I had many a movie and pizza night in mind while curled up in the luxury of your fine and warm establishment.' Sabrina paused, before reluctantly adding, 'And things were crazy. I just threw whatever I could get my hands on into the suitcase.'

A small snort escaped Amanda's lips, but before she had time to ask what had been so crazy in LA for Sabrina to not have time to pack, when she was without a shadow of a doubt the world's most OCD packer, Louisa entered the kitchen. 'Lou, help me please? Go and push her off the balcony for me, will you?' Sabrina said slightly irked, though a smile threatened to light up her face as she took in Louisa galloping in.

'What's she said now?' Louisa asked, looking at Amanda and shaking her head, before walking to the kitchen doors and peering out.

'She's having a go at my attire,' Sabrina answered, picking at the edge of one of the tortes on the kitchen island and putting the crumbs in her mouth. She was trying to be discreet, but Amanda was aware of what she was doing. She could never withhold cake from anyone though and quickly retrieved a plate and a knife from the cupboard and placed it in front of Sabrina. Sabrina smiled gratefully.

'Ignore her, Brina. She doesn't know fashion,' Louisa said.

Amanda was not biting and continued with her cream caramels, her head down.

'Even in winter, it's beautiful isn't it?' Louisa continued when Amanda didn't talk back. She peered out through the glass kitchen door onto the balcony that overlooked the positively stunning Amalfi Coast. With the night sky well and truly pitch black and one or two streetlights present on the mountainside, you could make out speckles of lights as far as the eye could see. With the lights flickering diagonally, from the water up to the sky, the Amalfi Coast looked like one giant Christmas tree.

'Sure is,' Amanda replied, without looking up, concentration fully etched back onto her face as she hovered over the stove once more. The views of the Amalfi Coast were firmly embedded in her mind. Night-time was possibly her favourite time in Italy. The twinkles of light bouncing off the mountains made it feel like a magical faraway land. Every time she looked across the coast she imagined that's how Harry felt seeing Hogwarts for the first time, all lit up in the night sky, endless possibilities and that feeling of home.

'This smells amazing by the way,' Sabrina said through a yawn, as she carefully cut a slice of chocolate torte and carried her plate from the kitchen island and sat down at the square table in the centre of the room, tucking her knees to her chest and pulling her jumper over them, before digging in. 'I forgot how chilly it gets in here.'

Their aunties' house was tucked high into the hillside. It was a humble home with wooden doorframes that lent themselves to draughts. It could do with renovating but lugging bricks and mortar up hundreds of stairs wasn't quite at the top of anyone's 'want to' list.

'Oh my God, this tastes incredible.'

'Ooh I want some and those cream caramels smell delicious too,' Louisa noted, steering her eyes away from the enchanting view and wandering over to see what Amanda was making.

'Now, that's more like it,' Amanda said, lifting her head from her mixture and noticing Louisa's outfit for the first time. Laughter barrelled out of her. Her little sister was wearing what seemed to be a Rudolph the Red Nose Reindeer onesie.

'What?' Louisa asked, her voice light and airy. She was acting oblivious to how ridiculous she looked as she helped herself to a plate from the cupboard and began cutting her own slice of cake.

'I think you need to get Brina one of them,' Amanda replied, removing the mixture away from the flames once more and whisking in the eggs.

'It looks cosy and she looks cute,' Sabrina said, stifling yet another yawn.

Amanda made a mental note to have a word with her sister, to check in on her and life in LA, as she picked up an oven glove and took the first batch of cream caramels out of the oven and replaced them with the new batch. Her chest rose with pride as she took in the light golden colour of the caramels, how they jiggled just right. She might have just done it. All those years watching Grandpa and finally she had done it.

'Wow, something smells good in here, girls,' came Mum's soft voice as she appeared in the doorway.

'Amanda's made cake and now she's making cream caramels,' Louisa said, nibbling on her rather chunky slice of torte.

'Grandpa's favourite,' Mum said, smiling as she walked over to Sabrina at the table and gave her a kiss on the forehead, before sitting down next to her. 'Thank you, girls, for being here.' All three girls looked over at their mum, whose eyes had begun to water.

Wiping her hands on her apron, Amanda stopped what she was doing, carefully placing the boiling pan on the counter so as to not let it burn. She walked over to her mum and enveloped her in a giant hug. Her tears wet Amanda's cheek. 'Of course we would be here, Mum. We wouldn't miss it and leave you to go through this all by yourself.'

'I know, I know, but you all have busy lives and I didn't want you to have to stop all the important stuff to have to come all the way here. Sabrina, you must be shattered with all the travel.'

'Mamma, don't you worry about that at all. I'm fine and I wanted to be here. Work will be there when I get back. It's family time now,' Sabrina said, putting her arms around her mum and resting her head on her shoulder.

'We love you, Mum. We wouldn't be anywhere else right now.' Louisa paused from reading Amanda's recipe book that lay open on the counter, wiped her cake-covered hands, and walked over to wrap her arms around her mum's neck, completing the bear hug their mum was now squished in the middle of. 'Grandpa taught us that nothing is more important than family. He deserves the best send-off and we wanted to see that he got home. He's the best grandpa there ever was. I miss him so much,' she added, her voice catching at the end.

'Me too. Thank you, girls.' Mum squeezed them all tight, not wanting to let her girls go.

'Well, now I feel left out,' Dad announced. He was leaning against the doorframe, smiling at all four of his girls. 'Any room for me?'

'Always, Daddy,' Louisa replied, running over, antlers bouncing up and down, to give their dad a cuddle.

'Do you need some help in here, Amanda, sweetheart?' Mum asked, releasing Amanda from her grip and looking over to the pots and pans.

'I mean, if you would all like to help, sure,' Amanda replied, getting reacquainted with the milk mixture and giving it a stir to see if it was still good, having cooled down.

'Ooh yes please, I'd like to help,' Louisa said, excitement in her voice. She ate the last of her slice of torte and picked up a spoon.

'Someone has a pep in their step this evening,' Amanda said, pleased to see that Italy was having a positive effect on her baby sister. She knew Louisa was hurting. She and Grandpa had been as thick as thieves. Louisa being the baby and all, they'd had a special bond. Amanda had worried that she was going to find this harder than most.

Before they arrived in Italy, her baby sister had quit her job via email and not left their nanna's side. Louisa had been moody and quiet and though the girls were used to Louisa's odd snappy remark regarding their love lives and such, it hadn't been pleasant under the circumstances. But, both Amanda and Sabrina allowed their sister room to grieve. They knew the pain was causing much of the anger and that Louisa simply needed to vent.

However, the sparkle in Louisa's eyes told Amanda she was finding her way and Italy had its own special healing powers. 'I'll have whatever she's having,' she added, smiling at Louisa and passing her the whisk, for her to finish up combining the rest of the ingredients.

'You don't know the half of it,' Sabrina piped up, with a laugh. Amanda sent a quizzical look her way.

'Are you two not telling me something?' Amanda asked pointing a spoon at both her sisters, who had matching mischievous looks on their faces. Louisa hadn't taken her eyes off the bowl in front of her and beneath her reindeer hood, her ears were glowing red.

'Now is not the time for gossip, dear sister: you are supposed to be teaching us how to bake this fine dish,' Sabrina teased.

Shaking off her sister's toothy grin and focusing on Mum and Dad waiting for instructions in front of her, Amanda got to work, teaching them all how to make the best cream caramels they had ever tasted. Grandpa's recipe, of course.

Chapter 9

Grandpa's Chocolate Pastry Filling

Ingredients (Check measurements with Grandpa):

Eggs (Both yolk and white?)
Flour
Milk
Vanilla essence
Perugina dark chocolate

What to do:

Make a roux, like how Nanna makes her custard, with eggs and flour first.

Pour milk and vanilla over roux. Allow to simmer first, then break up the chocolate pieces and leave to melt, stirring constantly and keeping an eye on it so it doesn't burn.

Usually takes a good thirty minutes till thick and cooked.

The evening had been a huge success. San Francisco Beat's first album had officially released to the world with a triumphant bang. Thanks to the undeniable charm of all four band members, Levi's ability to woo everyone he came in contact with and Dan's knack of leaving everyone in his presence in awe, all in attendance at the party, and all those who had tuned in via social media, were well and truly under the band's spell.

Sabrina gave herself a pat on the back for hosting and putting together such a winner of a launch party. She looked around and noticed everyone was smiling. Dylan was chatting away to a small group of music executives, with a huge grin on his face. James was entertaining a handful of women on the dance floor. Dan was sat in a far corner of the room holed up with his phone, a megawatt smile lighting his face. That smile could only mean one thing – he was talking to Amanda.

Sabrina scanned the room, unable to spot the charming drummer, and wondered if he had got lucky with one of the groupies already. The thought made her reach for a glass of champagne from a passing waiter. Lydia had said her goodbyes earlier, so she felt it was safe and well deserved for her to help herself to a glass or two. The cool bubbles fizzed on her tongue. She let her shoulders roll back as two hands reached around her waist, making her simultaneously jump and tingle from head to toe.

'You are amazing,' Levi whispered into her ear. She spun around to face him, pulling away ever so slightly. His touch felt incredible, but she couldn't help but glance around the room to see who was still there. She didn't want to come across as unprofessional.

'Thank you,' she stammered. 'You're not half bad yourself,' she added, watching Levi's reaction as his face creased into that boyish smile. He was staring at her with a look that she had only experienced once before, the day they met, six months ago. For fear of being mistaken as a groupie, she gently pushed his hands away from her hips and turned so she was standing with her side to him.

He watched her for a moment, then did the same. They both

stood facing the dance floor, their elbows skimming each other's. Sabrina threw back the rest of her champagne and instantly scolded herself for being so stupid as the bubbles reached her brain and her cheeks burned.

'So, are you looking forward to the tour?' she asked, feeling the need to break the silence, but not looking at him.

'Yeah, of course. It's a dream come true,' Levi responded with a casual shrug, watching her closely.

'Good, good, I'm glad,' she said, braving a sidelong glance his way. That was a mistake. Levi always looked good in his signature blue jeans and assortment of designer tops. But tonight he practically looked edible in his tailored suit. He was tall and lean, but the suit showed off his muscles in all the right places.

A moment passed before Sabrina realized that Levi was looking at her. She had, once again, been caught ogling him. She looked up catching his eye and gave him an apologetic, shy smile. A waiter wandered by with the last few glasses of champagne. Levi took two from the tray and handed one to her. She took it with a polite nod, before scanning the room. It was near empty now.

She watched James leave with one of the girls he had been dancing with before and spotted Dylan still engaged in shop talk at a nearby table. Dan hadn't moved from his spot in the corner. He had a faraway look in his eyes that made Sabrina smile. He was clearly in love with Amanda, but the daft pair were too stubborn to admit it.

'Would you like to go outside and get some fresh air?' Levi asked, pulling her out of her reverie.

'Sure,' she replied, careful not to keep eye contact with him for too long. Levi stepped behind her and gestured towards the patio doors. Outside, the balcony had been decorated with lanterns, twinkling lights and the same black and gold balloons as inside. There were benches placed around a still-blazing fire pit, which eased off the midnight chill. It looked beautiful and sophisticated, with a touch of rock-star elegance.

Sabrina smoothed out her black skater dress and sat down close to the fire. Levi settled in beside her. She watched the orange and yellow flames sway in front of her and couldn't help let out a laugh. She had been bossing Levi and his bandmates around for the best part of six months. She never shut up when it came to meetings, ideas, public appearances and telling them where to be and when. As for her and Levi, they gave each other as good as they got with their effortless banter. Yet tonight she had suddenly become a mute.

'What's so funny?' Levi asked, a mischievous sparkle in his brown eyes.

'Oh nothing,' she managed, taking another sip of her bubbly and giving Levi her best puppy dog smile. His breath caught and he let out a low groan before leaning in to her and cupping her face, his eyes staring straight into hers. He gave her time to pull away, but she didn't. Levi's lips were now on hers and Sabrina found herself kissing him back, hard.

Her hands found their way through his hair as he caressed her cheeks. All she wanted to do was kiss him; her mind had gone blank of everything else. She grasped his biceps as he pulled her onto his lap, not breaking the kiss.

Suddenly, a balloon popped against one of the lanterns and Sabrina's eyes flew open. What was she doing? She was being completely unprofessional. What happened if she and Levi didn't work? What would it mean for the band? What would Lydia say? How would she ever be taken seriously? She pulled back, their foreheads resting against each other's, both a little out of breath.

'Levi, I can't,' she whispered, and then stood up and ran away.

***

The skyline was a mix of orange and purple hues. A slight hint of grey was forcing its way in, trying to darken the spectacular vibrant colours. Sabrina was sitting on the balcony swinging back and forth on the outdoor swinging sofa. She twiddled her sandy blonde hair and gazed into the distance, watching as the sun rose above Sicily.

It wasn't until Amanda stepped out into the morning sun that Sabrina realized just how long she had been sitting there. She shivered as the morning chill suddenly hit her. Sleep had eluded her again last night. She rubbed her tired eyes.

'Hey, everything OK?' Amanda asked, catching her eye before putting on a red oversized jumper and throwing a grey one at Sabrina.

'Huh?' Sabrina started as the jumper hit her in the face. She quickly grabbed it and put it on, trying not to act dazed. 'Oh, yeah, it's as good as it can be, I guess,' Sabrina continued, with a shake of her head, trying to dispel the negative thoughts twirling round inside it. She patted down her static-affected hair and pulled at the cuffs of the jumper, warming up her hands.

Then she looked from her sister to the magnificent view. The sea stretched out for miles, glistening gold with the sun's strong rays. Off in the distance you could see the faint edges of Sicily. She took a deep breath, overwhelmed by its beauty, as Amanda sat and joined her in her swinging.

'So, besides Grandpa having the nerve to up and leave us at this wonderful time of year, what else seems to be bothering you?' Amanda asked, kicking her feet to move the swing back and forth.

'Your humour knows no bounds,' Sabrina replied, letting out a chuckle and pulling a face.

'What can I say? He taught me everything I know.'

'Then aren't we in for a treat for the rest of our days: delicious food with a side of sarcasm and terrible jokes.' Sabrina tutted.

'His jokes weren't all bad – he actually had some really good ones,' Amanda responded.

'I can't argue with you there.'

'So, what has you squinting and giving evils to the sunrise?' Amanda said, stopping the momentum of the swinging to curl her legs up underneath her. Sabrina did the same. It wasn't exactly warm in Italy in December and she could have done with bringing out an extra blanket for her legs. She was grateful for her sister's jumper.

'Uh, nothing much.' Sabrina paused, uncertain as to whether it was the right time to delve into her thoughts. She had managed just fine over the past few days not thinking about Levi. Her sisters were her priority and then Grandpa had well and truly gone and pushed any feelings for anyone outside the family right to the back of the line. But the sleepless nights were starting to make her eyes more weary and as the reality was settling in about Grandpa, Sabrina had felt more lonely than ever.

In turn this caused her mind to drift to Levi, leaving her feeling guilty and confused. She was his manager; he was a drummer in a rock band. She couldn't fall for him. That would be stupid.

'You can either sit and listen to more of my bad jokes or you can talk.' Amanda softened, gently nudging her sister.

'I saw Levi with Lydia as I was leaving the other night. They were getting quite cosy with each other in her office. I don't know why I'm acting all stupid over it but she's just so horrible. He can do better than her and he's never shown any signs that he likes her – though I know she is always drooling over him whenever she's in the same room – so I just don't get it,' Sabrina said, her face scrunched up in disgust.

'Ahhh, that would explain the dire wardrobe choices … and eeww gross. I feel your pain. Have you asked him about it?' Amanda said, making the swing rock back and forth again while she was thinking.

'Why would I do that? He can date whomever he wants. It's really none of my business. I just wish it wasn't my bitch of a boss. And it hasn't exactly been my top priority.' Sabrina fiddled with her sleeves.

'Brina, being your wise older sister I have the ability to know what you're thinking so here's my advice: one, you talk to him, because yes it is your business. You're looking out for the band's best interests after all and, well, because clearly you like him. And I know timing sucks but it's just going to keep eating away at you,' Amanda said, patting Sabrina's hand.

'I didn't say anything about liking him,' Sabrina noted, a little too forcefully, now playing with the hem of her shorts.

'Were you not listening? It's a gift, a skill, call it what you will, hey, that rhymed. But I know what you're thinking,' Amanda said, while performing spirit fingers around Sabrina's head.

'You are a nutter and anyway, how is you being best friends with Dan supposed to help me?'

'Oh yeah, well, advice part two: I can just have Dan fire him so you don't have to see him any more,' Amanda replied with a shrug and a sly raise of her eyebrows.

'Do you have any words of wisdom that will actually help me, oh wise one?' Sabrina said, rolling her eyes and playfully shoving her big sister. The sun was high in the sky now, yet Sabrina felt it was deceiving them. The fresh air hit her skin causing goose bumps to rise and the hair on her arms to stand tall.

'Look, I know what you saw probably sucked, but if I know Levi he wouldn't do something like that. I know he can be quite the flirt, but he's loyal and he knows how that woman treats you. I really think there's more to the situation that you don't know. In all seriousness you should speak to him,' Amanda said, her eyes boring into Sabrina's.

Sabrina wasn't fond of her big sister being right, but she knew it didn't make sense to run and hide. She had done that before and it hadn't worked out so well. In addition, she had to work with Levi. The band was her responsibility. She had to keep up with their lives and make sure nothing affected their work. If Levi was dating Lydia, she needed to make sure it wouldn't affect her position. She suddenly had the urge to be a little more honest with her big sister. She squirmed in her seat.

'Uh, we kissed – a long time ago, but we kissed,' she blurted out.

Amanda gasped and threw a hand to her mouth. 'No way, you didn't.' But one look at her big sister and Sabrina was fully aware she already knew.

'Is there anything you and Dan do not tell each other?' Sabrina asked, mock annoyed, tilting her head back on the seat cushion.

'Not much.' Amanda shrugged and laughed. 'From what Dan told me, Levi was crushed when you ran away from that kiss. Granted the idiot then chose to play rock star rather than talk to you, but even Dan said you very clearly put him in the friend zone after that. How come I had to hear it from Dan anyway?' Amanda asked.

'I was scared of what it was and I was terrified Lou would add it to her list of reasons she hates me and my perfect life. If I had a rock-star boyfriend, she'd just think I was living it up and having the time of my life and that I'd never come home,' Sabrina answered, with hurt in her tone.

'Look, I'm sorry about Lou. I hate you being gone too, but Dan can't stop talking about how amazing you are. In fact, that's all he talks about sometimes. You've worked so hard. She just misses you, that's all; but she will come round,' Amanda noted, pulling her jumper higher around her neck to keep the breeze at bay. 'Now, what are we going to do to fix the situation with you and Levi?'

'Lou did actually apologize to me earlier, so things might be looking up. Uh, I don't know about Levi. I don't even know if he likes me any more, and I did promise myself I wouldn't get taken in by his charm. Some professional I am. The first major band I take on and I immediately get a silly crush on the cute drummer. I'm just going to make a fool of myself,' she whined. Her voice sounded childish, even to herself, and she hated it. She was a grown-up, she was a professional, she could handle this. Heck, if the past few days were anything to go by she knew she was strong. If Levi had moved on, then so what? The pain could be nowhere near what she was already going through with her grandpa, surely?

'They are a pretty special group of guys. I imagine their faces adorn the walls of many teenagers' bedrooms right now and I can guarantee there's a woman swooning over their ridiculously handsome faces right this second. And you're not being unprofessional – this is how people meet. You've been working together for, what? Nearly two years now. You've spent a lot of time together. It happens. Plus, as far as Dan is concerned, the chemistry between you two every time you're in a room together is through the roof, so I don't believe it's just some silly crush on a hunky rock star. Something like what you have with Levi can't just fizzle out, no matter how much you try and bury it,' Amanda said, with a wink.

Sabrina watched as her big sister got up to stretch her lean legs. For all the food Amanda cooked and consumed, Sabrina was always impressed with her sister's athletic physique. Unlike herself and Louisa who were petite all over, Amanda had a few more inches on them in height and had inherited the same bust Mum and Nanna had. She was a knockout in a deep-cut neckline. It wasn't over the top but just enough to where she was sexy yet classy. Team that with any dress that showed her stunning legs and forget about it.

Growing up Amanda had been Sabrina's role model. To this day she felt the same. She adored her big sister's outgoing personality and laid-back, yet glam fashion sense. Amanda very much inspired her to be confident in who she was and with every aspect of life really. She had never admitted this to her big sister and there were many moments when Amanda drove her nuts and she wished her older sister would be more like Louisa when it came to love, rather than being so scared – something she herself ought to take into account too. But nevertheless, Amanda was strong and fierce and Sabrina loved that about her.

'Well, that's embarrassing,' Sabrina said, standing up to join

Amanda in looking out across the waters and the view of Positano to the right. You could see everything from their aunties' house: blue houses, pink houses, yellow houses all dotted along the mountainside, trees covering every inch, rocky pathways and steps upon steps upon steps that made it all seem like a secret maze, each road leading to its own unique and glorious haven. 'Thanks, Amanda. Oh and speaking of Dan and talking about being open and honest with people, have you been in touch with him recently?' Sabrina asked casually, hoping her sister wouldn't put her walls up again.

'I've spoken to him every day since Grandpa died.' Amanda let out a little sigh and then laughed. Sabrina studied her big sister's features closely. 'I can barely go two days without talking to him about something or other.' Sabrina knew this to be true; however, she was of the understanding that Amanda hadn't been keeping to that schedule in recent months. Dan had voiced his concerns whenever he hadn't heard from her in more than four days and those concerns had been voiced every week for the past three months. Sabrina felt hurt that her big sister wasn't being one hundred per cent truthful.

'You say that like it's a bad thing,' Sabrina noted, choosing to move past her sister's dishonesty when she saw that Amanda's face wore a worried expression. A frown crossed her older sister's face when she spoke.

'Well, it kind of is. He has his own life and people to deal with. He can't be speaking to me all the time or rushing to my aid when I need him.' The fact that Amanda had just mentioned needing Dan caused Sabrina to forget about her own job and Levi worries. This was a big step that Amanda was, again, oblivious to. Excited that her big sister was opening up to her she subtly pressed on.

'I'm sure Dan doesn't see it that way. I bet he's more than happy to help when you need him. And you know, speaking of telling people how you feel, you do know he's good for you. You're 'more lovable when he's in your life,' Sabrina said, giving her big sister a cheeky wink and a nudge in the side of her hip.

'He's my best friend, Brina – there's nothing more to tell.' And just like that Amanda closed up. It saddened Sabrina that Amanda's past had caused her to be so sceptical towards love when all signs clearly showed Dan was her meant-to-be. One rocky relationship and one disastrous break-up and her confident superhero of a big sister had built a wall. 'Hey, don't you dare go telling him that. He'll have a field day and get the wrong idea. I'm lovable all the time – just a big ball of lovableness.' Amanda winked back.

'Do you think it's bad that I'm thinking about Levi when Grandpa's funeral is tomorrow?' Sabrina wrapped her arms tightly around herself. It was an attempt at comfort, having not gotten used to talking about Grandpa this way. The tiles at her feet suddenly became very interesting.

'Not at all. If anything, I can completely understand why you would be thinking about it. Life is too short to sit and wonder about what-ifs. If you have feelings for Levi, why waste time? You know Grandpa loved life. Just look at him and Nanna. He saw her and didn't even hesitate – he walked straight up to her knowing that she was the one. And think about it, even with food, if he wanted to cook you couldn't stop him. He went to the kitchen and cooked. Sometimes you just have to go after what you want and not be scared of the consequences. He lived every day doing what he loved, surrounded by the people he loved most.'

Before Sabrina could suggest that her big sister take her own advice, Louisa wandered onto the balcony, resembling a sloth. She had a blanket draped over her, her feet dragging across the floor. As the sun found her face she blinked, raising a hand to shield the unwanted wake-up call.

'Morning, munchkins, what do you want to do today?' she asked, sounding a little more enthusiastic than she looked.

'You seem full of life this morning. Are you OK?' Amanda enquired, half joking, half serious about the sprightly tone in which her baby sister had spoken and the sharp contrast in her appearance. Her hair was scruffy, her cheeks covered in creases from her pillow.

'I guess so. I still feel like this is all some nasty dream, but I feel closer to him being here,' Louisa said, pausing to take in the view that Amanda and Sabrina were still admiring. 'I feel like I want to make the most of being here. We've missed this place so much. Grandpa loved it with everything he had. I want to embrace it and celebrate him and where he came from,' she continued, making Sabrina smile at her positive outlook. Of course, Sabrina was also aware that a certain gorgeous Italian had given her baby sister this much-needed boost of positivity, not simply the fresh Italian air. But she knew Louisa was right about Grandpa too: she herself had indeed felt closer to him since they had arrived in Italy.

'Sounds like a plan,' Amanda said, putting her arm around her little sister. 'But first we need fuel and by the smell that's rising in the air – my gosh they should bottle that and make it a perfume' – Amanda tilted her head to the sky and sniffed the air – 'Zia Sofia is making *saccottino al cioccolato*.' With one last glance at the waking village below, the girls turned towards the wooden door and made their way down the white tiled steps and into the kitchen.

Chapter 10

Nanna's Chocolate-Dipped Oranges

Ingredients:

750g caster sugar
500g of orange segments (preferably Italian)
200g melted dark Perugina chocolate.

What to do:

Place sugar in saucepan with 500ml water. Allow sugar to dissolve and reach 110 degrees, stirring occasionally. (Invest in candy thermometer for when Grandpa isn't around to guess for you.)

Add the fruit to the sugar mixture and reduce heat. Let simmer for 5 minutes.

Take fruit out of mix and allow to cool on wire rack, while you pre-heat oven to 180 degrees.

Allow segments to dry in oven for 10 minutes, before letting them cool down.

Once cool, melt chocolate and dip segments in, before placing back on wire rack and allowing them to set. (You may add sambuca to chocolate. Pretty sure that's what Nanna added last time, even though she wouldn't admit it.)

'Wait for me,' Sabrina shouted to her sisters, as they raced ahead of her. It was late in the afternoon. The sun had decided to play a game of hide-and-seek. It was doing a far better job at the hiding part and from eleven this morning had not bothered coming back out at all. Instead the brilliant blues and orange glow had been replaced by a miserable grey and a fine rain that wasn't showing any signs of slowing down.

'Come on, slow coach,' Amanda shouted back.

Sabrina tiptoed carefully so as to not slip on any black ice that might be lurking on the cobbles. Her sisters didn't seem too fussed about the possibility of twisting an ankle and were merrily skipping ahead but Sabrina would not be so careless. She didn't fancy a trip to A & E so close to Christmas. It had got icier as the day progressed, but the girls had been determined to visit some of their favourite spots. Though some would call them crazy, they had bundled up and were making their way down the mountain to the beach.

'It's so flippin' cold,' Sabrina said catching up with the others. The pebbles became easier to navigate as they landed on flatter ground.

'It's nice and fresh, good for clearing the brain,' Amanda replied. 'Who wants an ice cream?' She wiped away the raindrops that got caught in her eyelashes with her sleeves.

'You've got to be kidding me,' Sabrina said, zipping her coat up a few more inches. Amanda laughed. Louisa continued up and down a few steps ahead.

'Aw it's closed now,' Louisa called out to answer Amanda's question in all seriousness, as they walked past the little ice-cream café that was hiding away in the corner of the moutainside. This was the place they used to run inside still dripping wet from the sea and order their gelato cones, before chasing each other back onto the cobbles, trying not to drop their ice creams from their sticky hands. 'Italy shuts down this time of year.'

'I know, I know,' Amanda replied. 'It's so calm at this time. I love it. And this cold weather wouldn't stop me eating one of Tony's gelato cones.'

'Me neither,' Louisa noted, peering in the window just in case there was a sign of movement and they could actually get their hands on one of Tony's incredible hand-dipped cones. Sabrina watched as her sister's eyes darted around the small café and then seemingly a tad deflated, she carried on walking ahead.

They walked past the café and onto the pebbled beach. In the summertime this place would be packed, full of people paddling in the clear turquoise water, fishermen lined up along the edge of the stone barrier, canoes and brightly coloured boats every-where you looked. Now, in the middle of the frosty December, it was deserted.

The girls made themselves comfy, pulling out their lemon-print blankets from the rucksack they had brought with them. Sabrina helped Amanda with pouring out cups of *pastina* from the flask she had prepared, just like Grandpa would have done on their fishing trips. She handed one to Louisa and held the other two tight, allowing Amanda to put away the flask and get situated, before passing a cup to her.

'Ooh thank you for making this, Amanda,' Louisa said, in appreciation. She wrapped her hands around the cup to warm them.

They sat in silence for a while just watching the waves crash against the rocks. Every now and again a bird would swoop low, testing the water for any signs of fish. The rain had slowed to more of a light dripping and occasionally a ray of sun would cast a shadow over their chosen spot.

'Do you remember that time we caught that squid?' Louisa piped up. It had been a beautiful summer's day, many years back. Grandpa had taken them fishing right along the very pier they were currently looking out to. They had all been thrilled each time they caught a teeny tiny silver fish. They would jump up and down on the spot proudly waving their catch in Grandpa's face.

He had laughed, telling them to look out for the big fish as those would make for a more hearty supper. But the bucket had been close to the brim with the tiny fish when Grandpa called out for them to make room. He swung around his fishing line, letting go and dropping a squid the size of his hand on top of the bucket. The girls screamed as it wriggled and slipped down the side, the little fish not leaving any room for the squid to fit.

'That was the scariest thing ever, all those tentacles. We didn't know what to do with it.' Sabrina grimaced. 'It was so slimy, spilling out of that bucket.'

'We just kept catching all those tiny fish. Not a big one in sight,' Amanda added.

'Grandpa would smile all the same. Whatever we caught he was always so proud.' Louisa sighed. Sabrina could see that tears were threatening to cascade down her baby sister's face.

'Hey, it's OK,' she said, rubbing her sister's arm. 'He's looking down on us. He's still with us every day, remember? We will have to come back in the summer and see what we can catch.'

'I'd like that,' Louisa said softly, taking a big gulp of the comforting *pastina*.

'See what kind of fishermen he raised, hey?' Amanda added, rubbing Louisa's shoulder.

'That will be a sight to behold, the three of us trying to get the squids off the hooks once we catch them, without Grandpa.'

Sabrina shuddered. 'I'll let you do that bit, Lou.' She shuffled on the cold rocks, her butt having started to go numb.

'Ha, I'd give it a go. He always made it look so easy,' Louisa replied, replicating Sabrina's action and tucking her coat under her bum to avoid the chill of the rocks.

'At least we will give him something entertaining to look down on. I'm sure it would have him rolling with laughter,' Amanda said, before looking from Sabrina to Louisa and back again. 'Now, are you two going to let me in on your little secret?'

Sabrina was grateful to her big sister for changing the subject and had to laugh at the fact Amanda hadn't forgotten their exchange from the other night when making cream caramels. Sabrina's lips were sealed of course. It would be up to Louisa if she wanted to spill the beans. So she faked innocence.

Louisa continued sipping on her *pastina*. Amanda glared at them both. 'If you ever want homemade pizza again … your choice?' Amanda shrugged, taking the last sip of her *pastina* and placing her cup down on a bunch of pebbles.

'Oh all right.' Louisa giggled, handing Amanda her finished cup. 'Follow me.' She jumped up and took off. Sabrina tried to help Amanda by grabbing the cups and carefully stuffing them in Amanda's backpack as they both awkwardly ran after their little sister while trying their best not to drop everything.

'Where are we going?' Amanda shouted. She had to shout to be heard over the car horns as they reached the village. Sabrina noticed she was panting too, having both sprinted up the ramps and leapt two steps at a time to see which direction Louisa had gone.

'I have an idea,' Sabrina replied, shouting above the noisy car exhausts and gasping for air. She felt a touch wheezy at the sudden shift in gear. She hadn't planned on a cardio session today. However, as she slowed down and the air returned to her lungs, she felt her heart expand with love as she watched Louisa skip ahead. That feeling combined with the look of confusion that had spread across Amanda's face had her feeling buzzed on happiness. She knew that this feeling of pure joy was one that only time spent with your sisters and seeing them finding their way could evoke.

As they reached a more crowded path, the air filled with the most heavenly vanilla fragrance. Sabrina watched as Amanda's eyes grew wide. She could see the cogs ticking in her big sister's head, the need to find out where the smell was coming from building inside her. Louisa turned to face them both. 'OK, so please don't embarrass me or say anything stupid,' she said. Sabrina was pleased to see that with the last words spoken Louisa had given Amanda a pointed glare.

'Why, where are we? And please tell me you are taking me to wherever that incredible smell is coming from?' Amanda asked, her nose pointed sky high and sniffing the air. This was a common stance for Amanda whenever they were near food.

'I met a boy,' Louisa said. Sabrina let out a squeal of excitement that Louisa was allowing them to meet her handsome stranger.

'You what?' Amanda responded. 'When did this happen?' Sabrina noticed that Amanda was smiling. No doubt the sweet vanilla scent was clouding any need for big sister, little sister talks, which came as a relief. Sabrina didn't want Louisa to overthink this situation or for anything to dim the light in her eyes. She wanted her to enjoy this moment and this feeling for as long as possible. If one of them could get this love thing right, Sabrina would be happy if it was Louisa. She wore her heart on her sleeve and deserved it.

'Please don't think I'm crazy, Amanda, but I only met him a day ago when I came out for a walk, and he's just lovely,' Louisa said, looking slightly anxious. Sabrina gave her an encouraging hug.

'I don't think you're crazy, Lou, not at all. This is so exciting, are we meeting him? Is this why you brought us here? Oh my God, does he work in that place?' Amanda replied, jumping on the spot and copying Sabrina in hugging their sister. Sabrina's mouth fell open at Amanda's new-found giddiness. Yes, the sugary aroma had worked some magic on their big sister.

'Yes, yes he does,' Louisa answered, her shoulders falling away from her ears, clearly relieved that her big sister was not about to get all overprotective on her and burst her bubble.

'I say he's a keeper. Whatever that is, it smells phenomenal,' Amanda commented, licking her lips and hoisting her backpack up on to her back, like a schoolgirl ready for her first day.

'Just wait till you see inside,' Louisa said, her smile now reaching all the way to her ears, as she took both her sisters' hands and led the way.

Sabrina felt giddy with anticipation at the thought of meeting the man who had swept her baby sister off her feet and put the sparkle back in her eyes after the heartbreak of the last few days. There were two men working behind the counter. It didn't take a genius to figure out which one was Luca. He was the one who couldn't take his eyes off Louisa. The minute he noticed her walking into the shop, Sabrina witnessed a dazzling smile appear on his face as he immediately stopped what he was doing.

'Is that him?' Amanda whispered in Sabrina's ear, as they walked behind Louisa. 'Jesus, he is divine.'

'I think so. He hasn't taken his eyes off her and bloody hell, you can say that again,' Sabrina whispered back. Well done, Louisa, she thought to herself.

***

'Oh my gosh, I'm in love,' Amanda said, through a mouthful of ricotta torte. Sabrina wasn't sure if she was talking about Luca or the third pastry she was currently demolishing. Luca had stepped away from the counter to say hello to the girls. Sabrina adored the way in which he had hugged Louisa and given her a light kiss on the cheek. He had been charming and sweet and

Louisa was clearly besotted. Now, it seemed, so was Amanda. He had certainly won her over when he sent them home with a box of cakes.

'So, do you like him?' Louisa asked, walking arm in arm with Sabrina. Amanda walked a step behind, cradling the cake box and licking her fingers.

'Do we like him?' Amanda said throwing her head back and shaking her head. 'Do we like him?' she repeated almost to herself this time, as though Louisa had just asked the most ridiculous question.

'I think that's a yes from the cake monster over there,' Sabrina said with a chuckle and a roll of her eyes as she squeezed Louisa's arm. 'He's a sweetheart, Lou. He seems to have a good head on his shoulders and – just like you – he seems to put family first and really care about them. You could tell that just through the way he spoke. He's pretty wonderful,' she finished, linking arms with Louisa and guiding her past the low grapevines and what remained of the shrivelled oranges still clinging on to their trees.

'Uh, I'm so happy you like him. That's such a relief,' Louisa said, squeezing Sabrina back. 'I'm not expecting much. We're only here for a few more days but just to have someone ease the pain for those few days will be nice. He makes me laugh and I didn't think laughing would be possible with Grandpa gone,' Louisa continued and it made Sabrina's heart ache. She rested her head against Louisa's as they walked.

'Seize those moments to laugh, Lou. Grandpa would want to be looking down on your smiling face every day. We will cope together as a family and if Luca gives you that sense of hope and happiness, you keep hold of him and enjoy him for however long you have, OK?' Sabrina said, clutching on to her baby sister tightly. A strong feeling of protectiveness washed over her. She would do anything to look after Louisa and make sure she always kept her sense of wonder and positivity that beautiful things were just around the corner, even when faced with obstacles and struggles.

'And, did either of you two notice that he looks like Giulio Berruti?' Amanda shouted from the background, her head buried in the cake box. She was walking like a drunk, more interested in the contents of the box than her own wellbeing as she zigzagged on the crazy Italian streets.

Sabrina and Louisa looked at each other and promptly doubled over with laughter.

***

Evening rolled around once more. The sky was awash with a pearl-like grey, threatening flurries of snow with its chill. Amanda had finished preparing the evening meal and the table was set. Feeling slightly warm from the heat of the oven, she stepped outside for some fresh air. Though it was terribly cold out, Italy was exceptionally dazzling at night-time. You could see stars for miles in the silvery sky. They cast shadows down onto the water, making it sparkle as though it were a bath full of glitter.

In the distance, lights shone from little windows as families sat down together to enjoy dinner. Your imagination could take you away, dreaming of the adventures you could have along the Amalfi Coast and the characters you would meet along the way.

'How are you feeling, sweetheart?' came Mum's voice, as she strolled through the balcony, past the potted plants, to find Amanda sitting outside by the small fountain the girls had loved playing at when they were kids.

'OK I guess, Mum. How are you?'

'I'm holding up OK thank you, sweet pea.' Mum paused as she looked around her. 'I remember the day we decorated these rocks. Mum, your nanna, just let us make whatever pattern we fancied. She loved the colourful crystals so much I don't think she would have minded if we had covered the whole house,' Mum said, with a small laugh as she sat on the small ledge next to Amanda. She was referring to the tiles and bright sparkling gems that shone from in between the stones around the water fountain. The same fountain, still in all its glory, that was in all Mum's old baby pictures and her childhood photos, and which the girls had been drawn to. It was a popular spot for all Mum's cousins, aunts and uncles to be snapped.

'I think you did a great job, quite the artist,' Amanda replied. She wasn't lying either. The gems almost looked like a rainbow as they curved around the tiles that depicted the Virgin Mary. It was rather beautiful and calming seeing them reflecting off the water as it splashed into the basin.

'Have you heard anything from work?' her mum asked. Amanda sighed. She had been distracted the past few days, with cooking alongside her aunties, Sabrina opening up about Levi, Louisa and her Italian stallion and the funeral preparations. Her aunties had been doing the majority of the preparations, as they didn't want the girls or Mum and Nanna to have to talk flowers and gravesites. Amanda appreciated this greatly.

The Amalfi Coast had magical powers that made her feel a world away from Jeff's snide glares and the stress of running a manic kitchen, but she wouldn't be able to ignore the messages on her phone for too much longer. If it hadn't been for the constant checking her phone because of the lack of messages from Dan, she would have happily remained distracted from work drama for a while longer.

'I wasn't going to say anything because it doesn't matter now, and I really don't want you to worry, Mum. So, please don't worry. But things don't seem good.' Amanda didn't want to go into too much detail, even if her mum promised. Amanda knew she would still worry and she couldn't do that to her, not now. Jeff might have turned one of the UK's finest food critics against her only four days after she had left, but it all seemed superficial and redundant in comparison to losing Grandpa.

'Anthony seems eager for me to get back but I'm sure it's nothing. He's probably just getting sick of Jeff.' She wasn't about to tell her mum that Anthony had informed her that it was in her best interest to get back soon if she wanted to keep her job and her reputation intact.

Apparently, everything had gone south when Jeff decided to cancel Amanda's food order and reconstruct the dining menu. Food hadn't arrived on time and Jeff had naturally placed the blame on Amanda, informing Anthony that she hadn't done her job properly before she left. It just so happened that with hardly any food and a disaster of a menu, a renowned food critic had come in and received a less than stellar dining experience, which again, fell on Amanda's shoulders.

'It will be OK. I'm sorry for all the extra stress this has caused. You try not to worry about them – they will figure it out,' Mum said gently, as she stroked Amanda's hair.

'Mum, please don't apologize for us being here. We knew when the time came we would be coming here. I'm happy Grandpa is home. I wouldn't want it any other way. And I'm not allowing Jeff to cause me stress; Grandpa would not have it. He would tell me to do what I have to do, no worries just follow your passion.' Amanda gave her mum a flicker of a smile.

'That's very true, chickpea. I'm so proud of you,' Mum said, leaning in to her to give her a cuddle. Amanda hoped all would be OK upon her return. She didn't want to lie to her mum, but she didn't want to make her more anxious than she already was about her girls being away from work.

'Thanks, Mum. We're lucky we have so many happy memories of him, you know. I'm here for you though – don't feel like you have to be strong for us kids. He was your dad after all. This can't be easy for you.'

Mum let out a sigh and a slight laugh.

'I have the best daughters anyone could ask for. Thank you, honey, but you are right. We are lucky for the wonderful memories and those are what I want to focus on. I got to have him for a very long time and I'm blessed that he still enjoyed life to the very end, still chatting away, mind fully there. I couldn't have asked for anything more. But he's not gone too far. I know he's with me,' she said, putting her hand to her chest, over her heart.

'That's true, Mamma, you are the best and always right. I love you,' Amanda said, wrapping her arms around her and embracing her mum in a hug. In all her uncertainty about work and Dan, she knew one thing was for certain: nothing beat a cuddle from her mum.

'I love you too. You know Zia Sofia hasn't stopped going on about your cooking and how incredibly special you are. She says Grandpa and Nanna raised you right. I think she'd like to keep you given the chance. She says it's nice having a young, fresh, enthusiastic cook around the house.'

'Ha-ha, thanks, Mum, that's nice to hear. I love cooking with them. I hope to be half as good as them one day.'

'Don't doubt yourself, honey. That pasta smells amazing. Now let's go eat before we catch a chill,' Mum said, grabbing Amanda's hand and leading her back inside.

Chapter 11

Cornetto

Ingredients:

¼ pint warm milk
1 tsp salt
1½ tbsps sugar
1oz yeast dissolved in warm water
12oz white bread flour
4oz butter
1 egg yolk beaten with a little milk

What to do:

Put butter in a bowl and pour on warm milk. Add the salt and sugar.

Allow to cool to lukewarm then add yeast.

Then add the flour to form a dough.

Cover dough with a damp cloth and leave for two hours.

Knead the dough then leave to chill.

Chill thoroughly. (Ask Grandpa how long thoroughly is? Maybe an hour or more?)

Roll out dough into rectangle and roll again, then chill.

Fold twice more then roll to ¼ thickness and cut into 4-inch squares. (Really need to make these with Grandpa again. The rolling and folding is confusing. Wing it?)

Grandpa said something about triangles and edges and rolling up into crescents. (Why do cornettos sound so complicated? Need Grandpa's help.)

Once they look like cornettos, place on baking sheet, brush with beaten egg and bake in the oven for 15 minutes at 220 degrees.

(What would Grandpa do? Think — you've seen him do it.)

Louisa shot up in bed. Her alarm felt deafening this morning. Its ringing caused beads of sweat to form on her forehead. She smacked the button with an anger that she felt was going to be present today, despite her best efforts. She wiped her eyes and quietly reached for the pile of clothes she had organized the night before.

Careful not to wake the others, she tiptoed to the bathroom to get dressed. She wanted some time to herself, to calm her nerves, before she had to engage in conversation. She closed the bathroom door behind her and threw cold water on her face. Looking at herself in the mirror she felt numb and barely recognized the girl looking back. Her eyelids were discoloured, red and yellow in colour. Her cheeks looked sallow.

She wondered for a second how Luca could possibly find her attractive. At once the waterworks erupted and tears streamed down her face. She was a different person now. But that was OK, wasn't it? Luca breathed life into this new person. It was understandable for her to change. That didn't mean she wasn't lovable and that she would always be sad. Luca made her happy and Grandpa would want that for her.

She sat down on the edge of the bath, focusing on steadying her breathing and getting her thoughts together. 'You can't do this today, Lou,' she said to herself, clutching on to the side of the bath when she felt light-headed. 'You have to be strong. I have to celebrate you, Grandpa. Please give me the strength to celebrate you because right now all I want to do is be sick,' she sobbed. Releasing her grip from the bathtub, she turned on the taps. The sound of the water eased her heartbreaking thoughts. Later she simply went through the motions to get herself dressed.

Her mind was still hazy as she stepped out onto the balcony with a cup of coffee in hand. What the day had in store for them was finally hitting her and it was hitting her hard. The rich, smooth taste of Lavazza soothed her scratchy throat. Looking into her coffee mug, a small smile escaped her lips. It's true what they say about enjoying the little things in life and appreciating what you have. 'This is a good cup of coffee, Grandpa,' she whispered.

She stood on the balcony until the moon had completely vanished from her line of vision. She chatted to her grandpa a while, looking out into the grey sky above, telling him that this wasn't goodbye, she would talk to him every day. She could see him smiling down at her. She knew he wouldn't want her to be sad, but she couldn't shake the numbness that not having him next to her had caused. She finished her last drop of coffee as the sky started to brighten, and the sun peeked out from the dull clouds.

Suddenly she heard the voices of her nanna and Zia Sofia in

the kitchen. The house was awake. She headed back indoors and found everyone bustling around inside, making breakfast and beginning preparations for the day. At the sight of her, Nanna began to scramble, being extra fussy about food, telling her to eat. She pulled out all the plates of leftover *cornettos* and *sfogliatelle* and started putting bread in the toaster.

Louisa's heart gave a tug as she could see Nanna was distracting herself. She looked terribly ruffled and fragile, her brows furrowed and her eyes unfocused, not full of their usual sparkle. Taking the toast from her nanna's quivering hand and placing it next to the jar of Nutella, Louisa hugged her tight before encouraging her to sit.

'It's going to be OK, Nanna. It is, I promise,' Louisa whispered, taking her hand and placing a *cornetto* in front of her. 'Eat, you will feel better.'

Nanna simply shook her head and gave Louisa's hand a squeeze. 'You, *mangia, mangia*,' she managed, her head hung low, waving her hand over the breakfast spread.

Louisa picked up the *cornetto* and cut it in half, placing one half back down on Nanna's plate and the other half on her own plate. She wasn't certain her stomach could handle the buttery breakfast, but she didn't want to make her nanna worry needlessly and so began munching on it slowly.

One by one her sisters filtered into the kitchen followed by Mum and Dad and Zia Emilia and Zia Rosa. They sat in silence before Louisa offered them all a *cornetto*. As they each took a bite Louisa noticed their faces flush with a little more colour. It was quite remarkable the way food could evoke so many special memories and how it could warm you and lift your spirits.

She forced herself to take another bite, knowing she would need the energy. Piece by piece the buttery flavour hit her tongue and she felt somewhat calmer. She could see Grandpa in her mind, busy in the kitchen, passion oozing from his every pore. Breakfast was one of his favourite times of the day.

Her eyes prickled as she longed for another morning where she would burst through her grandparents' front door, the strong smell of Lavazza in the air, Grandpa with his head over pots and pans, the oven already through half a day's work at seven-thirty in the morning, Nanna asking her what she wanted for breakfast, as she, Louisa, made herself comfortable at the kitchen table and watched her beautiful *nonni* live life to the fullest.

***

Louisa walked with her sisters either side of her. They each held on tight to a picture of the Madonna and Padre Pio, as they walked in step to the church. Nanna and Mum were holding up OK. The girls had given them a little space to grieve together, though they stayed close, so they could help Nanna down the slippery stairs. Dad was walking behind with their aunties, all of whom were dressed in black, heads bowed as they walked hand in hand.

There was a sprinkle of snow on the ground and on the trees around them, causing the pavement to glisten under their feet as the sun's rays moved with them. Louisa was grateful that the sun had appeared and was keeping the cold at bay for their walk. As they made their way past the corner shops and houses, more and more people joined their party. They nodded when they made eye contact with the family and bowed their heads with sympathy.

Louisa felt touched that these elderly men and women would brave the cold and the far from easy walk just so they could pay their respects to Grandpa. The knowledge that he had stayed in their hearts all these years, even when he hadn't always lived here, made her smile. She spotted Luca among the crowd and her heart skipped a happier beat at the sight of him. She waved, which caught the attention of both her sisters. They waved too, smiling from Louisa to Luca, before returning their sullen stares to the steps in front of them.

It didn't take them too long to reach the church, yet Louisa's thighs were burning. She tried subtly to rub them, allowing herself to bend over slightly and rest her hands on her knees to catch her breath. There must be something in the water, she thought, taking in the tanned and wrinkled faces of those around her. The Mediterranean diet certainly had a lot to answer for, as she didn't see any of the older men and women in attendance struggling to fight a stitch in their sides. Grandpa did make it to ninety-six, she mused.

Once the stitch in her side settled down she raised her head from the floor and uncurled herself, rotating her shoulders so she was standing up straight. Amanda gave her a quizzical look, her eyes narrowed, before they both smiled in understanding.

It took a moment for Louisa to acknowledge the spectacular sight before her. Then her mouth dropped open. The church stood grand, the architecture magnificent. The yellow and cream brick shone in the sunlight. The two turrets either side of the entrance loomed over them in a way so regal and proud. The detailing and craftsmanship was enough to take your breath away.

On each side of the square, colourful tiles depicting St Luca and the Virgin Mary added a touch of softness and spirit to the otherwise cold and dirty high walls. Off to the side a modest fountain blessed all who touched it with holy water as it ran from a small statue of Jesus and into a little dish below.

Louisa closed her mouth and gulped, her feet unsteady when taking a step. She linked arms with her sisters and led the way to the last bundle of steps that would take them to the church. When they reached the top of the stairs the girls gasped simultaneously. The square was packed with people. As the girls made their way past the friendly crowd, they were greeted with waves, hugs, handshakes and whispers of 'I'm so sorry.'

By the time they reached the entrance, Louisa was left gobsmacked. She stared at the grain in the giant wooden doors at the front of the church, opening and closing her mouth like a goldfish. She felt overwhelmed by the number of people who had shown up to be there for her grandpa. Of course, it wasn't too much of a surprise that he had made an impact on so many people's lives, but still, at that moment, she lifted her head high and couldn't have felt prouder to be his granddaughter. Likewise, she noticed her sisters were looking more confident, a determination suddenly etched on their faces as they too stood tall.

Louisa blinked back a tear and noticed a gorgeous wreath, adorned with shiny golden bells and vibrant red holly, hung in the centre of the giant oak doors. Louisa had almost forgotten that Christmas was in a few days' time. She looked back and searched the crowd for her parents and her nanna. From her viewpoint on the step, she found her nanna was busy stopping to speak and shake hands with the people as she passed.

One lady ever so gently grabbed her nanna's cheeks and kissed them, her hands shaking, tears glistening in her eyes. The lady's face bore a torn expression. Her eyes crinkled with kindness yet there was a sadness in her gaze. Louisa imagined there was a pain at seeing someone you love again after so many years. Maybe she was a best friend of Nanna's, since they embraced for longer than the others. Maybe the joy in seeing each other again was over-powering, thinking of the time together they had missed, while at the same time being grateful for another encounter.

Many people hugged Mum, clearly thrilled to see her, Louisa observed. Some of them probably hadn't seen her since she had lived here as a teenager. The sweet gestures and togetherness Louisa felt looking out to the sea of people made her eyes tear up and her mind wander to thoughts of the last time she stood in the same exact spot. It had been Easter and she had been six years old. She was wearing a pretty white and yellow collared dress with flowers embroidered on it and was holding a branch aloft with small parcels of cheese attached to it.

After the Easter mass, she had run around the square chasing her sisters, who were nibbling on the sugared almond branches they had been given. They looked more appealing than the cheese branch she was carrying, so naturally, they teased her, and a game of tag broke out, with the girls running in circles around Grandpa as he spoke merrily with friends.

The sound of the creaking church door interrupted her thoughts. Louisa felt both Amanda and Sabrina squeeze her hands tight. They stepped into the church as the church bells rang out. Looking back over her shoulder she spotted the pallbearers carrying her grandpa's coffin. Life would go on, but it would never be the same again.

***

The service was beautiful. Sabrina couldn't have been happier with the celebration of their grandpa's life. With him and Nanna being Catholic they stayed true to traditions as their grandpa would have wanted. The priest read Grandpa's favourite readings and did the traditional funeral mass. However, the girls also wanted to be able to talk and share stories about Grandpa and so stood up to address the congregation towards the end of the mass.

Sabrina felt a release in being able to laugh and joke and reminisce, being able to share her pain with others but also to share her love for the wonderful man she felt lucky to have called her grandpa. She felt Grandpa would have approved of their straying from certain traditional elements and recalling the odd humorous story. The girls took turns, picking up where the other left off, when their emotions got the best of them and the tears rushed down their cheeks, but they did well regaling the crowd with anecdotes and making them chuckle in memory. It was the next bit Sabrina wasn't sure she could handle.

Her eyes squinted in the sunlight and a dull ache settled in her stomach as she stepped out into the square. The sun peeked through the clouds, easing the chill of winter ever so slightly, and

Sabrina thought about how she needed to invest in some fashionable Italian sunglasses and could now understand the fashion statement. The sun could be blinding.

She moved away from the crowd leaving the church, checking over her shoulder that her sisters were safe with their dad, before she sat herself down on a bench that was tucked away in the corner. Her heart was hammering in her chest and she needed some privacy. She didn't want this day to be real. She rocked back and forth in her seat, willing the sickness that was rising in her throat to pass. She hated being sick.

For a moment, she got lost watching the cracks in the pavement and following their trails. Then she reached into her purse and pulled out her favourite picture of her grandpa. She smiled as his bright eyes and loving face looked back at her. This was the face she wanted to think about when she remembered him, along with the countless goofy and wonderful memories, not a vision of a box or a church. Raising the photograph to her lips, she kissed it gently and placed it safely back in the zip pocket of her purse.

Just then a shadow appeared at her feet. Raising her hand to her temple to shield the sun's beams, she craned her neck towards the sky to see what large object was causing such a looming shadow. If she hadn't been sitting her knees would have buckled and she would have fainted for sure.

She blinked and rubbed her eyes, not sure if her eyes were playing tricks on her and if sunstroke was a thing in the middle of winter. It couldn't be. But sure enough after blinking for the fourth time, she opened her eyes again to find Levi standing in front of her with tear-filled brown eyes, looking incredibly dashing in his black suit.

'Oh, my gosh,' she said, and without even a second thought Sabrina threw her arms around him and began to bawl.

'It's OK, I'm here,' Levi whispered in her ear, stroking her hair as he did so. Sabrina didn't have time to overthink her actions and contemplate her professionalism. She simply allowed him to soothe her. After a moment or two, she pulled herself away but kept him at arm's reach. She didn't dare look away in case she was dreaming. Instead she stood rooted to the spot just staring at his face, his brown eyes inviting and comforting. Another moment passed and once she was satisfied that Levi was not a mirage she turned to the tall, floppy-brown-haired guy next to him.

'Dan,' she managed before words escaped her and all she could do to express her gratitude at him being there was to hug him too.

'That was a lovely speech you did in there,' Dan said, his eyes glistening. Sabrina realized he had been crying too and though she would never wish for Dan to be sad or for anyone to ever experience the pain she felt, she couldn't help but feel a love for him right there and then. Dan had met Grandpa once but had Skyped with him and spoke on the phone with him on many occasions, and of course, he had listened to Amanda talk about him non-stop, but Sabrina had a feeling that as much as Dan thought highly of their grandpa and respected him, his tears were for Amanda and because in this situation he hadn't been able to protect her and no matter what he said, he wouldn't be able to take away the pain in her heart from losing someone she loved with everything she had.

'Thank you, it felt good to talk about him, you know? Wait.' Sabrina paused and tilted her head in confusion. 'Did you understand it?' she asked, remembering they had spoken in Italian and Dan did not speak Italian.

'I understood bits. Amanda sometimes forgets when she's speaking in Italian, so I've learnt the odd word over the years,' he said, his voice catching a little when he mentioned Amanda, then he smiled shyly. This was not the alpha male Dan Sabrina was used to being around. He seemed vulnerable, like he had let his guard down.

'Have you seen Amanda yet?' Sabrina asked, placing a hand on his arm. Levi handed her a tissue, which she gratefully took with her free hand.

'Not yet, we didn't want to interrupt anything. We got here just as it started,' Dan replied, clearing his throat and adjusting his suit jacket. 'How's she doing?' he added. His raspy voice sounded strained, like he couldn't bear the thought of his best friend in pain.

'It's been a rough day,' Sabrina said. 'But I'm sure seeing you will lift her spirits.' She patted his arm. Without warning the church bells chimed again, signalling the procession to the cemetery was about to start. Levi caught Sabrina's eye and he reached out to squeeze her hand. She leant in and gave him another quick hug, thankful to have his support both mentally and physically as the coffin came into view.

'I'm going to go find my family, OK?' she said, her voice a whisper.

'OK, sure. We won't be far behind,' Levi replied, his hand lingering on hers for longer than was professional.

Sabrina nodded gratefully before running off to find her family. Her heart suddenly felt lighter and though she had things to say to Levi, she couldn't shake her surprise at the fact that he was here. She hadn't even realized she needed him here but seeing his face had caused her whole being to relax. A calm had washed over her.

She only felt slightly guilty about the band's schedule and the fact that she was being a terrible manager, not shouting at them both and asking why on earth they weren't keeping to it. In seeing Levi, that had all gone out the window. There were more important things in life.

136

Chapter 12

Nanna and Grandpa's Lemon and Marsala Cheesecake/Tart

Ingredients:

For the filling:
2 x 8oz cream cheese
½ cup sugar
Rind of 1 lemon
1 tbsp lemon zest
2 tbsps lemon juice
½ tsp vanilla
2 eggs
For the crust:
½ cup of butter
10 digestives (Need to try with amaretti)
¼ cup of Marsala (It's more like a whole cup, see how you feel.)

What to do:

Crust:

Crush digestives.

Melt butter and add to crushed digestive mix.

Add Marsala and then press crust mixture into greased pie dish.

Chill in fridge while you make your filling.

Pre-heat oven to 180 degrees.

Filling:

Mix your cream cheese, sugar, lemon rind, lemon zest, lemon juice and vanilla till smooth.

Add eggs one at a time and mix after each addition.

Pour into crust and bake for 40 minutes.

Leave to cool and then refrigerate for 3 hours before serving. (Give to family first, as otherwise you and Grandpa will eat the whole thing.)

It took every bit of strength Amanda had left in her to not crumple into a heap on the grass as she watched the coffin being lowered into the ground. Her heart was beating manically in her chest. She was shaking from head to toe, holding on to her sisters as though they were her lifeline. She wanted to scream, run away, stop the coffin and see her grandpa's face again, all at the same time. Her whole body shook, not knowing quite what to do with itself.

She couldn't stop the buckets of tears that flooded her face and didn't know if she would ever be able to. The tissues in her hand were sopping wet and were no longer very useful to stop her runny nose. Once the coffin lay in its final resting place and the priest had said his blessing, Amanda watched as one by one Nanna, Mum, Dad and each one of her aunties threw a rose into the open earth.

When it was her turn she clung on to Louisa and stepped forward, kissing the beautiful flower before throwing it into the air. Some time passed before Amanda noticed the people start to move around her. Some were chatting to one another; others were making their way past the marble plaques, taking a moment to look at the picture and read the engravings about who lay behind it.

Mum and Nanna made their way over to the girls to inform them they were going to head back to the house. Amanda gave them both a huge hug and told them she'd catch up with them shortly. She listened as a few more people blessed and kissed the air, waving their hands to say their goodbyes as the formalities ended. Amanda was stood still, rooted to the spot, just staring at the ground where her grandpa now lay. Her sisters hadn't left her side.

'Well, Grandpa, you're finally home,' she whispered. She could taste the salty tears that pooled on her Cupid's bow and tried to dab them away with her dishevelled tissue.

'We love you,' Sabrina choked out, not having much luck with her own tissue either, Amanda noted.

'We'll talk to you every day,' Louisa mumbled, wiping her nose on her cardigan.

Amanda turned to her sisters and pulled them both into a group hug. 'I love you both so much,' she said.

'Love you too,' they replied in unison.

'Now let's go and drink all the Limoncello and make Grandpa proud,' Sabrina said clearing her throat. Giving up on her tissue she wiped away her tears on the sleeves of the black jumper dress Amanda had lent her.

'Sounds good,' Louisa replied, trying with all her might to muster a little laugh.

'You guys go ahead. I'll just be a minute,' Amanda said. She needed a little more time before she could walk away from her grandpa.

She watched as her sisters walked up the stone steps and receded into the distance, then she closed her eyes and began counting to ten in her head, in an attempt to steady her breathing. As she reached number eight, she felt a hand on her shoulder. She closed her eyes tighter, concentrating hard on the warmth that surged through her body at his touch. She felt it down to her very core.

Suddenly, every emotion for him, for her grandpa, the stress of work, of trying to bury her feelings, came barrelling out. She turned around to face him and he grabbed her and pulled her in to him tightly. Dan cupped her head with one hand and hugged her waist with the other. Tears were falling down his face too. She could feel them melt into hers as she buried her face into his solid, comforting chest.

'I'm so sorry, baby girl, I'm so sorry,' Dan whispered, his raspy voice barely audible through his own sobs. They remained in each other's embrace for some time, until Amanda took a shuddery deep breath and stepped back to look at him. His brown eyes were rich and wet, his cheeks blushed red and his jaw tense. As he met her gaze his jaw softened, and his full lips parted as he leant in to kiss her forehead.

With Dan she could let her guard down and be vulnerable and she knew that was the case with him too. He didn't act tough or claim to be tough but there was undeniable masculinity about him mixed with that poetic softness. Deep down she knew he would somehow be here, though she had tried not to think about it too much, knowing how rough his work schedule could be; but she had needed him, and he took his job as her best friend seriously and had never let her down.

At his touch, she realized that no matter her feelings towards Dan and whether he felt the same, he was always going to be her friend. At that moment, she felt grateful that Dan knew her well enough to not listen to her, when she had told him not to come. He knew her better than that. She didn't think she could push him away if she tried or at least she hoped that would always be the case.

She looked up at him. The golden light of the sun highlighted his perfect cheekbones and lit up his deep brown eyes; then she rested her head against his chest once more, not ready to move on just yet.

It was three years ago on her dream trip to San Francisco that Dan had entered her life. She had walked into the first coffee shop that had taken her fancy and been blindsided by the voice that had the small crowd engaged. The words he sang reached the very depths of her soul. When he had stopped singing it allowed her brain to function once more and she had got chatting to the stunning girl behind the counter. Within minutes they built up a great rapport. Her new friend, Nikki, informed her that the voice belonged to Dan.

***

'By the sounds of it I think I'm going to want one of what she's got.' The raspy voice made Amanda's insides flutter. She looked up to be greeted by the most soulful deep brown eyes she had ever seen. Time froze for a moment. Amanda searched his face. She felt as though she knew him, like she had seen him before.

'Coming right up, Dan,' Nikki said, causing Amanda to snap out of her trance and get back to her hot chocolate. She couldn't help noticing Dan's lips curve into a slight smile, his eyes still trained on her. 'Oh, and, Amanda, this is the famous Dan. Dan, this is Amanda,' Nikki added.

Amanda squinted carefully over her giant mug of heaven and took him in. He was incredibly well built, muscular yet somehow managing to pull off dark skinny jeans. How his legs fit in them

141

she wasn't quite sure. His shaggy brown hair was wavy, with a few tight curls here and there. He looked like he had walked straight off a movie set.

She looked to his face again, thoughtfully, intrigued by those eyes, eyes that were still looking at her. She looked away. He too seemed to be taking her in, figuring her out. Did he feel the same way she did? Had they met before? Nikki came back and placed a steaming mug of her delicious hot chocolate in front of him, putting paid to Amanda's thoughts.

'I have to warn you; this stuff is addictive,' Amanda said, taking another sip, her eyes peering over her mug, still watching Dan carefully. She chuckled inwardly. Not all tall, handsome, muscular men could pull off holding a giant mug of chocolate with a generous amount of whipped cream on top. Then again, she didn't think it was possible for Dan not to look cool and she had known him less than five minutes.

'What would you recommend eating?' Amanda asked Nikki, taking her attention away from Dan, whom she felt somewhat in awe of.

'I'm so glad you like the drink. Now let me see.' Nikki clapped her hands together and looked Amanda up and down. 'Hmmm...'

'One of your lemon tarts with fresh cream,' Dan said nonchalantly taking another sip of his hot chocolate before standing up.

'Lemon is my favourite,' Amanda said, with a big smile and a curious look at Dan. Dan simply smiled back, a smile that greeted Amanda with so much warmth and a sense of this is where she was meant to be. Could smiles do that? Could they really tell you this is where you were meant to be?

'You were right; this stuff is ridiculous,' Dan said, turning to face Amanda and holding the mug up, almost like a casual cheer. Then he turned back to Nikki. 'You're an angel, Nikki,' he added with a wink before walking back to his guitar. Amanda watched him as he carefully sat down, placed his hot chocolate on a small coffee table and picked up his acoustic Taylor.

While the memory played out in her mind, Amanda felt her light sobs begin to slow down. She straightened Dan's tie and lifted her head to greet him properly.

'Hi, baby girl,' he said softly, brushing the hair out of her eyes.

'Hey,' she replied. 'You came,' she added, attempting to dry her eyes with her soggy tissue and chuckling to herself as she did so. 'You really came.'

Dan handed her a handkerchief from his pocket. 'I told you I would. I'm so sorry, baby girl,' he said, running a hand through his Pantene-advert-worthy locks. Amanda considered him for a moment before taking a deep breath.

'I know, me too,' she replied, taking his hand in hers. 'Come on, I'll show you round,' she said to Dan. 'I'll be back soon,' she whispered to Grandpa's final resting place. Turning on her heels she began walking slowly through the cemetery. She stopped every few steps to point out a family member or to show Dan where, in the summertime, the multicoloured flowers would grow. Now though, the beds were home to many a green bud and a buddle of green leaves waiting to bring life to the spot. The cemetery was empty now. Everyone had gone back to her aunties' house for food, but Amanda was in no rush.

For a while they walked around in a comfortable silence taking in their surroundings.

'It's even more breathtaking than you described it to be,' Dan said, his all too familiar low voice wrapping her in a blanket of comfort. She stopped at a short stone wall that looked out across the cemetery. The cemetery itself was a thing of beauty: white marble headstones, whitewashed walls, fresh flowers of every colour as far as the eyes could see, crisp bright green grass dusted with snow, and if you looked beyond all this, you saw the sea. The clear blue water glistened under the sun. It looked to be something out of a fairy tale.

Amanda looked at Dan out of the corner of her eye and smiled. 'Would you like to see where Nanna grew up and where I spent my summers as a child?' she asked.

'I would love to,' Dan replied, smiling back. Before he could turn away, Amanda threw her arms around him and squeezed him tight.

***

As she walked back through the tiny village, after the funeral, after the cemetery and now with Dan by her side, it felt like Amanda's eyes had opened to the winter wonderland around her. Twinkling lights shone from every window. The grand nativity scenes that Nanna had told her about took pride of place in shop fronts. They were exactly how Nanna had described, each magnificent, each unique. The detail, the craftsmanship, you could get lost looking at them, almost like if you stared at them long enough they would come to life.

'Dan, look at this one,' Amanda squealed with glee. 'It's a little baker man with a pizza.'

'Wow and look at this one. They're amazing,' Dan said, pointing at a man sitting on a chair, his eyes closed and strumming his guitar, completely lost in the music.

'That one's unreal, Dan. You can feel his emotion while he's playing,' Amanda said, her eyes following Dan's finger that was pointing at the wooden music man. 'I thought Orzoro was paradise in the summer, when the lemon trees are in full bloom, a sea of yellow everywhere you look, Zia Rosa's balcony full of blossoming tomatoes and *carciofi*, but now, now it's so serene, so peaceful like you're inside a snow globe that no one has touched, like you have your own piece of heaven on earth.'

'That sounds pretty spot on to me. You could be a poet,' Dan said, following Amanda's gaze as she looked around the village not wanting to miss a thing.

'I'm a woman of many talents. Are you hungry?' she asked, with her hands on her hips.

'You are indeed and aren't I always?' he replied. Their easy banter made Amanda's heart feel lighter than it had done in days.

'Well, Mr Muscles, you're in for a treat. I can't take all the credit as my aunties cooked most of it, but I did make the pizza.'

'Why are you still talking? Show me the way.'

Amanda laughed at Dan's response. 'All right, patience, mister. I certainly created a monster when I introduced you to Grandpa's pizza. You're addicted to it,' she said, and then began walking up the steep steps to her aunties' house.

'That's not what I'm addicted to,' Dan said softly from behind her, causing her to pause at the top of the steps and turn to look at him. She stared into his chocolate-brown eyes, eyes that could see right into her soul and were filled with so much honesty, they made goose bumps appear on her skin. She rubbed at her forearm, the words Dan had muttered lost on her. In that moment her whole being simply felt elated that he was here with her now. The she cocked her head to one side making Dan laugh as she looked him up and down.

'Is everything OK, baby girl?' he asked, sweetly, standing perfectly still, almost like he was allowing her to go over her thoughts and whatever reason she had for giving him the once-over.

'Oh yes,' Amanda said, her quizzical look turning into a soft smirk, 'it seems to be. I thought by now you might have changed somewhat, grown two heads maybe, but you haven't changed a bit. Though, we might have to have words about the supermodels. I mean come on, Dan, you could be a little more creative, date an astronaut, a philosopher, a …'

'… chef?' Dan finished her sentence, matching her cheeky grin.

Amanda looked at his mischievous face. 'Ha-ha, very funny.

I'm being serious, Dan, don't tease me, this is serious stuff,' she stated sarcastically, and continued walking up the steps.

'Well do excuse me. But if we are getting serious, you do realize that many of those pictures just happen to be me coming out of a building at the same time as a model?'

'Oh of course, I have that same problem all the time,' Amanda said, turning back around and meeting Dan's gaze. A laugh escaped her as Dan stood shaking his head and rolling his eyes. 'Do any male models ever venture to these places? I might need to come with you next time,' she asked.

'Not a chance,' Dan said, pushing her gently up the stairs in an attempt to leave this conversation behind.

'Spoilsport,' Amanda huffed, turning back around, smiling to herself.

'Speaking of pictures, that was a nice Insta story you shared a few weeks back. I didn't think you had it in you to show cleavage for likes, buy hey I'm not complaining,' Dan's slow confident voice piped up.

Amanda snorted and continued walking, not wanting to give Dan too much satisfaction, though she couldn't help respond, 'OK, firstly, since when do you use social media? Secondly, when did you start using social media lingo? Thirdly, you know without a shadow of a doubt I did not do that on purpose. You press one button on your phone and suddenly you're live to the world. What's that all about? And, don't laugh.' She paused, turning to see Dan's face crease into a grin. 'It wasn't funny. Do you know how hard it is to clean yeast off a phone? I don't know how these food bloggers do it. My phone needs a better insurance plan if I'm going to have it near boiling pans and sticky ingredients.' Dan shrugged and nodded in mock sympathy. 'And fourthly, don't be looking at my cleavage.'

'Well, you press one button innocently and there it is – not my fault, baby girl.' Dan continued walking, meeting her on her step and towering over her. She didn't move, challenging him for a minute and staring at the dimples in his cheeks that appeared when he grinned. She sure had missed him. She decided the only adult way to win the conversation was to mess up his hair and run.

Chapter 13

Torrone

Ingredients:

3 large egg whites
1 cup of honey
½ cup of icing sugar
cup of cornstarch
3 cups of sugar
2 cups of pistachios
½ tbsp of vanilla extract

What to do:

Combine honey and sugar in a medium saucepan. Cook until it starts to bubble, stirring regularly.

Attach a candy thermometer to the side of the pan and keep on the heat till it registers 315 degrees Fahrenheit. (Play music to keep you entertained. Patience is not yours or Grandpa's strong point, but you need to keep an eye on the thermometer. You can't guess with this recipe — you will burn it, like you did the first time.)

Then remove from heat. The temperature may rise a few degrees but then will drop. You want it at 300 before using.

While your honey and sugar mixture is still cooking, beat your egg whites in a mixer till stiff peaks form.

Add the icing sugar to the egg whites till combined.

Keep the mixer running slow and pour the honey mixture into the egg whites. They may double in size, so let stand for a few seconds and they will return to normal. Add vanilla.

Beat until mixture thickens and sticks to the beaters. Around 20 minutes. Fold in nuts.

Sprinkle cornstarch on a clean surface, then pour your mixture onto it.

Listen to Nanna and be sure to put some cornstarch on your hands too, as you will get VERY sticky. Knead the mixture until it's firm.

Stretch the mixture out and roll it to the size of your pan.

Leave the tins on a wire rack to cool and firm completely, for up to 8 hours. (Don't listen to Grandpa and eat it before ready — you will be trying to get torrone off your hands for weeks.)

Cut into pieces.

The fresh aromatic smell of coffee was prominent in the air, mixed with a sweetness that tickled Sabrina's nostrils. Plates of *panforte* and *torrone* littered the small living room as a silky darkness quilted the sky outside. Praiano was lit up with a rainbow of Christmas lights.

The family were gathered in the living room to decorate a humble tree, now feeling ready to sprinkle a touch of Christmas over the house that they hadn't been quite so up to before. Dan had joined in too, which made Sabrina feel thrilled for her big sister. Dan and Amanda made such a gorgeous couple. They could star in their own Hallmark movie the way Dan looked at Amanda; but give it time, Sabrina thought, smiling knowingly to herself. Happily, she drew her eyes away from her sister and got back to the decorating at hand.

The modest assortment of Christmas décor didn't require too much time to put up, but with the girls awing and oohing at every item, it prolonged the evening's events way into the night. Each bauble and ornament that emerged from the wooden box brought with it a story that the girls' aunties lovingly shared.

Sabrina took her time emptying the box she had chosen to unpack. She wanted to hear every memory, every story that the decorations evoked. It warmed her heart that they had kept hold of the precious belongings all these years and still treated them with the utmost delicacy. Many brought Nanna to tears, with her having not seen the treasured heirlooms for twenty years, but clearly remembering the value they held. The powerful vocals of Andrea Bocelli and fresh *panzerotti* brought the evening to a close as the whole family and Dan sat back to admire their hard work.

They had placed the Christmas tree in the corner of the room; gold angels and robins adorned the branches. The girls had also added Baci stars and empty panettone boxes, just like they did at home, as that always made their nanna laugh.

The nativity took centre stage on a small table in the middle of the window. It was a beautiful piece of art that Italians took very seriously and had to be displayed as such. Her aunties had Mary and Joseph and baby Jesus, along with the shepherds and a few impeccably carved animals. Zia Rosa had explained how

Jesus mustn't be placed in the scene until Christmas morning, and so she put him on a shelf across from the window. He would be moved closer each day until the time was right for him to enter the nativity.

Sabrina wished Levi could have been a part of the festivities, but she understood that work was work. She picked up her fifth piece of *panforte* and curled up next to her nanna on the couch. Nibbling on the spicy traditional Italian dessert, that tasted like Christmas in her mouth, she looked at the white lights that glittered from the tree and her heart fluttered a happy beat. Her stomach was full of the most fabulous food and she felt that a week after Grandpa's funeral, the darkest of days were over.

Nanna kissed the top of her head as Louisa danced around trying to persuade everyone to indulge in a game of charades before heading to bed. One game wouldn't take too long, Sabrina thought, even though her bed was calling her name. Instead of succumbing to its cosy temptation, she sat up and joined in with the others shouting out guesses and laughing at Louisa as she paraded up and down the living room.

'I might need another coffee,' Sabrina noted, with a chuckle, pulling a blanket off the couch and draping it around herself.

'Make it an espresso,' Amanda added. 'We might be here all night.'

'Come on, it's not that hard,' Louisa muttered. She was now hunched over, scratching her armpits, making O shapes with her mouth.

'Hey, no talking,' Dad said, his face creased from laughing.

'Kong,' Dan said, calmly. He was sitting on the armrest next to Amanda and looked effortlessly handsome. Sabrina enjoyed every minute of getting to work with him; he was ever the gentleman. He was also a perfectionist, which meant they often had late nights in the recording studio and early starts as the sun rose, when he had ideas and needed to get a track down.

It was a privilege to watch him and his band working together, seeing their chemistry and how they fit. The others gave Dan their utmost respect and never once complained or argued about the late nights and early mornings. They were a dream to work with, but seeing Dan away from work was a treat – watching him now, seamlessly fitting in with their family and taking part in goofy activities made him more appealing. Sabrina couldn't understand why Amanda constantly protested the idea of even looking at Dan in a romantic light. He was a catch.

'We can't play this game with this one,' Amanda said, playfully pushing Dan off the armrest. 'He's always right.'

'Yes, Dan, it's your turn,' Louisa shouted, pointing at him with great enthusiasm.

'Oh, this should be good,' Amanda noted. The admiration in her eyes was obvious to Sabrina.

The way her big sister looked at Dan was endearing and made her thoughts drift to Levi. She wondered what he was up to tonight and why he hadn't come over with Dan. She hadn't seen him much since the funeral. Dan had mentioned that he was working, and Sabrina trusted Dan, but she couldn't help her mind from running away with her and conjuring up images of Levi and Lydia together. Maybe he was missing Lydia and hiding out at the hotel talking to her on the phone.

Sabrina shuddered and took a big sip of coffee, shifting her mind to focus on the entertaining, and rather adorable, performance that Dan was giving them. She made eye contact with Amanda, then looked at Dan and back to her big sister, offering her a wiggle of her eyebrows and a cheeky wink, which only resulted in Amanda throwing a pillow at her and almost making her spill her coffee. The joys of love, she thought.

***

The family had called it a night as the clock struck ten-thirty. Dan had fallen asleep on the couch and, not wanting to disturb him, Amanda had retired to the kitchen. She knew jet lag must be catching up with him but she herself felt wide awake. The kitchen was cooling off after an evening of cooking up a storm with her aunties and Nanna yet again.

Amanda was getting used to cooking alongside them. She wasn't looking forward to getting back to working with Jeff. Maybe she could bring her aunties home with her and ask Anthony to hire them; then she could cook with them every day, revamp the restaurant and serve Italian food. She'd much prefer that than the blend of hip pub fare they served, she thought. That's if she still had a job and any respect.

She gazed through the kitchen windows and sighed at the view. No matter how many times she stared out across the balcony, the magnificent Amalfi coastline took her breath away every single time. The stars burned bright. The biggest, boldest gold star blinked when she spotted it and Amanda wiped a lone tear from her eye. She didn't want to be sad; she really wanted to make her grandpa proud.

The thoughts of serving Italian food were stronger than ever and she knew, just like him, she couldn't ignore the passion deep inside her. She would have to follow her gut sooner or later, no matter her fears. And maybe her sisters were right, maybe she needed to take this blogging thing seriously and have a little patience. She knew her recipes were out of this world and she certainly got excitement from sharing them with others.

And it's not like she was a complete fossil: she could figure out Instagram and post more frequently on her Facebook. People loved Italian food. Once they knew of her blog she was sure they would love it. Though the likes of Snapchat would have to wait until she was a touch more competent, the whole live to the world thing twisted the knob of self-doubt in her stomach, which she didn't care for. It was better to leave that for now.

Feeling the draught from under the doorframe Amanda got up and grabbed her cardigan from the back of the door, where she'd hung it while she was cooking. The white fleece instantly warmed her. She pulled it up tight around her neck, the smell of mint hitting her nostrils as she did so. They had whipped up a delicious chocolate and mint pudding for dessert and the smell lingered in the air and on her clothes. Her aunties could make a fortune making perfumes, she thought, chuckling to herself.

The smell brightened her sombre mood and her thoughts turned to Dan. He loved everything she cooked and tonight had been no exception. He had inhaled the chocolate pudding and she didn't think there was another person she enjoyed cooking for more. She twiddled her thumbs, thinking about when he came into her life.

After becoming acquainted with him at a cute café her first day in San Francisco, she had been in awe. It was like she knew him already. He seemed to know her too when he picked out a lemon cake for her to try. Lemons were her favourite and he had grinned at her with such knowing. She wasn't sure she would see him again after that encounter, but the universe had other plans. She sighed at the memory and followed her feet in the direction of the cafetière … Coffee, she wanted coffee but maybe decaf at this time would be sensible.

***

It was day two of Amanda's trip to San Francisco and it didn't take long to reach her destination; the walk had been slightly cool, but it was a gorgeous morning in San Francisco, with the sun shining through the fog. Taking in the fresh air and creativity of the city, she wandered down Columbus Avenue, past Bruno's Deli until she was standing outside the bright red and brown building.

Her stomach took another lurch as she took in the bold white letters that read 'The Beat Museum'. She had meant to get here yesterday but had got caught up talking to Nikki and it had got too late. She took a deep breath and stepped inside. The musty

154

smell of decades-old paper and dusty first edition books filled her nostrils.

She couldn't believe it. She was here, at the home of the Beats, where the likes of Jack Kerouac, Allen Ginsberg and William S Burroughs lived on through their works and memorabilia. Her pace was slow as she read every poster, every article that her eyes met. Goose bumps rose upon her arms and she felt a chill of excitement.

Ever since she was sixteen years old and read On the Road *for the first time, she'd felt a connection to Jack Kerouac. His passion, his outlook, the way he thrived on life and learning, it had inspired her so much when working towards her own dreams in the kitchen. Her recipes were her road. In the kitchen she relaxed, followed where her heart took her and got lost in the ingredients. Food was her adventure, and she was always wanting to learn more, experiment with different flavours and try it all.*

'If I had to guess, I'd say On the Road *brought you here, but that it's not your favourite.' Amanda delighted at the sound of the familiar husky voice, but she kept her eyes trained to the letters on the wall.*

'And what makes you say that?' she replied, slowly turning to face Dan, the mysterious musician she had met just yesterday. He was leaning against the brown worn-looking counter, wearing a light denim jacket with a faux sheepskin collar. He was tall with broad shoulders and thick legs, yet he wasn't intimidating.

'Forgive me for being judgemental but you seem like the type of person who has devoured his works and found solitude in many. On the Road *brings out the dreamers, the people taking a chance, believing in themselves to do something out of their comfort zone. You've travelled if I remember correctly.* Tristessa *speaks to the lovers, those who search for that unequivocal love, though I have yet to find out about your love life. And the likes of* The Dharma Bums *grabs those who seek more from life, who are always searching to find meaning and reach a peace within themselves.' With that Dan met her eyes and gave a shy smile.*

'Do you work here? Because if you don't, you should – that was impressive,' Amanda said, slightly awed by the speech he just gave. She also couldn't help but laugh. He was an interesting character for sure.

Dan simply watched her. 'Would you like to grab a coffee?' he asked, brushing a hand through his hair.

'Sure,' Amanda replied, without much thought. She felt compelled to talk to this man. She tightened her blue woolly scarf around her neck and watched Dan as he placed a book he was holding back on the shelf. His movements were slow and he was very sure of himself. He didn't seem to rush through life.

With a slight nod to the man behind the desk, Dan led her outside. They walked in comfortable silence for a few moments before entering a small café. Amanda caught the name on the door, Caffè Trieste, and her smile grew larger. She had read about this place. The Beats would often come here. She had just walked inside a building that Jack Kerouac himself had visited.

'I'll grab us coffees if you find seats,' Dan said casually. Noticing the bubbling excitement about to burst from within Amanda, he smiled before turning towards the counter. Amanda snapped out of her reverie and pondered for a moment that he hadn't asked what she would like, before she spotted a cosy-looking booth at the back of the quaint café and made her way towards it, still jumping up and down inside.

She took off her light jacket and made herself comfy. A few minutes later Dan walked over, a small mug in one hand that was filled with rich black liquid, and in the other, she noticed the mug was bigger and piled high with what could only be whipped cream with some sort of crumbs or cookies placed on top. She hoped that was hers. It looked like one sip and she'd be away with the unicorns and fairies on a sugar high.

She felt pleased and slightly giddy when Dan placed the colourful mug in front of her. He looked pleased at her reaction, as she let out a faint 'Eeeek' and clapped her hands together.

'What is it?' she asked, keen to find out more about this exquisite-looking coffee.

'It's your coffee,' Dan replied, his eyes wide, his mouth turning up into a grin as he bent to sit down.

'You're hilarious,' Amanda said, still staring at her mug, deciding whether to try drinking it or eating it first. She decided on the eating first, of course, so she pinched a biscuit and dunked it into the cream. 'Oh, my God, that's not whipped cream, that tastes like custard, but it's so airy and light and amaretti – these are my favourite.' She dunked in another biscuit.

'I thought you might like it. It's a little twist on your normal Italian coffee. We have a lot of Italians around here. You might have noticed the delis and restaurants.' When Amanda nodded, Dan continued, 'It's more of a hot chocolate really but they mix it with Lavazza. And you're right, it's not whipped cream, more of an Italian vanilla frosting with crushed amaretti.' He smiled, and Amanda smiled back. She liked his description of the extraordinary hot chocolate meets coffee drink and felt there might be a foodie sitting opposite her.

Amanda's eyes widened as she scooped up more of the frosting with a spoon, so she could get to the hot chocolate. Dan was gaining best friend points fast. Taking a big sip, she squealed rather loudly. 'Sorry,' she whispered. 'Have you tried this before? I've been making Italian hot chocolate for years, but this takes it to the next level. I never thought to add coffee.' She took another sip, slurping past some of the remaining frosting.

'I have indeed – it's pretty incredible,' Dan replied, squinting his eyes and taking a sip of his plain, boring-looking coffee and leaning back in the booth. For a moment Amanda took in the café. It was filled with people, a mix of young and old. There were groups of people chatting, to-go cups ready in their hands, men and women batting their eyelashes at each other as they shared desserts, desserts that looked just as wonderful as her coffee, and naturally, what she would expect in a place that had been frequented by such iconic *writers, there were people tucked away at tables, heads down and scribbling in notebooks.*

'So, which book do you think is my favourite?' Amanda asked, squinting back at Dan. She felt intrigued by this man who she had now stumbled upon twice in two days. She was also curious, after his Jack Kerouac analogy monologue, as to what type of person he pegged her to be.

'If I had to take a guess I'd say – and this is just a wild guess – The Dharma Bums. *You're searching for something,*' he said, casually lifting his coffee to his lips and looking rather pleased with himself.

'OK, smarty pants. I'd say Tristessa *for you. You're searching for someone,*' she said confidently, matching his cocky smile from over her own coffee.

***

The whistle of the cafetière broke through Amanda's daydreams. She began pouring herself a tiny espresso in her zias' ceramic espresso cup, when she sensed him.

'Is there enough there for two?' Dan asked, his voice soft and low.

Amanda smiled and reached for another cup. 'Always,' she replied.

Dan's hair was unruly at the best of times. But now his brown waves were sticking up every which way. He caught her looking at it and in one cool and swift movement he ran a hand through it. It, of course, did exactly what he wanted and now looked smooth and bouncy, slicked back, his waves grazing his shoulders.

He stood close to Amanda, watching her carefully pour the coffee. When she had finished he took the small cups and walked over to the kitchen table, where she followed him, grabbing a bag of biscotti on the way. They proceeded to drink their coffee in a comfortable silence while watching the sky fade from charcoal grey to an inky black. It was reminiscent of her daydreams, sitting with him enjoying the simple pleasures of a coffee, though this time they weren't getting to know each other, they were very much acquainted, and their view was less San Francisco hippies and more peaceful Italian skyline.

'Would you like to go for a walk?' Dan asked, breaking the silence and getting up to place their finished cups in the sink. He began washing them as Amanda jumped up and walked to the coat rack to get her coat.

'What's going on in that wonderful brain of yours, baby girl?' Dan asked, joining her at the door and putting on his thick brown jacket. Amanda shrugged. She realized she wasn't her usual chirpy self, but she wasn't ready to unload her thoughts on Dan just yet. Her deepest, darkest secret could wait. She loved having him around and couldn't possibly bear an argument or rejection after the past few weeks. She didn't think her heart could handle it.

Furthermore, she didn't want to come across as ungrateful for what she had in her life. Dan wouldn't be here much longer. She had to make the most of the time she had with him before he was off on tour again and it would be another year before she saw him. As she thought about this, it occurred to her that three days had passed, and she hadn't asked Dan when he was leaving.

'So, I was thinking,' he said, putting an arm around her shoulders as they descended the steps that would lead to the main road, 'I don't want to impose on your family, but would it be OK if I stayed for Christmas?' It was as though he had read her mind.

Amanda stopped in her tracks, her heart beating a little faster now. 'Of course it's OK.' She tried to sound nonchalant, but her voice came out a touch higher than normal. Looking up into Dan's eyes, she added, 'You wouldn't be imposing. I like having you here, but is it OK with your mom? She's going to miss you.'

Dan pulled her closer to his side and kissed her hair. 'Yes, she will, and I will miss her too, but she understands; in fact she very sternly told me to make sure I look after you.' He raised his eyebrows and gave her a sidelong glance.

Amanda let out a laugh. She loved Dan's mom. They had hit it off right away when they met in San Francisco. She shared Dan's passion for art and books and, like Dan, she enjoyed food. She and Amanda had plenty to talk about. They had stayed in contact over the past three years too and Amanda longed to hang out with her again.

'She messaged a few days ago – it meant a lot, her thinking of me,' Amanda said, watching her feet, her shoes leaving prints in the dusting of snow. 'I will have to text her tomorrow,' she continued, wistfully, 'just to make sure she doesn't think I've kidnapped you and am holding you hostage.' She smiled though not quite feeling one hundred per cent bubbly.

She needed Dan now – that she could very much admit to, at least to herself and herself only, but it was easier said than done focusing on the present, being grateful that she was getting to spend Christmas with him for the first time, when her brain wanted to drift to images of him getting on a plane. While Amanda was battling the secrets in her head she could sense Dan was watching her closely.

'So,' he began, 'I think when you were in San Francisco I was the best tour guide there ever was. What are you going to show me?' he finished with a hint of mischief in his voice that Amanda was more accustomed to hearing from Levi's mouth. She glanced up at Dan and couldn't help a grin. His full lips were slightly parted, and he gave her a flutter of his curly long lashes. He was certainly a welcome distraction and a light her heart needed when it came to work problems and missing her grandpa; however, not so much with her whole Dan being the problem, problem.

'Oh, I don't know, Dan,' she said feeling a little stumped. She hadn't been thinking too much about being a fantastic tour guide. Sensing she wasn't acting like her fiery self, Dan grabbed her mitten-covered hand and picked up the pace.

160

'You know what? I have the best idea. Now, it's not something for the faint-hearted but I know my best girl is tough and the bravest I know,' Dan said. She cocked her head and gave him a quizzical look. He stepped in front of her with a skip in his step. When he looked at her, Amanda got lost in the depths of his soulful brown eyes.

'I think we should go skinny-dipping, get rid of all these clothes and jump straight into that water,' he finished, with a smile that undoubtedly would have any girl doing whatever he wished. They had been walking for a good twenty minutes, their feet having led them down to the beach. It was deserted, unsurprisingly, as the wind had picked up and there was a strong icy nip in the air. They were the only two daft enough to be out this late at night, Amanda thought. She took a moment to register Dan's very out of character suggestion and let out a bark of laughter then slapped him hard in the chest.

'Who are you and what have you done with my best friend?' She guffawed, poking him as he walked backwards getting closer to the small waves lapping over the cobbles at the water's edge. 'Does that work for all your usual suspects and you thought you'd try it on me? Or, has hanging out with Levi for the past twenty-eight years just started to rub off on you?' She punched him again, in the shoulder this time.

'Are you a chicken?' he asked, his cheeks flushed red from the cold chill.

'No, Dan.' She pushed him, and he caught her hand and pulled her into the path of the waves, the water splashing against her boots. She screamed. 'I am not a chicken, but you are joking, right? The last thing I need right now is frostbite and least of all to see my best friend naked.' She laughed, then worried for a second that that might offend him, but looking at the coy grin on his face, it hadn't. Why would it? she thought, remembering he had a million girls lining up to see him naked. It wasn't like she could bruise his ego.

Dan stepped out of the water and walked to a spot nearer the high rocks, which blocked some of the wind, and sat down, pulling Amanda onto his lap.

'Well, that's not very nice is it?' he said, his low and raspy voice back to its usual octave. She could feel his warm breath on the back of her neck.

'What's not nice? Me not wanting to see you naked? I'm sure there are plenty of girls out there who would be happy to kiss your ego better,' she replied, leaning back into him. He wrapped his arms around her waist as they both looked out across the sparkling sea.

'Yeah, I guess so,' he said. She could feel him smiling behind her. It crossed her mind that this had all been an act to make her laugh and get her to loosen up. Dan was good at that. Him acting completely out of character had definitely done the trick. Work seemed miles away and though she missed Grandpa, having Dan around and her family together, she knew there were still happy things to come. Though to her dismay, she now had the image of him skinny-dipping in her mind, which was, again, not really helping the Dan problem that she was trying to bury deep down inside.

She let out a low groan.

'Someone's thinking naughty thoughts,' Dan said, laughing. He squeezed her tighter.

'I hate you,' she replied, unable to wipe the grin from her face.

Chapter 14

Nanna's Insalata

Ingredients:

Burrata (Orzoro have the best, will need to import it if I ever have my own place)
Homegrown tomatoes (Get tips from Grandpa on growing the juiciest ones)
Olive oil (Preferably homemade)
Salt
Basil

What to do:

Simply plate burrata whole.

Slice tomatoes and drizzle with olive oil and salt. Arrange alongside the cheese.

Garnish with lots of fresh basil.

Sabrina could hear Nanna was enjoying every minute with her sisters. They were laughing away in the kitchen and whipping up another something delightful in preparation for lunch. Dan and Amanda had been catching up after not having seen each other in months, though Sabrina wondered what they possibly had left to talk to each other about, and Louisa had been spending her days and nights exploring Italy with Luca. Something told Sabrina that Luca was a keeper, if Louisa's blushing cheeks and delirious smile were anything to go by.

Sabrina had enjoyed Levi's company when he was around, but she hadn't seen him too much due to work calls and him needing to take care of business. This she understood to mean his mind was occupied by other more important women. She hadn't found the right time to bring up Lydia or tell him how she felt, but it seemed that him taking care of business said it all. He liked her as a friend – she knew it. He flirted with everyone and Sabrina was no exception. How could she have been so silly to think that he could possibly fall for her when he had groupies and celebrities galore to choose from?

She pondered this thought for a moment as she sat in her aunties' living room. She was nice and toasty, having remembered her slipper socks and Amanda's sweatpants this time. In addition, she had on her Zia Emilia's baggy Christmas jumper, which had become her favourite piece of clothing – it did such a wonderful job at keeping away the chill and it felt vintage.

With Levi and Dan now present she felt she best get caught up on how things had been going at work while she was away. She hadn't had chance to talk to Dan and Levi about any gigs or radio shows yet, so having avoided all things work-related for the past two weeks, she braced herself and nervously switched on her laptop while looking around the room.

There was nothing but pictures of her family adorning the walls. In a beautiful white rustic-style frame, there was Grandpa beaming down at her, just Grandpa stood with his hands on his hips, his head thrown back in laughter in the kitchen. Someone off camera must have told him a joke. Sabrina smiled at the thought. Another gorgeous golden frame saw Zia Emilia on her wedding day. Next to her Zia Sofia stood with her late husband, whom the girls had never met. A bright baby blue frame showed their mum as a baby playing outside with her toys on the balcony and a bigger deeper blue frame displayed Mum and Dad sat together with all the family around them having a feast at the very table they sat at every night here.

She even noticed a picture of her and her sisters standing tall and proud holding a fish that they had caught with Grandpa one summer. The wall was one of Sabrina's favourite things about the house. Off to the side the Christmas tree they had put up last night stood elegantly in the corner of the room. It added a special glow to the room and emitted a lovely fresh pine scent. She sighed. She sure did love this place.

She smiled at the candles and religious statues on the shelves near the nativity before bringing her attention back to her laptop. It pinged to life with an email, from Lydia Jones. 'Oh crap, what does she want?' Sabrina said out loud, scared to open it up. Her hands trembled slightly. Her stomach did a flip as she double clicked the email and on the screen staring back at her were the words: 'You're fired. Sincerely Lydia Jones.' Followed up with a bunch of more formal-looking words and phrases.

In an instant she felt sick. How could she possibly fire her? She had told her why she was going away; did she not have an ounce of compassion in her? It took a minute before the words sunk in, her usual laid-back demeanour completely diminished as Sabrina started to panic. She couldn't go back to LA without a job, she couldn't afford her apartment without a paycheque and oh my God, what had she done? Who would take over San Francisco Beat now?

She had made a promise to the boys and now she was leaving them with she didn't even know who. Her mind raced as to what she was going to say to Levi. Would he hate her? She was sure the boys really liked having her as a manager. Now she'd messed it all up. She loved her job.

***

Sabrina had always loved music. When she was younger she would often sit by the fire in the living room with Nanna, singing along to the most beautiful melodies and powerful vocals of Frank Sinatra, Andrea Bocelli and Pavarotti, while Amanda was busy cooking with Grandpa and Louisa busied herself with sewing and designing. Sabrina had loved sharing this time with Nanna. Many times they would get up and sway to the music, not a care in the world, just the music leading the way.

That feeling stayed with her throughout her teen years. She embraced everything she heard from pop, to rock, to punk. She even tried getting into heavy metal, though admittedly that wasn't quite her scene, but she respected and appreciated it all. At sixteen she got a job in HMV and whenever she had free time she would be at gigs or buried in a book, learning her music history and how the music business worked.

At twenty-one she had a lucky encounter with John Mayer, OK maybe not that lucky. She had finally bumped into him after she had been stalking him for several days. He had taken a liking to her and expressed his amusement at her boldness, and indeed bravery, for following him into the men's bathroom at Leeds Music Festival. He liked her bubbly, flirty nature and suggested she spend the summer on tour with him.

Sabrina jumped at the chance and spent the rest of her summer holidays basically playing cheerleader, keeping him caffeinated and occasionally supplying interesting conversation. And she enjoyed every single minute. She loved being behind the scenes and made sure to speak to every member of the crew, picking their brains along the way.

It was after this stint that she felt confident to push herself in the direction of the big leagues. She had no desire to leave home but when an opportunity arose at one of California's top record labels, she immediately jumped at the chance. It had been four years and she had worked her way up from office runner to manager's assistant, to manager.

And thanks to Amanda's trip to San Francisco three years ago, and Amanda's encounter with Dan, she had been able to step out from under Lydia's Dolce & Gabbana heel and become manager to the hottest band the world had seen for some time, in San Francisco Beat. Now all her hard work had gone down the drain and for what reason? Did she get fired because Lydia knew Levi had come to see her? Would Lydia really do that out of jealousy? She guessed now was as good a time as any to talk to Levi.

'Levi, I've been fired, I've been fired,' she shouted down the phone, slightly irked at herself that her usual problem-solving, calm and collected manner had been completely tossed out the window.

'I'll be right there,' Levi replied. She heard him grab what sounded like his hotel keys and slam a door behind him.

The boys were staying at the renowned Hotel Stella just minutes from the house, so Levi burst into the small living room before Sabrina had figured out exactly what she wanted to say to him. She was shaking and tugging on her jumper, confused as to how she was going to fix this.

'Levi, what happened? I thought you guys said you would be fine without me when I spoke to you on the phone? I sent you all the schedules – did something go wrong? Did I do something wrong? Why did she fire me by email?' she asked, still tugging on her jumper, her eyes searching Levi's face for a clue.

'I'm sorry that she emailed you like that. She really is heartless but it's going to be OK. You were too good to work for her anyway,' Levi said, in response to her flustered mumblings. He had joined her in pacing the room, though his strides were much larger than hers. He cleared the room in two steps. His constant turning around was making her dizzy. She plonked herself back down on the couch.

'Levi, it's not about me being too good for her. I need a job, I need to pay my bills. That's what adults do, and I worked so hard to get to the position I was in. It's been four long years and now it's all gone. What happened? I had everything planned for you guys – you promised me it would be OK. You said it was all about the music. What scandal did you guys get caught up in? What hotel room did you trash? Uh which celebrity did you sleep with?' Sabrina asked, head in her hands. The thought made her stomach turn. Though she didn't truly believe that the boys were capable of such awful acts of pretentiousness, she was out of options and way past freaked out.

Her voice turned soft. She felt drained and hurt. 'What happened? How could she do this?' she repeated, in a hushed and deflated tone.

'It's not like that, Brina. It's nothing like that at all. Jesus, we're not exactly your typical rock stars, are we? Look, we were all a bit out of it when you rang. It was hard to think about work when you were in so much pain. Dan was a mess and couldn't focus on anything. He just wanted to be with Amanda. We had been following your schedule up until that point and it was going great. The interview segment went well on *The Late Late Show* with James Corden and we played those two awesome pub gigs you set up. The radio DJs were cool and loved the new stuff. It was great, Bri, you did great.

'But then after hearing the news about Grandpa, our heads weren't really into it and Lydia showed up on Monday night when we were in the middle of an interview. She was a huge distraction and kept feeding lines to the DJs or interrupting. Then she informed us the schedule had changed and that we would be following her schedule for the remainder of the media tour.'

Sabrina was trying to comprehend everything that Levi was

telling her. She was pleased that her spots had gone down so well but she couldn't believe the nerve of Lydia. She ran a hand through her hair and tugged at her bottom lip, thinking.

'Wow,' she exclaimed allowing Levi to pause for breath. He seemed flustered, trying to get everything off his chest. He had stopped pacing now too and stood in front of her.

'We turned up on Tuesday morning and she had us at some sort of photo shoot for boxer briefs, some designer brand or something I don't know – well you know Dan wasn't going to have that. Everything you set up she basically changed. No more gigs just photo opps and fragrance commercials. She kept telling us that if we thought album one was a hit then we were out of our minds and that if we listened to her, album two would be bigger than our little minds could dream of.' He shuddered. 'So …' he paused causing Sabrina to feel queasy '… so, so we walked,' Levi finished, shrugging his shoulders while putting one hand through his windswept hair.

'You what?' Sabrina said, her jaw dropping in shock. Her brain felt scrambled as she struggled to comprehend just how little Lydia had really thought of her. How could she possibly have thought for even a second that she would make her proud through hard work and all that she was doing with San Francisco Beat. She would obviously never be good enough in Lydia's eyes, especially if Lydia was always going to treat her as competition instead of an equal and try and screw with every band that worked under Sabrina's management. The thought that the boys had stuck up for her clawed at the tiny thread of confidence that she had left.

'We walked. James told her how we felt, and we left,' Levi said, squatting down to make eye contact with her.

'That's why you could be here,' Sabrina said, putting two and two together.

'Well, it made things easier, but we were always going to come. I'm sorry I didn't tell you, but I didn't want you to worry about us missing dates or to tell you and then have something come up, though that wouldn't have mattered. I wanted to be here, Brina, and like I said Dan has been a mess not hearing from Amanda as much lately. He couldn't get here quick enough. You should have seen the look he gave Lydia as we left.' He smirked ever so slightly at the memory.

'So, there was no big celebrity fight or drama that's caused her to fire me?' Sabrina asked, feeling slightly ashamed that she had thought that of her boys.

'Not to my knowledge,' he said, with a shake of his head. 'And look, I'm sorry for acting like your job doesn't mean anything. I know how hard you've worked. I didn't mean it like that but the thought of you working for someone like that when you are so talented, well it just gets on my nerves,' he added, suddenly finding the rug on the floor fascinating.

'So, let me get this straight. She fired me because you wouldn't strip for her and she's jealous I get to work with you?' Sabrina said, catching Levi's eye, a flicker of playfulness back in her gaze.

'Well, I guess, if you put it like that, yeah.' He half chuckled and shook his head, embarrassed. 'I'm sorry that she fired you. I will help you sort it out.'

Sabrina looked at Levi. She couldn't help but feel he was being honest with her as that had to be the first time she had ever seen him get embarrassed. Then her breath caught as she remembered seeing him in Lydia's office that night before she left.

'I saw you,' she whispered, now too finding the rug incredibly interesting.

'Saw me where?' Levi asked, his eyes narrowed, and his brows creased in confusion.

'With her, in her office, before I left for the UK,' Sabrina stammered. She closed her eyes. Was she really about to tell him how she felt? This had gone way past professional.

'Oh, God, Brina,' Levi said. He placed his head in his hands. He looked ashamed. 'Brina, that was nothing. I didn't know you were there. I'm so sorry. But trust me, I was an idiot. It was my fault.'

'Do you like her?' Sabrina couldn't help but ask. Her eyes found their way back to his. This would tell her everything. She needed to look at him, to know if her feelings would mean anything or she had missed the boat with Levi. After all this time, had he moved on?

'After everything I've just said you think I like her? Of course I don't like her. She's horrible and the way she has treated you is appalling.' He stood for a moment and stretched out his legs before kneeling down in front of her and continuing, 'She sent an email calling for an urgent band meeting or something, said it was important, something about the new album. I was out so didn't get chance to clear it with the boys. Being the fool that I am, I didn't think to text. I thought I'd meet them there on the way home, then I turned up to find no one else there but her. I'm sorry. I didn't see your light on.'

'Did anything happen? Not that it's any of my business anyway,' Sabrina said, getting lost in his soft brown eyes and simultaneously trying to stay focused. She wasn't in the clear yet; she had no idea if Levi liked her the way she still liked him.

'No, nothing happened. She tried it on with me – it was pretty creepy. I told her no a few times and made it clear that nothing like that would ever happen between me and her and I left.' Levi's eyes stayed with Sabrina's and his lips curled into a grin. 'What do you mean it's none of your business?' he said with a nudge. 'Do you want to try saying that without pouting? It would make it a tad more believable.'

'You can sleep with whoever you want, I don't care,' Sabrina replied, though her smile didn't reach all the way to her eyes and she was still very much pouting.

'I think I've been making it pretty clear over the past few years who I'd like to sleep with and I have to say that she's been a pretty good flirt too; though, I don't know if she knows that? I thought I had read her correctly. And, when we kissed, I wanted her more than anything and not just the sleeping with her part. I thought we could have thrown dates in there too.' The way he scrunched up his nose and his eyes twinkled as he said this caused Sabrina's insides to somersault.

She hadn't realized she was holding her breath. With Levi's words she let out a sigh of relief, but it caught again just as quickly as she released it. It was her fault that those dates hadn't happened. She had to face her fears and be honest with him, like he was being with her.

'I know. Oh gosh, I know, Levi and I'm sorry. It's all my fault. I didn't want to push you away, I wanted you too, but oh…' She pushed a hand through her hair and broke eye contact. Levi took her shaking hands in his. 'I shouldn't have listened to her. Lydia threatened my job. She said you needed to date models and celebrities. And I didn't want to come across unprofessional, so I pushed you away. I wasted time. I'm good at my job, I could still be professional, but I didn't want to harm the band or do anything to hinder your success.' When she finally looked up at him, Levi was smiling at her.

'Babe, you are amazing at your job and while I admire your dedication to the success of my band, who I date has nothing to do with Lydia. And from the moment I walked into your office I had a feeling work and pleasure would mix rather nicely.' He cleared his throat and gave her a small wink. Then his eyes fell serious. 'But I am sorry too. I didn't chase you. I didn't tell you how I felt. I admit to getting a little caught up in this fame game and the attention and I just settled with our flirting, unsure what you wanted, instead of asking you.' He squeezed her hands.

Sabrina felt the tension in her shoulders ease. There was a comfort in knowing they had both made the same mistake, and a relief in finally knowing he felt the same way. She smiled. This time it reached her eyes. She didn't want Levi to feel bad. They had wasted too much time already. She was just glad they were now on the same page.

'I have not been flirting with you, Levi. I am a professional and it was my job to take care of the talent. I was only being nice.' Sabrina's heart was beating with a flurry. She had missed her banter with Levi. She wanted to get back to that.

'Taking care of the talent, huh? Well what was that kiss all about? What would you call that?' He was back to being his charming, cocky self and it made Sabrina feel like a hopeless romantic. It felt out-of-this-world good.

'Taking really good care of the talent.' She laughed, and Levi wiggled his eyebrows at her. 'Oi, the Virgin Mary will have something to say about your naughty thoughts – stop it,' she added, laughing and pointing at the living-room décor. He laughed with her and sat himself on the couch next to her, facing her.

'I'm sorry that I cost you your job and caused you to worry. The past few days have been rather hectic. I haven't wanted to be away from you but with Dan distracted I've had a lot of work to do. And, I'm sorry I didn't tell you how I felt sooner, but are we good now?' he asked, his eyes wide, pleading.

Sabrina laughed. 'So, this is what I get for finding a band with a hot and irresistible drummer? I'd hate to think of what she would have done to me had I brought in Niall Horan. Yes, we are good,' she said with a nod.

Not showing a care in the world at being listed as second best to Niall Horan, Levi – with all his confidence and charm – cupped Sabrina's face and kissed her like he had been waiting to do for the past two years.

As soon as Levi's familiar lips touched hers, Sabrina felt at home. She kicked herself for having run away from this for so long. How silly she was, she thought. She would not make the same mistake twice. She kissed him back, matching his need and urgency. After a few moments and feeling suddenly bold, she pulled away, her lips tingling from his touch.

'Without meaning to sound too forward, would you like to stay for Christmas?' she whispered, his face mere inches from hers.

'I would love to,' he whispered back, then leant in to kiss her again.

After a few minutes, Sabrina pulled away, breathless once more. 'Are you sure? Will your family be OK with it? Italy isn't exactly like LA or San Francisco. It's a lot quieter and ...' Levi placed a finger on her lips.

'My mom has the whole family with her this Christmas – my brother and his kids, my grandparents – she won't be on her own. I could do with quiet, no paparazzi coming down my chimney pretending to be Santa. And most of all, yes, I am sure. I want to be with you.'

In that moment Sabrina felt eternally grateful for the magic of Italy and the *amore* that it unleashed.

Chapter 15

Nanna's Zeppole

Ingredients:

Yeast (Need to double-check with Nanna how much yeast)
Flour (I'm sure it's about 6 tablespoons)
Sugar (How sweet does it need to be, Nanna?)
1 egg
Pinch of salt
Orange and lemon zest (Only Italian lemons and oranges)
Powdered sugar (Use the millions of packets you have in the cupboard from all the pandoro cakes — it's amazing)

What to do:

Dissolve the yeast in warm water, add three tablespoons of flour and leave in warm oven to rise overnight with a cloth over bowl.

Add egg, sugar, salt and 2 tablespoons of flour and mix.

Keep adding flour until you have a dough.

Make into ring shapes and fry until golden brown. Dust with powdered sugar and the orange and lemon zest.

The air smelt rich and thick as the aroma of roasted vegetables wafted through the kitchen. It was getting rather stuffy as Amanda weaved back and forth around Zia Sofia as they prepared the dinner.

'Isn't she beautiful?' Zia Sofia asked Dan as she waved her right arm in the direction of Amanda, while at the same time roasting peppers over the stovetop with her left. Her Italian accent was thick and strong.

'And she cooks,' Dan replied smiling shyly at Zia Sofia, who immediately burst out laughing and started pinching his cheeks with her pepper-free hand.

'You are a very smart man. You are lucky to have such a beautiful girl, who can cook too,' she said in a mix of Italian and English while tapping him on the head and still laughing.

'Be careful with that pepper, Zia – come here,' Amanda said trying to ignore her auntie pawning her off to Dan. She walked over to her and prised the now very crisp pepper from her hand. 'Sit down and I will finish the rest,' she said and then turned to Dan. 'You don't even know what she said,' she whispered.

'I'm pretty certain it had something to do with your beauty,' he replied, with a wink. Dan, ever the charmer. Amanda had been helping Zia Sofia in the kitchen all morning. They were preparing the roasted peppers for the risotto they were making for dinner. She and Dan had gone to pick them up from the fresh market, just a stone's throw away from the house, just this morning as the sun came up.

Amanda loved showing Dan round Orzoro and telling him stories from when she was a child. He'd probably heard them all before, but he listened intently all the same. The weather had been getting cooler. Snow flurries came and went but she was happy being outdoors, breathing in the salty air and getting lost in the Christmas lights that hung from the streetlamps and houses.

She would never get tried of the mesmerizing view of the water. Time stood still on the Amalfi Coast. One look at the water and hours could pass by without you ever realizing it. There were so many views in the world but none could hold a candle to this coastline.

'She's taking over my job now. She's better than the teacher,' Zia Sofia said with a chuckle as she sat down at the kitchen table opposite Dan. Amanda felt a tug at her heartstrings as she watched her. Like her nanna, her zia was short with soft grey curly hair that came to her shoulders. She was strong and had so much gumption. She could do everything by herself, but she was ageing. She couldn't be on her feet for too long, though she tried when she had company, always up, cooking this and that; but Amanda could see the pained expression as she bent to sit down. She admired her and loved her so.

'I doubt that very much, Zia. I try, but your food – there is no comparison anywhere in the world,' Amanda informed her, opting to speak Italian to make it easier for her auntie to relax.

'Ahh, sweetheart, it makes me so proud. One day you will have your own restaurant, you'll see.'

Amanda walked over to her auntie and gave her a big hug. 'Thank you, Zia. Maybe one day. Then you can come to England and make sure it's up to standard,' she said, giving her a kiss on the cheek.

Out of the corner of her eye, Amanda caught Dan looking at her. She smiled. He had told her on numerous occasions that she should have her own place. They often got carried away discussing what it would look like, what she would make. Together with Dan's added enthusiasm, she had envisioned this magical place of her own and spent many a day daydreaming about it one day becoming a reality.

She would import everything from Italy and serve nothing but fresh Italian cuisine right from her grandparents' cookbook. It wouldn't be fancy; it would be simple and made with pure love. Catching Dan's eye again as she stood, his bright smile and understanding of her when she spoke Italian caused a flutter of butterflies in the pit of her stomach.

She sharply turned her back. Dan didn't make her nervous. Dan did not give her butterflies like this. What was wrong with her? She haphazardly diced the tomatoes. She was aware that her feelings for Dan were getting stronger, but she couldn't deal with the frenzy of fluttering in her stomach. Wiping beads of sweat from her forehead she wondered if she was she getting sick. Maybe that was the reason for the sudden knot in her stomach. Her emotions had been a mess lately and she had been stressing out more than ever about work and her struggling, somewhat non-existent blog, but she didn't want to get sick. She absolutely could not get sick before Christmas – there was so much to do.

***

The risotto was a hit. Everyone had had seconds and thirds and was now enjoying relaxing at the table, talking about their days, nibbling at the breadsticks and *taralli* that were scattered over the table. Amanda sat back feeling proud. She looked over at her nanna and despite everything she had been through lately, Amanda was thrilled to see her face filled with joy, engaged in conversation with her sisters. The laughter lines around her eyes were more prominent. She imagined coming to terms with Grandpa's passing was made just a little easier by having her sisters by her side. Sisters she had missed for twenty years. They were making up for lost time, that's for sure, shouting over one another, holding hands and giggling like teenagers. It was a pleasure to watch.

Levi and Sabrina were looking rather cosy at the other end of the table. You could clearly see their attraction towards each other. Amanda hadn't had chance to speak with her sister to see if she had cleared the air with Levi, but by the looks of things, she must have. Everything certainly looked to be OK as they huddled in close together, Levi whispering into her ear in between giving her pecks on the cheek.

She knew they had both liked each other forever. Dan had mentioned there being an attraction there from the moment they met, but Dan, himself, had warned Levi to concentrate on his work and not meddle with his best friend's sister. Dan had assured Amanda that he would kill Levi if he hurt Sabrina. Amanda was grateful for Dan being protective, although she would probably get to Levi first if he ever broke Sabrina's heart.

Watching Levi's face, she knew it was genuine. All his focus was on Sabrina as he playfully stroked her hair. Amanda had never seen him so relaxed. Amanda cared for him, like he was an older brother. He had always been good to her. They got on like a house on fire and she couldn't imagine Dan being friends with someone who wasn't trustworthy or loyal. She was happy for her sister and proud of her too for going after what she wanted and putting her feelings on the table.

Louisa sat with Luca. They were talking with their mum and dad at the end of the table. Luca spoke with ease and fitted in seamlessly. Amanda loved the way Louisa's eyes sparkled as Luca spoke. Her little sister was smitten, and Amanda knew with all her heart that Grandpa was looking down on them all.

'I'll grab dessert,' Amanda announced, standing up from the table. Out of nowhere, she felt a rush of longing and a sense of hopelessness inside her. She made her way to the kitchen and got herself a glass of water. She downed the glass and leant on the sink, giving herself a minute to compose herself. Then she collected a tray of *zeppole* and a tub of custard from the kitchen island and rounded the doorway, bumping right into Dan and hitting her head on his chin. 'Ouch,' she exclaimed, unable to rub the sore spot with having her hands full of dessert.

'Are you OK?' Dan asked reaching up and touching her cheek.

'Yes, I'm fine,' she replied, moving backwards and placing the custard back on the island so she could rub her forehead. 'Do you need something?' she asked. Her voice sounded irritated. She hadn't meant for it to come out like that, but the butterflies were back and she didn't care for them. Seeing Louisa all loved up with Luca and Sabrina all cosy with Levi made her beyond glad for her sisters, but it had caused an ache in her own heart, one that seemed to get worse when Dan gave her one of his all-encompassing looks.

'Who's Luca?' he said, with a slight frown.

'He's basically Thor, with an Italian accent and dark, shorter hair. Why do you ask?' she said, her voice coming out a little testy. She leant back on the island to steady herself, the bump on the head, combined with the butterflies, making her feel slightly dizzy.

'Because I care about Louisa and you hadn't mentioned she had a boyfriend. In fact, you haven't been telling me much at all lately.' It seemed Dan had noticed her lack of availability. Besides the phone calls since Grandpa had passed, she hadn't been calling him or answering his calls as often over the past few months. The two of them stared intensely at each other, both a little agitated all of a sudden. Amanda knew where to place the blame for her frustration: it was standing right in front of her. Dan on the other hand rarely got vexed. What on earth could be bothering him? He didn't have the right to be cross. She was the one dealing with a swarm of butterflies in her stomach.

She had to be careful – one soulful look from Dan and every secret she harboured would come floating out, and damn it if her feelings weren't confusing the heck out of her right now. She simply stared back at him, not trusting herself to speak. Dan continued, his voice back to calm and raspy. He didn't stay vexed for long. Well that's good, Amanda thought. You don't deserve to be irked – you have nothing to be irked about. She squinted her eyes, giving him a slightly evil glance as she took in his sweetness. 'Look, I know you're going through a lot right now, Amanda, but if I'm not mistaken I felt you could always talk to me, about anything.'

'I do talk to you, Dan. I talk to you all the time and even if I don't talk to you, you somehow know what I'm thinking,' she said, in a voice that made her sound like a spoiled three-year-old.

'Well, you seem to have me stumped this time, Amanda. What's wrong?' Dan said, stepping forward and leaning against the island close to her. Louisa had been right: he did resemble Harry Styles. Dammit, that did nothing to help her feelings right now.

'Boy trouble, Dan, OK? Just boy trouble, it's nothing,' she said with a sigh, not taking her eyes off his reaction. His dark eyes grew tense, a shadow casting a darkness over his pupils, but his voice remained calm.

'Who is he?' he asked, shoving his hands in his cardigan pocket and looking to the door for a brief moment.

Feeling dumbfounded by his blunt response, she couldn't help the words that came out next. 'No one, just someone from work. He's wonderful, sexy, he completes me, so yeah, there's no trouble really. I'm just being silly. Everything is pretty darn swell and I'm fine,' she lied. There was another painful silence. Had Dan truly not read her this time? Now, she truly felt stupid. She did not like this childish attitude she was displaying. It wasn't like Amanda to lie, let alone to Dan. And it certainly wasn't like Amanda to say daft things to make him jealous. She rolled her eyes at her own awkward behaviour. Dan was not the jealous type, especially when it came to her, and who she dated. Protective, yes. Jealous, no.

'OK. Well, I guess congratulations are in order. He sounds great,' Dan said before pausing. His brow arched and his eyes drifted to the floor. A look of confusion crossed his face, which

181

Amanda found intriguing. Dan was a master at concealing his emotions and he rarely dropped his gaze when speaking to her. 'I'm happy for you,' he continued, which was then followed by another thoughtful pause. Then he collected himself before bringing his steely gaze back to her. 'You know, if he doesn't treat you right and there are any troubles, you need to tell me. If you need me to speak to him or sort him out I will.'

Amanda blinked her eyes hard in frustration, completely thrown off by this whole conversation and the fact that she was not acting like herself at all. Why was she doing this? OK, so she knew why, and she didn't like it one bit.

'Oh he treats me just fine. He's the perfect gentleman, always there for me, always ready with compliments, most definitely marriage material.' What was she saying? Dan remained calm though his gaze grew more intense and Amanda sensed a hurt in his eyes. Could he tell she was lying? It was a few moments before he spoke again.

'Well that's great. How come you never mentioned him before?' he asked, standing up straight, hands still in his pockets. He towered over her once more, his wavy hair catching the corner of his left eye.

'A lot has been going on with work, Dan, and family – you know all this. I didn't think it was important, you know.' She was lying to him and it didn't feel good. She could feel her palms beginning to sweat and she prayed she wasn't about to drop the tray of scrumptious desserts she was still holding in one hand.

'Yes, OK, of course, it's not important for you to tell me something like this. That's fine.' At this he looked down at the tray of *zeppole* and brushed a hand through his unruly hair.

'Can we drop it now, Dan? Now you know and everything is superb,' she said picking up the jug of custard once more.

'Amanda, could you do me a favour?' He leant in close to her ear. She could feel his warm breath on her neck. In that moment she was angry with her body for betraying her as her knees buckled slightly. This really was getting ridiculous.

'What, Dan?' she said, aware her voice sounded hard yet out of breath, not at all how she was accustomed to speaking to Dan, on either account.

'Don't go getting engaged to this Mr Perfect, marriage material guy without telling me first, OK?'

At the risk of another eye roll and asking Dan why on earth he would ask such a stupid question, when he knew she always told him anything and everything important, except things like this because they were utterly scandalous and completely not true and she had just made it up on the spot. She took a deep breath, resisted the strong urge to stomp her feet and throw the whole tray of *zeppole* out the window and made her way back into the dining room, quickly. How could he not see what was going on? What was wrong with him? What was wrong with her? She needed a *zeppole* or five.

***

The room was quilted in darkness, the faint scent of coffee still lingering in the house. Amanda lay in bed staring at the ceiling. She felt ridden with guilt about lying to Dan, but she just didn't get it. Their emotions, their mind frames, everything had been in sync from day one. She didn't like having these feelings alone and she couldn't understand how Dan could be so calm when her insides were squirming.

She willed her brain to switch off so she could get some rest, but instead it decided to play a highlight reel from one of the most perfect days she had shared with Dan when she had been in San Francisco.

***

The fog had cleared up by early Friday afternoon. The sun was high in the sky making San Francisco beautifully picturesque and rather toasty. It wasn't a scorching hot day and there was a light breeze that made it the perfect day for further exploring the city and for eating ice cream. Each day there had been new things to discover. Amanda was blown away by the culture, the art and most importantly the food.

Every night when she got back to her hotel she would take out her notebook and write about all the flavours, the combinations, the unique dishes she had devoured. She rang her grandpa every other day to run dishes by him and inform him of all the new recipes she was creating. She had her spark back, her ideas and creative juices were flowing, and she owed Nikki the world for letting her experiment in the kitchen at Bruno's. She didn't know how she would have coped if she had had nowhere to turn to make these ideas come to life.

'Ooh they have Red Velvet and Peanut Butter, ooh and Rocky Road. What are you going to get?' Amanda asked Dan, the words spilling out fast, as they stood in line at The Baked Bear, a newly opened ice-cream sandwich shop. Dan had brought her here, enticing her with talk of ice-cream sandwiches that were so good you would be back for seconds the very same day. He didn't seem to be lying. The queue rolled out into the street.

Amanda hadn't needed too much convincing. He had her at the mere mention of chocolate chip cookies. Now, the sweet smell of those freshly baked cookies was tickling Amanda's taste buds, making it harder for her to be decisive. The corner of Dan's eyes crinkled, his rosy lips relaxed and slightly parted, a barely there smile permanently played at his lips. He stood with his hands in his jeans pockets and though people glanced his way, his eyes stayed focused on Amanda. His attention never faltered from her. She had a slight flush in her cheeks from the gentle heat and the fact that she felt frazzled at trying to decide on which ice-cream sandwich to get.

'I tell you what, how about I choose for you? It will be the best ice-cream sandwich you've ever had and if you don't like it, then we'll just have to keep trying until we find your favourite combination,' Dan said softly. She looked up into his soulful brown eyes. Her own features softened as she relaxed at the decision being left up to Dan.

'You sure know the way to a woman's heart,' she said, playfully shoving him. 'What if I say I don't like it just so I can eat more ice cream and cookies? How much ice cream and cookies do you think you can handle, Dan?'

'Oh, I know you'll like it.' He paused to chuckle and shake his head, then draped an arm over Amanda's shoulder. 'But if that's a challenge, Miss Amanda, bring it on.'

***

Amanda closed her eyes, licked her lips and breathed out a satisfied breath, as she savoured the last bite of her oatmeal and cinnamon cookie sandwich with coffee ice cream inside.

'So, you liked it then?' Dan enquired with a cocky smirk. He had already finished his red velvet cookie sandwich with strawberry cheesecake ice cream. Amanda liked his healthy appetite.

'It was terrible. I think I might need to test another,' she answered giving him a small wink. She halted suddenly, the view in front of her stopping her in her tracks and she grasped Dan's arm. They had been walking a while chatting easily about ice-cream flavours and what cookies and ice creams worked best together. She hadn't realized they had been walking in the direction of the San Francisco Bay. The fog lay low and the Golden Gate Bridge looked positively enchanting in the distance.

'You're going to want to save room. I'm not done with you yet,' Dan said, a butter wouldn't melt smile spreading across his face. 'This place is a foodie's heaven.' He nodded towards the sign that read 'Pier 39'. 'And if it's the view you love, then I know just the place too.'

Amanda smiled as she linked her arm through Dan's. As they walked she stole glances at the bay. A few weeks ago, the wind had been knocked out of her sails when Jason broke up with her. She didn't think she would ever find happiness again. She could never have imagined the feeling she had now, walking side by side with this man she had only met three weeks ago, but whom she felt had been her best friend forever. Her heart felt light as a feather and she had a strong feeling of contentment.

'Dan, do you think you could ever leave this place?' she asked, curious.

'It's drawing you in, isn't it?' he replied, still focused on walking ahead.

'It just has so much about it, I couldn't ever imagine wanting to leave.'

'I'm glad you feel that way and that you appreciate the beauty and culture we have to offer. Don't get me wrong, I love it, it's home, but I'd like to see the world. I hope that I get to travel more with the band and you never know, maybe I'll like someplace else better or just want to experience living somewhere new. You never know what the future may hold. Emily may want to move; work might take us to different places. Sure, I'd miss this place, but I'm open to adventure and the idea of home being somewhere else. I think it's invaluable to experience other cultures and it interests me. Are you planning on moving here then?'

He had stopped walking now and turned to look at Amanda, his eyes sparkling with hope. Did he want her to stay? Amanda had fallen head over heels for the Bay and the people she had met here, in such a short amount of time. She didn't believe they could possibly feel that way about her. She was probably one of many quirky wide-eyed travellers that crossed their paths every day.

Amanda laughed as she looked up at him, trying to suss out whether he could feel their connection too. The sun was making her squint slightly but through the gaps in her fingers as she raised her hand to avoid the blinding rays. That same feeling she had when she'd walked into Bruno's for the first time hit her. Dan's eyes were intense, like he understood everything about her just by looking at her. His voice spoke to every part of her being and she knew he felt it too. She giggled to herself as her brain computed this new information.

'What's so funny?' Dan asked, though he was grinning too.

'Oh nothing,' she responded as they walked towards Luigi's Pizzeria. 'I've travelled quite a bit over the years perfecting my craft and I've lived away from home before, but home to me is always when I get to see my nanna and grandpa morning, noon and night and when I can have my mum over for a cuppa. So, I don't think I could ever really live anywhere too far away. This place is everything and more. I will be back, but my sisters and I have a pact that one day we will all live on the same road as each other. That might sound crazy to you I know, but I'd be lost without them. Sabrina just moved to LA and I worry constantly – I don't know how my parents do it.

'When I lived in London for work my parents could visit and Louisa and Sabrina liked to come up and stay with me on the weekends, so I got to see them in one piece each week and knew they were OK. With the time difference and her work schedule it's harder to keep track of Brina and I hate not being there for her if she needs anything.' Amanda stopped talking, suddenly aware that she had started to ramble. Her worries were spilling out of her as she found Dan so easy to talk to.

'You know I don't think you're crazy. In fact, I think it's awesome that you and your family are so close. Family bonds are special ones and it's a beautiful thing that you appreciate it and what you have with them. But you know I also think it's great and so important that you are travelling and seeing the world on your own. It allows you to find yourself outside of your comfort zone.

'Are you always right?' Amanda laughed, happiness flooding her once more, as she gently nudged Dan.

'Not always. After you,' he said as he opened the door to Luigi's Pizzeria.

'Thanks. Oh, my goodness, it smells amazing in here,' Amanda said taking a deep breath in, the aroma of fresh dough filling her senses with gratitude.

'I thought you'd like it. Now what did I say to make you giggle before? You are aware, Miss Amanda, that you actually giggled?' Dan raised his eyebrows as he led her to a cosy booth by the window that looked out across the magnificent San Francisco Bay.

'I didn't giggle. And it was nothing.' Amanda looked him up and down, his dark eyes staring deep into her, exposing her white lie. 'Uh, it's just I never believed in soulmates before,' she started, reluctantly, with a roll of her eyes, 'but San Francisco has been calling to me for the longest time and now that I'm here I feel it was meant to be, like I was meant to find you.' As she said this she felt heat rise to her cheeks. It sounded silly saying it out loud and Dan sure was taking a long time to answer back.

Feeling foolish she picked up a menu and gave it her full attention, hoping he didn't think she was a crazy person. After what felt like forever, Dan spoke.

'I know exactly what you mean,' he said, dazzling her with a soft smile as he picked up his own menu.

***

'OK, I don't think I have ever been this stuffed and that's saying something if you know my nonni,' Amanda said, leaning back and rubbing her stomach. After demolishing a medium size Fisherman's Wharf Pizza from Luigi's Pizza at lunch, they had stopped by Crepe Café and walked and talked while nibbling on the silkiest, lightest, melt-in-your-mouth s'mores crepe Amanda had ever tasted.

Dan had been a fantastic tour guide pointing out famous places along the harbour and filling her in on interesting facts about Pier 39. They ducked in and out of the gift shops, Amanda favouring

The Fudgery and Chocolate Heaven the most. She made a mental note to nip back and pick up some treats to take back to her family in a few days, though she would have to resist the urge to buy one of everything in both places. Everything had smelt and looked divine.

'You can't possibly be full.' Dan laughed, as he patted his own stomach. 'I have one more place to take you, if you're feeling up for it?' Dan challenged, his eyebrows raised.

'I see you're dishing out the challenges now. Well, I can always just look and save the eating for another day,' Amanda said, knowing full well that never worked. She had never been able to say no to food.

'I'm going to hold you to that. I should place a bet. What would I win if I bet that you won't be able to resist another San Francisco treat once you step inside the place?'

'Well, I don't think that's very fair. You know where we're going and seem to know my weaknesses – I don't stand a chance,' she said, doing her best fake pouty face.

'You're cute when you pout,' Dan said, hands in his pocket, as he casually leant against the railings overlooking the docks. 'I'll give you a hint,' he continued and nodded towards the café straight ahead of them on the corner. A squeal escaped from Amanda's lips.

'No way, they actually have their own café?' She couldn't believe it. 'No, Dan, it's too dangerous. All bets are most certainly off – I love that stuff.' She had automatically began skipping towards the white-panelled shack with a gold, white and red sign that read 'Biscoff coffee corner.' Dan walked slowly behind her, watching her as her eyes lit up when she reached the door.

'We'll just take a quick look around,' Dan whispered, his lips curling into a mischievous grin.

***

Back then of course, that day had all been innocent. Now she cringed. Had she felt more then? But Dan had had a girlfriend,

189

Emily, and she hadn't felt jealous. She didn't look at him and swoon or want to kiss him or anything of the sort. They had talked about how they felt. They had bonded over that instant connection that they both knew was special.

Besides, Amanda had read in a women's magazine once that soulmates didn't have to be lovers and that's how she felt towards Dan. They were meant to find each other but it wasn't a romantic thing – she knew that much. No matter how often her friends teased her and queried their friendship, asking if they were together or telling her that they should be together, she always stood her ground.

Even when her sisters couldn't quite understand their relationship either, she stood her ground. She had boyfriends, she went on dates and Dan never got in the way of any of that. They were friends in the purest form, good old-fashioned friends. They didn't sleep together or want each other in that way. Those thoughts hadn't even crossed her mind, well, not until recently.

When putting down the phone after their nightly phone calls, she felt empty. She suddenly felt like she wanted more. She wanted him to be by her side every day, like she wasn't whole without him any more. But she was determined to not screw this up. She didn't want to confuse the emptiness over losing Grandpa with a sudden longing for Dan. It was for this reason she didn't want to make one of the most important relationships she had ever had complicated, or worse still, non-existent.

Tonight it had all gotten too much, seeing Levi and Sabrina happy together, seeing Louisa chatting away to Luca – she wanted that too. But she didn't want that with Dan, surely? And he obviously didn't think of her that way. She knew that based on the countless girls he was linked with every week in the media and the conversations they had had over the years. Dan wasn't the settling-down type. He wasn't a womanizer by any means, but he saw the beauty in everything, women being one of them. She needed to get out there and start dating again and just have some fun. She was not about to get the whole love thing wrong, again.

'Breathe, Amanda, breathe. This is stupid – you're a big girl, you can handle yourself. You're probably just emotional after everything that's happened. You love Dan, but not in that way at all. That would just be stupid, and just gross,' she said to herself, scrunching up her nose, as if the thought of Dan, six feet three inches, muscles to rival a wrestler and shaggy brown hair, wasn't attractive to her, at all.

Chapter 16

Grandpa's Wine

Ingredients:

Grapes (Check with Grandpa if a certain kind is best)
Possibly some sugar (Really need to ask Grandpa)

What to do:

Place grapes in bucket.

Make sure feet are impeccably clean.

Proceed to stand on and squash grapes.

Once squashed, pour into huge fermenting jars and leave to ferment.

(But again, ask Grandpa and this time take notes as you make it.)

A stillness washed over Orzoro. The cars had disappeared, and the locals were all nestled in their houses. It was late in the evening when family meals were coming to an end. *Nonnas* were helping the *mammas* clear the table and tidy away the dishes, while the *nonnos* and the *papas* entertained the children.

The night sky twinkled with gold specks. Louisa heard voices out on the balcony. It was dark and freezing outside now the evening had settled in. She peeked through the window, naturally checking if whoever was out there was dressed appropriately for the weather conditions. She didn't want her nanna or zias catching a cold right before Christmas.

She needn't have worried about that for underneath the glow of the lanterns she spotted two men with their hands casually dug into their pockets and one frantically waving his hands around as he spoke. The contrast in their actions told Louisa who the men were. Dan and Levi, naturally laid-back in their stances and Luca … Italian.

'Lou is like a little sister to us. We don't want anyone messing her around or hurting her. She's a sweet girl – she deserves the best.' That would be Levi's voice.

Not to be outdone: 'What are your intentions?' Dan asked next. Oh God, she thought to herself, rolling her eyes. She pulled her oversized jumper tighter around herself but found her hand pausing on the door handle, suddenly curious to hear Luca's response.

'My intention is not to hurt her. She is beautiful, and I like being with her.' Luca's accented English made Louisa's heart flutter.

'Just to be clear when you say being with her, you mean talking, having coffee, not …'

Louisa cleared her throat, interrupting Levi and stepping into the night to make herself known. She immediately regretted this decision as she was only wearing socks and her toes instantly turned into icicles.

'Everything all right out here, boys?' she asked, shooting an apologetic smile at Luca. Levi jumped back a little surprised. Dan didn't move and remained calm, as always.

'Everything is great thanks, Lou,' Dan said, with that handsome smoulder that was turning women's brains to mush everywhere.

Looking at Dan and back to Louisa, Levi relaxed and sent a smile her way, no longer looking so guilty.

'We were just getting to know your man, Luca, here,' he said, patting Luca on the arm. That's exactly what she had been afraid he'd say. Though she was incredibly touched that they would want to protect her, she didn't want them to scare Luca away. At least not until after the holidays when Luca realized she would be going home and he probably wouldn't want a long-distance relationship. For now, she felt she was deserving of a little Christmas romance.

'Dan,' she protested, staring him down and waiting for more information on what they had been discussing. Luca put an arm around her and covered his mouth with his hand as he whispered in her ear, '*Va bene, capisco che siano protettivi.*'

She laughed. Of course Luca would be fine with this. She turned to look at him and gave him a quick peck on the cheek before turning her attention back to Dan. Dan was still looking at her. His stance screamed alpha male, yet he wasn't intimidating, not when you knew him.

'Am I free to take Luca from both of your mitts now?' she asked sweetly, a broad smile on her face.

Dan matched her smile recognizing the false innocence. He shrugged. 'Sure,' he said with a wink. Louisa laughed and linked arms with Luca, guiding him inside so she could grab her shoes and jacket. As she walked away, she heard Levi comment to Dan, 'We'd better start learning Italian.'

***

Inside the house Louisa quickly located her shoes and a thicker jacket before signalling to Luca, with a nod, that she was almost ready to go. He had been coming over to surprise her with a date when he had been ambushed by Dan and Levi.

Luca took her hand in his and the excitement in his eyes over taking her out and the feeling of his hands entwined in hers caused a warmth to spread through her body. Though her body temperature was on the rise, she still wasn't looking forward to facing the chilly Italian air again this evening. Putting it off for a few more minutes she walked towards the living room, where her family were enjoying the night's quiz show. She spotted her big sisters, Sabrina curled up next to Nanna and Amanda wrapped in a blanket in the chair.

'Are you two aware that your other halves are harassing people on the balcony?' she said, mock seriously. It took her sisters a minute to register what she had said. She watched as they both looked at each other and then back to her. Sabrina shot up first. Amanda stood in a calmer and much slower manner.

'What on earth are they doing out in the cold?' she muttered. 'Idiots, the pair of the them,' she added, wandering out of the room after her sister. Louisa laughed as she watched her sisters grab coats from the coat rack by the door, before she herself informed the room that she was going out, with a chant of '*Ciao*' and '*Ti Voglio Bene*,' in everyone's direction.

***

A few moments later and Louisa was panting slightly, trying to keep up with Luca's pace.

'Where are we going?' she queried. From the steep decline of the paths on which they were walking, Louisa knew they were heading in the direction of the beach, but she didn't want to believe it to be so. She remembered this route from when she was a child, trudging behind Grandpa, doing her best not to get her fishing line caught in any of the olive branches that peeked out over the garden walls. At this time of night and the fact that it was December she also knew that nothing would be open.

'It's a surprise,' Luca answered, his Italian sounding so beautiful it made Louisa's cheeks flush. Spending time with him was certainly sharpening up her own Italian. She had very much enjoyed conversing with him and getting to exercise her bilingual skills.

The sound of soft waves crashing against the rocks drew nearer and the wind was picking up a few notches the closer they got to the water.

'*Ferma*,' Luca said, turning to face Louisa and taking her hand. They were at the edge of the beach now. Pebbles lined the path and a few feet ahead tucked into a small cave at the bottom of the mountain was a wicker basket lit up by candlelight. Louisa gasped.

'*Amore mia*, this is for you,' Luca said, his voice gentle and sweet. He took both her hands and led her to the light.

Louisa walked into the warmth of the cave and noticed a big woolly gingham blanket at the entryway. Seeing her shiver, Luca bent down, picked up the blanket and wrapped it around her shoulders. Immediately she stopped shivering as the blanket locked in her body heat.

'*Grazie*,' Louisa whispered. She didn't know what else to say. This was the most romantic thing anyone had ever done for her.

'Please sit, *mia amore*,' Luca said gesturing towards the picnic spot where two fluffy cushions lay. 'I've prepared a special feast just for us,' he added with a mischievous glint in his ocean-blue eyes. Slowly he opened the top of the wicker basket and pulled out two plates covered in foil. Before unwrapping them to reveal tonight's main course, he pulled out some grapes, olives, *taralli*, his homemade biscotti and a small bottle of what looked to be homemade wine.

Amanda recognized the cork job and label to be homemade,

thanks to her childhood years whipping up batches with her aunties and Grandpa when they visited Italy in the summer. Luca poured them each a glass before it was time to unveil the dinner that was causing the mischievous glint in his eyes. His eyes were making Louisa blush before she had even tasted a sip of wine.

'Tonight's specialty,' Luca began. His eyes were playful as he unwrapped the plate to reveal two slices of fresh margherita pizza. Louisa let out a roar of laughter, bringing the blanket up to cover her mouth as she tilted her head back.

'My favourite,' she exclaimed, clapping her hands together. 'Luca, this is incredible. *Grazie mille*. I've never eaten pizza under the stars before, but how utterly perfect and romantic,' she said, looking into his eyes, the candlelight reflecting in them, making them glisten.

His handsome face bore a bashful grin, as though he knew pizza wasn't the most extravagant meal and she was just being kind.

'You're too kind, *amore*. I hope you will like it. I wanted to prepare you the finest meal but the *pasticceria* was busy today. I could not get away. So, I instead give you Sabino's Pizza.' His eyes wandered to the floor.

Lifting his chin up with her hands, Louisa said, 'Luca, this is more than a fine meal – this is the finest of meals. I adore pizza and under the moonlight, it's magical.'

'You are a special woman,' Luca replied. Louisa's cheeks burned a bright shade of red.

There wasn't a crumb left over from their moonlight picnic. Louisa loved that Luca made her feel so content. He had smiled when she reached for another *taralli* and had clapped when she dipped the hard bread into her wine. Whenever she had been on dates before she had felt her date's eyes boring into her with judgement when she ate quicker and more than they did. She could never understand it. She was grateful for the freedom and

197

understanding she saw in Luca's eyes. In addition, with Luca, the conversation flowed freely.

'I'm sorry if this is a difficult question, *amore*, *ma* what your plans are now?' Luca asked, covering Louisa's toes with the blanket.

Louisa wriggled her toes against the softness of the blanket and placed her now empty wineglass down. 'Hmm, I don't really know,' she mused, crinkling up her nose. 'Grandpa left me with folders full of designs and sketches – the man knew fashion.' She laughed. 'Mind you, I don't know if it's that he knew fashion or that he just loved everything I drew and never said a bad word about any of my designs.'

Luca leant forward and kissed the tip of her scrunched-up nose. As he slowly moved away Louisa kissed him on the lips. They both let the kiss linger for a few moments, the sweet taste of red wine present and delicious. A hiccup caused Louisa to pull away. She laughed as Luca passed her a bottle of water from the basket. She took it with a grateful nod, took a sip and then held her breath, all while Luca looked on, amusement swimming in his piercing blue eyes. Once her hiccups had settled, Louisa continued with her thoughts.

'I might consider one of the Manchester fashion courses or look for an internship somewhere and get experience out in the field. It's not that I don't like school, but I would love to get stuck in and learn as I go. Plus, I must do something now. I left work rather unprofessionally after Grandpa passed. I know I shouldn't have sent an email about my quitting, but I just couldn't face going in,' she finished, the guilt of having not turned up at work on the Monday after Grandpa passed still weighing in the back of her mind.

She had worked as a receptionist at her local dentist since returning from her failed attempt at living in London. It wasn't what she wanted for her life or work, but she had wanted to prove to her parents that she wasn't a complete failure and that she had a plan. And so, she had found a job, put on a happy face and looked the epitome of girl boss in their eyes. They of course still encouraged her to draw, but Louisa could see they were rather proud of her working in such a fine establishment that was the dentist's office. Receptionist was a pretty sophisticated title.

'Do it, *amore*. Your designs are magnificent – you can do it,' Luca said, encouraging and bringing Louisa back to the present. He didn't seem fazed by her immaturity of quitting her job. He smiled and handed her a chocolate Baci.

Louisa emitted an excited gasp. 'My favourite, thank you,' she said, unwrapping it immediately and forgetting about her job woes. 'What about you, Luca? Will you stay at the *pasticceria* forever?' she asked, before taking a small bite of the dark, hazelnut chocolate.

Luca played with the wrapper of his own Baci. He had his knees propped up and was leaning on them. He would make a fine model, Louisa thought, taking in his baby blue eyes and five o'clock shadow. He wore a long-sleeved dark grey jumper with black jeans and black dress shoes and in his relaxed state, Louisa felt he wouldn't look out of place in a Levi's magazine ad.

'I love the *pasticceria* and would I be happy to take it over, *ma* I'd like to travel and see the world. Italy is beautiful and it's my home, *ma* there are more beautiful countries to see, no?' He tilted his head with a gentle shrug.

Louisa's heart beat a little faster. She could sense they were one and the same when it came to family. She had no doubt that Luca had had a desire to travel his whole life, to explore and get away from the tiring grind of the *pasticceria*, but she knew all too well the importance of family and wanting to stay close by to look after everyone. She often got mad at Sabrina for moving to LA and when Amanda used to jet off to multiple destinations in her quest for culinary perfection and cultural adventure, she would huff and puff, stating that she had everything she needed right there in Manchester.

Now, though, at twenty-two, as the swirl of butterflies floated round in her stomach, she felt she was beginning to understand their forays into other countries and she made a mental note to apologize again to Sabrina for being so harsh on her over recent years. For, if Amanda had never gone to San Francisco, she would never have met Dan and, in turn, Sabrina would not know Levi. Whether her sisters admitted it or not, Louisa knew they were both smitten.

Sabrina seemed to be on the right path and it certainly looked like she had finally jumped in head first with Levi if their canoodling around the table was anything to go by. Amanda remained stubborn and kept her heart under lock and key, but Louisa felt there was more magic to be revealed in Italy yet. As for her, had she not been in Italy at this time, had her grandpa not encouraged her in spirit to hold her head high and get out of the house, she would never have met the beautiful man in front of her.

'You are right,' she said to Luca, brushing her hand over his. 'The world is full of beauty. Sometimes you just have to look a little harder for it and step outside your comfort zone.' They smiled in understanding of each other. Luca needed to know that his family would be OK if he left them for a little while, just as much as Louisa needed to know that too.

When the light wind picked up, Luca placed the dishes and bottles back into the basket. Louisa snuggled further into the thick blanket, her eyelids becoming heavy. The wine and food had made her sleepy. She lay back on her cushion, eyes closed, and pulled the blanket up to her neck. When she opened her eyes, the moon made her breath catch. Its pearlescent glow lit up the night sky. Her eyes searched for the boldest, brightest star in the sky. When she spotted it she let out a deep sigh and forced herself to smile.

'*Sei la stella del mia cielo*,' she whispered, tears pooling in her eyes.

'*Amore*,' Luca said, placing a hand on hers. Louisa realized he was sitting near her feet watching her, his features relaxed, taking her in. She patted the blanket next to her. Luca gave her a shy smile before lying down beside her, taking her hand once again in his. She leant in to him, laying her head near his neck. He smelt sweet yet manly, a mix of Acqua Di Gio and biscotti. Her heart warmed at his gentleman-like nature. She didn't feel intimidated or threatened.

'You have good friends,' Luca said, playing with her hair. 'I like you, Louisa, very much and my intention is never to hurt you,' he added softly, kissing the top of her head.

At that moment Louisa felt at home. 'I believe you,' she replied.

Chapter 17

Grandpa's Christmas Biscotti Recipe

Ingredients:

4 eggs
4 tsps baking powder
3½ cups flour
1 cup sugar
4 tsps vanilla
½ cup butter
2 cups icing sugar
6 tbsps water

What to do:

Sift together flour and baking powder, then set aside.

Cream together butter and sugar. (Use machine or hand-held whisks.)

Add eggs, one at a time.

Mix in vanilla and add flour mixture.

Knead until you have a dough.

Refrigerate for 1 hour.

Roll out dough into little balls. (Press middle down with your thumbs, like when you make gnocchi.)

Place in oven at 375 for 8 to 10 minutes.

Place on cooling rack to cool completely. (Don't show Grandpa until cool – he will eat them. They're not too bad warm but better served crisp. Work on a warm biscotti for Grandpa?)

Once cool, mix your water and icing sugar (add a drop of vanilla to icing too or even sambuca) till you have desired consistency, and drizzle over cookies.

Out of nowhere a car screeched to a halt in front of the girls because of what slowly came into view a few moments later. Sabrina gulped as the bus blared its horn to warn any other cars of its presence as it manoeuvred round the rocky bend.

'I think this is ours,' Amanda shouted, her words muffled by the blush pink scarf that was snug over her mouth, trying to thwart the sharp wind.

'That's what I was afraid of,' Sabrina answered, sticking her hand out to signal to the bus that they would be getting on, and quickly pulling it back in and tucking it straight back into her the pocket of her borrowed coat. She hadn't brought gloves, or a coat, with her and the weather had been growing wildly colder.

The rickety old bus came to a stop and the girls quickly got on. It wasn't much warmer on board. The windows needed sealing, and many had cracked glass, but the few people inside gave off enough body heat that the girls stopped shivering. They paid the driver and made their way to the back of the bus where three seats together were free.

Sabrina tapped her black pumps on the dusty bus floor as it pulled away from the stop. Driving in Italy made her nervous. She looked out of the murky windows attempting to distract herself with the Christmassy view. The bus ride to Amalfi was going to take thirty minutes. Maybe counting Christmas trees and string lights would keep her anxiety at bay.

Before long, and thirty or so Christmas trees later, the bus came to a road Sabrina recognized. Just opposite the bus stop was a rather prestigious jewellery shop and next to that one of the girls' favourite places for pizza by the slice: Gennaro's. Celebrities would frequent this famous jeweller's whenever they bragged of visiting the ever growing in popularity town of Amalfi. Often, they would then be papped dining at Gennaro's because of course shopping for expensive diamonds made you hungry.

Sabrina couldn't complain about the paparazzi ruining their coast, or their home away from home becoming an increasingly hot spot for tourists, because it was good for the families and the small businesses. In addition, the girls enjoyed celeb spotting while tucking into Gennaro's prosciutto and artichoke pizza. Her stomach rumbled just thinking about a warm slice.

'Are you thinking what I'm thinking?' Amanda said, stepping down from the bus behind Sabrina.

'If you're thinking salty melt-in-your-mouth prosciutto and the juiciest *carciofi*, then yes,' Sabrina replied, shoving her hands into her pockets as the cold froze her fingers instantly.

'You know it,' Amanda said cheerfully, wrapping her scarf around her ears and clutching on to Louisa. Sabrina wanted warm food in a hurry, but she also figured this would be the perfect time to get away from her sisters for more than five minutes to get them their Christmas presents.

'You go ahead and order the biggest pizza and I'll catch up with you in ten minutes,' she said, waving her hand in the direction of the restaurant. She watched Amanda and Louisa look at each other before they turned to look back at her.

'OK.' Louisa shrugged, turning towards Gennaro's.

'Buy me something nice,' Amanda said to Sabrina before following Louisa's path. Sabrina watched them go, until they disappeared through the restaurant doors. She didn't want them spying on which shop she was going into. When she felt the coast was clear, she wandered into Angelina's Jewellery Shop.

***

If Sabrina hadn't checked her watch, she would have thought time had sped up while they were inside Gennaro's. Admittedly they had been completely lost to the world, with only one thing on their mind, pizza, but as much as she loved pizza and savouring every bite, she was pretty sure they had inhaled it in a matter of about twenty minutes, so the darkness that had settled around the square confused her for a minute. Her watch did indeed read three p.m., but the night sky had her feeling like it was bedtime. Snow was definitely on the cards tonight, she thought.

She patted her stomach feeling content and satisfied with their late lunch and linked arms with her sisters. The yellow streetlamps cast a glow over their faces, which Sabrina watched as they each took in the way the square was lit up for the holidays. Amanda's eyes were wide, but her lips remained closed, pursed together. She did this when she was thinking. Louisa, on the other hand, had her mouth wide open, gazing at the giant Christmas tree with pure excitement and wonder. Sabrina didn't know what she would ever do without them. Not even the bickering, the teasing or the odd full-blown argument would make her feel otherwise.

They walked arm in arm up the cobbled path. The people had dissipated now, the cold getting too bold for most. But the girls had a special place to visit that even Jack Frost's worst would not keep them from. Amanda grasped hold of the golden handle and pulled open the wooden door. Thanking her sister and stepping inside, Sabrina's nostrils were met with all her favourite flavours.

'Oh my gosh, I think I'm just going to get one of everything,' Louisa squealed. Sabrina shook her head and laughed at her baby sister.

'Lou, I would give you a medal if you ate one of everything in this place right now,' Sabrina teased. Shopping in Amalfi was always fun, but this was the reason Sabrina put herself through the ordeal of the treacherous bus ride; to visit the most magical place on earth, Pasticceria Pansa. You'd have thought this was their first time visiting this award-winning establishment, with the noises escaping from their mouths and the joyful expressions stamped across their faces, but it wasn't. They had spent countless summers eating cakes in the square outside, while Nanna and Grandpa sipped coffees under the canopy, but each time they visited, it elicited this type of reaction.

'I think I've died and gone to heaven,' Amanda said, her eyes growing wide as she took in the rows and rows of *sfogliatelle, le scorzette*, biscotti, and *torroncini*. 'Can I just live in here?'

'I'd happily leave you here if you so desired,' Sabrina said. She was getting better with the sarcasm, having spent so much time with her big sister these past few weeks. She tried to wiggle her way through the crowd. It seemed there was no one in the square because they were all in the bakery.

'Very funny,' Amanda replied, her eyes still bulging at the cakes before her, while trying to stay trained on both Sabrina and Louisa.

'I learnt from the best. OK, what are we having, girls?' Sabrina asked, trying to bring her sisters back down to earth while sending a playful look Amanda's way. She had made it to the counter, only having gotten stepped on once.

'Eeeek,' was all Louisa managed back as Sabrina watched her take in the gleaming golden and brown cabinets, the enchanting white marble floor and the mirrors that made it feel like the quaint *pasticceria* went on forever.

'I think I'll have our usual,' Amanda replied pointing at the swirls of almond cakes dusted in sugar and decorated with coffee beans, chocolate drops and candied peels. These were the cakes that made their hearts sing with jubilation, the cakes that their grandpa would bring home to them after his trips to Italy.

Sabrina smiled at the memories of rushing to the door to greet their grandpa, squeezing him tight and eagerly awaiting him unpacking the delicious treats. The house would fill with the most divine aroma – vanilla, almonds, coffee – some sort of magical scent that would bring your taste buds to life in anticipation. They would each take a cake and sit by the fire with a milky coffee as Grandpa told them how the family were doing and about the fish he had caught.

'*Ciao, bella,*' the cashier said, bringing Sabrina out of her reverie. 'What can I get for you?'

***

Sabrina wandered through the crowd of people bustling round the little shop with panettones and chocolate Santas in each hand, and made her way outside to find her sisters sitting on the edge of the fountain. She had told them to go ahead of her and find a seat outside as the bakery was heaving. The air was still chilly, the fountain now dusted with snow and iced over, but the excitement of being at one of their favourite places in the world was keeping them warm and toasty.

'So, how are things with Levi?' Louisa asked, the moment Sabrina sat down next to her. Sabrina couldn't help the toothy smile that spread across her face at Levi's name.

'Things are pretty great, thank you,' she replied taking a sip of coffee. The snow was calming down ever so slightly, though the air remained nippy. The hot coffee was a welcome shot of warmth through her veins.

'All right, don't overindulge us with too much information,' Amanda said, sarcastically, shooting her a side smirk.

'Well, what can I say? I haven't been able to wipe the smile off my face since he kissed me and when I'm with him, life is just happy. He makes everything fun,' she replied, thoughtfully, biting into a *cartucci* she had unwrapped. Her eyes drifted to the fountain as she thought about Levi's boyish grin and the way he could have her howling with laughter at the silliest of things. She caught her reflection in the ice and brought herself back to reality in time to see Amanda raise her eyebrows playfully.

'OK, enough about me. How's everything going with Luca?' Sabrina asked, turning to face Louisa, and helping herself to another cake.

'You know the other night he took me down to that little cave on the beach and had a candlelit pizza dinner prepared for me. Pizza under candlelight,' Louisa responded. 'Could a girl possibly wish for anything more?' she added. 'Mind you, he might do that with all his holiday romances and I would be none the wiser.'

'Hey, don't be like that,' Amanda said, suddenly very serious. 'Zia Sofia knows his family and thinks extremely highly of them. He's got a reputation for being quite the gentleman around here and I trust Zia Sofia. I don't think you have too much to worry about,' she finished, handing Louisa another cake and then wrapping the tray up. Sabrina knew this took some effort on Amanda's part; she was clearly doing her best to not devour the whole tray of cakes before they got home.

'He is rather old-fashioned in how he treats people, always holding open doors, very polite and the effort he puts into dates is pretty cute,' Louisa said, with much more enthusiasm in her voice. 'We'll just see where it goes. It's not like I was expecting him or waiting for him, so I'm just going to enjoy him while I'm here. Plus, I'm not about running away from love.'

Louisa paused and Sabrina felt a little taken aback by her little sister's dig. She thought they had patched things up and had come to an understanding, but before she could argue with Louisa's comment, Louisa continued, 'I'd be a bit of a hypocrite to do so after all I have said to you two over the years. I must admit when I am wrong – this kind of all-encompassing feeling of love can be a little scary.' Louisa fluttered her lashes at her big sisters.

Sabrina couldn't help but laugh. 'Well, at least you can admit when you are wrong, unlike some,' she said, nodding in Amanda's direction, in jest, 'but, Lou, you were right too. It feels so amazing to have opened up to Levi, so please don't be scared with Luca and go with your gut,' Sabrina added.

'That sounds like a plan. Right, I don't want to hear any more about your Mr Giulio Berruti lookalike, making pizza more bloody amazing and being the perfect gentleman.' Amanda laughed. Having ignored Sabrina's teasing, she shoved Louisa with a loving wink. 'We best get these pastries home now if anyone else stands a chance at having some,' Amanda added, standing up and dusting off some *pasticceria di mandorle* crumbs off her pale pink pea coat.

'Wait, wait, wait, not so fast, missus – you're the only one that hasn't been interrogated. Now it's our turn to ask you the questions,' Sabrina said, tugging Amanda's coat and pulling her back down on the fountain edge.

'If my brain serves me correctly, you two are the ones with the boyfriends and therefore I get to avoid being interrogated, as the last time I checked, I don't have one,' Amanda answered back as casually as can be, before standing up again and reaching for the cakes. Sabrina pulled her down once more.

'No, no, you're not getting away that easily. Have you and Dan figured it out yet?' Sabrina asked, keeping hold of Amanda's coat sleeve.

'What do you mean?' Amanda asked, innocently, though Sabrina was not convinced. She didn't want to push too hard. Her sister was not one to be pushed if she didn't want to talk about something. She and Louisa had tried over the years to encourage Amanda to talk to Dan about their relationship, but Amanda had always expressed that she and Dan were friends and that they were more than happy staying that way. On numerous occasions she would tell them that soulmates didn't have to be lovers and then proceed to cringe at the thought of Dan in that way. However, Sabrina and Louisa weren't buying it. They figured in time they would both realize that they should be together.

'You do realize that you and Dan are like every cliché in the book, like every romance story ever written, but it's real, it's in front of you, like you can actually reach out and grab it, yet you both choose not to. I just don't get it,' Sabrina said, softly. Not to pressure Amanda too much with all eyes on her, she looked away and busied herself with tying the bow on the cakes.

'Sabrina, love doesn't always work like that. Dan is awesome but he's my friend,' Amanda replied, fiddling with the shiny pink buttons on her coat. Louisa seemed to be on the same wavelength as Sabrina and was focusing on draining the last of her coffee, scared of overdoing the eye contact.

'Do you not see the way he looks at you, Amanda, and the way he calls you beautiful?' Sabrina responded, still at work on creating a pretty bow with the ribbon.

'Brina, he's called me beautiful since day one. That means nothing. Dan calls everyone beautiful. You know what he's like with women.' Amanda would always have an answer for every-thing, Sabrina thought.

'It's different this time – it's the way he says it. It's not the same as before. I know you've noticed,' Louisa said. Sabrina could sense her baby sister trying to keep the lightness in her voice too, not wanting to scare their big sister with heavy and deep conversation. Louisa made her eyelashes flutter, knowing full well Amanda would never get mad at her own baby sister. Sabrina tried hard not to laugh.

'Guys, look, I know you don't understand it, but I can't explain it. I'm super happy that you are both loved up and have faced love head on – that's truly wonderful. I'm not running away, I'm not wrong. Dan and I, we just fit together as friends. And besides the other day I told him I had a boyfriend and he was totally cool with it,' Amanda said, shrugging her shoulders.

Sabrina looked at her big sister. Amanda's eyes were darting around the square, avoiding eye contact, telling Sabrina that she was lying and that something had shifted in her thoughts. At the risk of being shoved into the freezing cold fountain, she jumped up.

'You, my friend, are lying. You love him – I can see it in your eyes. That delightful brain of yours has finally clicked. Ahhh, and that's why you haven't been speaking to him. You're scared. It all makes sense now,' Sabrina said. She was unable to stop the words coming out of her mouth. Her smile was beaming. Maybe it was the Italian cakes. Maybe it was Levi. Maybe it was Grandpa giving her the go-ahead from above, but love was in the air and there was no time like the present to get her daft big sister to realize it.

'This is like the best news ever.' Sabrina paused and threw her coffee cup into the nearby bin, allowing herself a second to think. Turning back to her sisters she continued, 'You, you are an idiot if you think Dan is fine with the idea of you having a boyfriend. You know Dan: he just wants you to be happy. And, why, might I ask, did you have to go and tell him that? It was all going so well,' she said, bending over slightly to catch her breath.

'Excuse me? What was going so well? I do not love him,' Amanda said, more firmly. Her hands were squeezing the life out of her own now empty coffee cup.

'You were spending time together, instead of always talking on the phone. These past few days I could see it in his eyes. He knows it too and then, clever clogs, you go and tell him you have a boyfriend. Why on earth did you do that and what exactly did he say to that?' Sabrina asked, flailing her arms around. She was asking questions for the sake of it, simply to make Amanda realize what she was doing. But Sabrina knew it didn't matter. Whatever excuse Amanda came up with and whatever Dan had in fact said were proof of nothing. There was no way Dan believed Amanda had a boyfriend and no way Dan would be fine with it.

'You are completely off your rocker, Bri. Uh …' Amanda paused. Sabrina was not about to drop the conversation this time. Even though it saddened her to watch her big sister shift uncomfortably in her seat, she couldn't give in and allow her to keep her heart locked away any more. She kept her eyes locked on Amanda's. There was an excitement bubbling inside her this time that overshadowed the tiny worry in her mind that her sister might possibly slap her in the face. Instead a few moments passed before Amanda let out a frustrated sigh and stuffed a whole *cartucci* in her mouth from the parcel that was still unwrapped. Sabrina didn't break eye contact.

Louisa looked on in amusement from one sister to the other. Then, finally, a few more seconds passed before, with a mouthful of cake, Amanda muffled, 'I said it because he doesn't get it. He doesn't like me in that way. Everything is just normal to him. He doesn't see me like that and I was in some sort of carb coma. And his stupid response was: "He sounds lovely. If he treats you bad I'll sort him out and don't go getting married without telling me" or something to that effect.' Amanda huffed, spraying *cartucci* crumbs everywhere.

Louisa and Sabrina remained silent. All of a sudden, a light bulb went off in Sabrina's head as though it took a second for her brain to realize she wasn't dreaming and that their big sister had finally admitted to what they knew to be true all along.

'Eureka!!! See, all is not lost. He wants to marry you. Don't you get it?' Sabrina yelled for everyone in Pasticceria Pansa and the square to hear.

'I feel like we have been waiting for this moment for light years,' Louisa added, joining Sabrina in standing and flailing her arms in the air.

'Jeez, stop it. You two are worse than me. Arrrrghhhh, he does not want to marry me,' Amanda said, kicking her feet in frustration. 'And fine, so what if I think for a brief, tiny, inkling of a moment I'm actually in love with him, it's horrible – it will pass. I'm just confused with everything that's been going on,' Amanda said, looking every bit a two-year-old who just spat out their dummy.

'I knew it. You've got it bad, dear sweet sister. I wondered why you had been avoiding him these past few months. And then telling him you have a boyfriend – you're an idiot but a clever idiot. Don't you see? You're testing him. You might not have realized it, but your heart spoke for you. It was trying to find a way. By the sounds of it, you have nothing to worry about,' Sabrina shouted. She was pacing back and forth in front of Amanda, doing her best Sherlock Holmes impression.

'How can you possibly think I have nothing to worry about given everything I just said?' Amanda asked, her face bearing a look of bewilderment. 'I have been best friends with this man for three years, he has been linked with numerous, and bloody gorgeous, might I add, models and celebrities and I'm just a chef from Manchester, not even a celebrity chef at that. He's always so bloody calm and collected and can always tell what I'm thinking. Yet … yet, this time he doesn't have a clue, unless he's trying to ignore me because he so obviously does not feel the same and feels bad for me and hopes it will go away. And, my God, how am I supposed to kiss my best friend? People don't do that. I don't want to think about whether or not Dan has a bloody six pack.' Amanda was standing now. She let out a huge breath. Sabrina had never seen her big sister so conflicted.

'I have no doubt that beautiful rock god best friend of yours has a six pack,' Sabrina teased, making Louisa laugh and succeeding in lightening the mood. She noticed Amanda's eyebrows relax as she tossed back her tousled brown hair. Amanda took a deep breath in. Sabrina watched as she let it out along with a high-pitched laugh. Sabrina imagined Amanda felt like the weight of the world had been taken off her shoulders.

'Bri, please, it would make things so much easier if you could just set me up with Harry Styles and leave this Dan thing alone,' Amanda said, with a twinkle in her eye. Yes, Sabrina had no doubt her big sister felt like a million dollars getting this off her chest.

Sabrina chuckled. She grabbed Amanda and Louisa's hands and began twirling and dancing around the fountain, the ice in the air being forgotten as the joy of the conversation warmed them up. 'I think Dan would fire me if I set you up with Harry Styles. That man adores you and has been going crazy not hearing from you over the past few months and you throw a nice cherry on the top of the cake by telling him you have a boyfriend. Poor Dan, he must be going stir crazy.'

Amanda scrunched her nose up at Sabrina and gave her a look that said 'don't be daft'. Then she said, 'I do not believe for a second Dan has been going crazy. Dan doesn't do crazy. Dan doesn't let anyone in.'

Sabrina stopped dancing to catch her breath. 'Our big sister, so young and naive. Dan may not let just anyone in, but you, it so happens, are not just anyone. And, FYI, I happen to know his best friend rather well,' Sabrina said, turning the tables on Amanda from their previous conversation on the balcony.

'Please spare me the imagery of that sentence quick and tell me what that has to do with anything?' Amanda said, making Louisa chuckle.

'Just like you drive us mad when you haven't heard from Dan, Dan drives Levi up the wall when he hasn't heard from you – that's what that has to do with anything. I have the inside scoop,'

Sabrina noted, her energy coming back to her as she began twirling once more. Amanda seemed frozen to the spot at this new-found information. Sabrina chuckled and grabbed her sister's hands. Drops of snowflakes caressed her cheeks as she looked up to the sky.

'It's a Christmas miracle, Grandpa,' she shouted up to the stars. 'She's in love with him. And it's only taken three bloody years for her to realize.'

Chapter 18

Nanna's Christmas Cake

Ingredients:

One pandoro (any brand, but Bauli are really, really good)
Marsala or sweet wine
Strawberries
Nanna's custard:
4 tbsps sugar
4 tbsps plain flour
4 egg yolks
*Skin of lemon and orange (Amalfi lemons and oranges are best; they
don't have so much pith)*
2 pints of milk

What to do:

*Stir together all the custard ingredients, whisking on a low heat until
thick and cooked.*

Slice pandoro into star shapes and drizzle with Marsala.

Once custard is cooked and cooled, layer the cake together again with custard in between each slice.

Decorate with strawberries.

Christmas morning arrived and brought with it a crisp air and bold orange and purple sunrise. There had been no snowfall during the night, which meant Louisa could see small specks of green peeking from the plant pots. The balcony was littered with pots of every size. Though nothing much was growing at the moment, in summer they would be blooming with artichokes, oranges, tomatoes, lemons – you name it, her aunties would grow it fresh, right here amongst the rustic tiles and weathered house.

As she looked around, tears threatened her face as she thought of her grandpa's green house, how over the years he would try and grow the artichoke but to no avail. The British summer wasn't quite right for such delicacies.

'I'm thinking of you, Grandpa,' she whispered, tracing her hand over the stone wall. 'I wish you were here.' Louisa had woken up at the crack of dawn, having been unable to sleep due to a small amount of magic that came from it being Christmas Eve and a whole amount of anxiety of what the day would bring without her grandpa.

'Nice outfit.' Louisa jumped out of her skin at the sound of Levi's voice. She hadn't heard them open the gate. She hastily wiped at her tears with her Olaf onesie, as Levi embraced her in a giant friendly hug. 'Merry Christmas, Lou,' he added, stepping back and catching her eye.

'Thanks, Merry Christmas, Levi. Everyone's inside if you want to go in. There should be plenty of breakfast left if you guys are hungry,' she said, forcing her voice to sound normal and pointing to the kitchen doors. Levi released her and walked off, eager to see Sabrina no doubt. Dan didn't seem in such a hurry as he took in her watery eyes. He wandered over to her and stood by her side, looking out in the same direction she had just been looking.

'How are you holding up?' he asked, his voice ever so kind as he turned to look at her, his eyes deeply rich with interest and concern.

Jeez, Amanda better hold on to this guy and never let him go, and soon, before he got snapped up by someone else, Louisa thought, as Dan's voice nearly melted her own heart. Though she knew that Dan getting snapped up by someone else was not possible, as she was certain the man in front of her only had eyes for her sister. She took in his tall, muscular frame. He was wearing tight black jeans, with a white shirt peeking out from under a thick woolly cardigan, a look that she felt only Dan could make look hot on a rock star. She cleared her throat.

'I'm good thanks. Sorry, Dan, I didn't mean for you to catch my blubberfest,' she said, feeling a little embarrassed all of a sudden. She played with the tassels on the end of her red and green scarf and thought for a moment how lovely it had been to spend more time with Dan and Levi over the past week. She knew them reasonably well through Skype calls and all that Amanda had said about them, but getting to hang out with her big sister's best friends had been a treat.

Louisa almost forgot that they were international rock stars, as they were incredibly grounded, but just being stood next to Dan and the aura of an enigma he embodied made it impossible to completely forget. He was a striking human and Louisa had seen the way people gawped at him. Here on the Amalfi Coast it was ever so subtle though and they hadn't been bombarded with fans like they were elsewhere. Had they been in Milan, Louisa didn't think they would have enjoyed the luxury of a cosy, quiet Christmas.

'Sweetheart, I think you have every right to a blubberfest. I'm sorry we barged in on your time,' he said, rubbing her shoulder and putting paid to her thoughts of what it was to live a rock-star life.

'No, it's OK. I was just taking a minute to say hi, you know? I'm trying so hard to be cheerful and thankful. I'm surrounded by my family and I want to enjoy every minute, but then it hits me that he's not there, just like that … I don't want to be ungrateful.' Louisa's bottom lip trembled. She tried to fight it, but it was no use. She knew Dan understood and felt grateful for him being there as the tears rushed once more. He stepped forward and put his comforting arms around her. After a minute, she sighed deeply. 'Uh, he sure is going to be a tough one to miss.'

'You miss him all you like, hon. Never feel guilty for talking about him or taking a moment to yourself. Everyone in there understands. It will take time to heal, but it will become less painful as you remember all the incredible times you had with him. We can mourn them and celebrate them. It becomes a balance and you will find that balance when the time is right. In the meantime, sweetheart, don't forget those in front of you. Talk to them and share your feelings. They are there for you. You will get through it together while still living life and creating memories with them also.'

His words came out slow and soft, like he knew no amount of words could truly take away the pain, yet he could only try, and that's what mattered: to understand the love someone had for a person and to simply be there for them and support them.

'Dan.' Louisa turned round to look at him, taking in everything he said and feeling a lot lighter for it. 'Thank you, you are right. It's important we make the most of every single second with those we love; therefore, when they are gone we have a book full of wonderful memories that we can read from every day, almost like we can live and experience them all over again. Grandpa gave me a hundred books full of amazing memories that I will think of every day, but I must also continue writing the chapters with my family and not miss a single second with them.'

She paused and took a step back, feeling grateful for this new philosophical outlook. 'Dan?' she said again, looking him in the eyes and dabbing at the wetness of her cheeks with her onesie. She cleared her throat once more. 'Dan, make sure you grab hold of those you love and make those memories and not just the fly-by memories but the out of this world, most incredible, magical, heart-soaring memories that would almost seem like a Disney fairy tale if you read it back. OK? Oh, and if gorgeous, funny, talented chefs go around making up daft stories about made-up boyfriends and perfect men, don't let them stop you going after what you want. Don't miss out on opportunities or waste any more time. Go and write those chapters you want to read, right this second.'

Dan looked at her, a smile appearing subtly on his ruggedly handsome face, his cheeks slightly flushed. Louisa hugged him for a second time. She knew Dan was a smart guy and was more than confident that he knew exactly what she was referring to. 'Grandpa liked you very much, Dan. No doubt Amanda told you he always asked about you and would have loved to have seen you again. Life is short – there's no time to wait.'

Without waiting for him to reply, she made her way back into the dining room, walking past the rosemary plant, grabbing a handful and taking a big sniff as she stepped through the door.

***

The lanterns were in the shape of tiny stars. They hung from the orange trees down to the gate below. By the door a ceramic blue and yellow pot held a bunch of long twigs, each glistening with gold flecks under the moonlight. There were three windows at the front of the house, the centre ledge of each one boasted its own bright and colourful Christmas ornament.

The first window Louisa looked at had a red and gold arch that was home to three long stem candles. The second window displayed a small gingerbread house made out of porcelain. The lights bounced off it giving off a disco effect on the rose curtains beside it. In the third window above the door, a baby tree twirled around playing a soft Christmas tune. Louisa felt like she had walked into Santa's grotto and she was only in the garden.

'It's just through here, *amore mia*,' Luca said. She looked over to him to see him standing on the spot watching her. He had his hand out in the direction of the front door yet didn't seem in a hurry to go inside. His features softened and a light flush rose in his cheeks, highlighting his perfect cheekbones when she looked at him. He smiled, dimples appearing either side of his gorgeous lips, making Louisa's knees wobble. She could stand here and stare at him all night and happily risk frostbite, she thought.

'You're telling me this is where your parents live? Luca, it's like a Christmas wonderland,' she breathed, feeling like she had walked into something straight from a Pinterest board. She walked over to Luca, and taking his hand she stepped up to the front door and was greeted by a stunning twine wreath dusted in fake snow with sprigs of holly leaves sticking out of the top.

'*Si, Signorina*. My parents are big fans of this holiday,' he said, bringing her hand up to his lips and kissing it gently.

'Do they decorate inside too?' Louisa asked, turning to face him, her eyes wide with excitement. Out of nowhere, Luca cupped her face and kissed her sweetly. His lips lingered on hers for a moment when he slowly pulled back.

'You look beautiful when you are excited,' he said. 'You have eyes like a Disney princess,' he added, tracing his thumb over her cheek. 'Are you ready to go inside?'

Louisa hesitated for a moment. For one she was trying to compose herself after Luca kissed her. His kisses tasted like the mouth-watering cakes he made at his family's shop. Needless to say, he tasted yummy. And two, though Luca made her feel so welcome with his warm features and kind heart, she still felt a nervous flutter in her stomach that she was about to meet his whole family.

The door creaked open and Louisa was instantly hit with the smell of almonds and cocoa. She had barely placed one foot inside the house before an older lady, a touch taller than she was, with bright blue eyes and long, wavy, dirty blonde hair ambushed her. She could only be Luca's mother. The lady embraced her tightly for a good minute before stepping back, still holding on to Louisa's arm, and introducing herself as Rose, Luca's mother.

Rose guided her through the hallway, past the gallery of family photos Louisa really wanted to look at, and into the living room where two people sat chatting away by the most spectacular Christmas tree Louisa had ever seen. Her jaw dropped as she took in this dazzling six-foot tree adorned with gold and silver tinsel and every ornament she felt had ever been made. From wooden Santas to felt gingerbread men and tiny red robins, to glass angels, candy canes and pasta, it was a beautiful explosion of Christmas spirit dangling from every branch.

Louisa was mesmerized. She took a step closer wanting to examine each bauble and was caught off guard with a running hug as two little arms wrapped round her legs. Luca was quick to catch her just before she hit the floor.

'*Mamma mia*,' a voice shouted out. 'Matilde, Matilde, *stai attento, stai attento*.' A gorgeous blonde woman with a red skater dress and matching red bow in her hair ran over and scooped up the little girl, the culprit behind the hug attack. The woman bounced the girl up and down in her arms and looked at Louisa. 'I'm so sorry,' she said. 'She seems to like you already,' she added with an apologetic chuckle.

Louisa straightened up, patting Luca on his arm, thanking him for catching her, then she bent slightly to look Matilde in the eye and offered her a smile. The girl's eyes were crystal blue like Luca's and she had the prettiest face. 'Hi, Matilde, I'm Louisa. Thank you for my hug,' she whispered, then raised her eyes to meet the woman's. 'Hi, I'm Louisa and please it's no problem at all – she's a sweetheart,' Louisa said, shaking her head to signal it was nothing. Hugs were more than welcome.

The lady balanced Matilde on one hip and reached out a French-manicured hand. 'It's a pleasure to meet you, Louisa. I'm Giulia, mum of Matilde and sister of Luca,' she said, nodding in Luca's direction before turning to a man sat by the fire smiling up at them. 'And this is our papa,' she added pointing at the man, who promptly stood up and embraced Louisa in a hug. He patted her on the back as he squeezed her.

'*Ciao, bella,* welcome to our home. I'm so sorry to hear about your grandpa – please if there's anything you need, our home is your home. You and your family are always welcome. Oh Luca, she's more beautiful than you described,' he gushed, turning to look at Luca. Louisa had a feeling Luca got his sensitive side from his dad. She also felt bad for having not been more aware of her surroundings when she walked into the living room and introducing herself first, but the tree had totally absorbed all her attention.

Smiling at everyone, she took a seat on the cloud-like sofa by the tree as Rose wandered back into the room with a tray of the cutest assortment of Italian Christmas cookies and a jug of hot chocolate.

'Thank you all so much for your kind words and hospitality. Your house is magical,' Louisa noted, waving her hands around the room and then settling them on Luca's knee. Her initial nerves had evaporated and she felt at home. At that moment Matilde got up, picked up a snowflake-shaped cookie and plonked herself on Louisa's knee.

'Matilde, you must offer Miss Louisa a cookie,' Giulia said, gesturing towards Louisa. Matilde shuffled on Louisa's knees until she was sat facing her, holding up her own cookie and offering Louisa a bite.

'Thank you, sweetheart, but that's OK. That's your cookie, you eat it,' she said. Matilde smiled up at her with her ocean-blue eyes and happily took a big bite. Luca laughed and picked up the tray of cookies and placed it in front of Louisa. She chose a chocolate reindeer and relaxed, leaning back into the sofa. The chocolate melted in her mouth. She chatted with Luca's family and watched Luca play a game of tickle monster with little Matilde. He seemed too good to be true.

'So, what do you do?' Giulia asked, her Italian rolling off her tongue in the most musical and eloquent way. Louisa envied her accent and hoped with more practice now that she was here in Italy itself that she too might sound as beautiful as Giulia one day. She swallowed another scrumptious bite of a cinnamon Santa cookie, which she told herself would be her last one – she didn't want to spoil lunch in an hour's time – before speaking.

'I hope to be a fashion designer one day. There's been a few bumps in the road so far, but Italy has inspired me all over again.' Louisa watched as Giulia clapped her hands together with a delighted expression, her stunning highlights glowing from under the trees lights. This woman could be a movie star. Everyone in Luca's family was gorgeous.

'*Mamma mia, perfetto, oh perfetto*, Louisa,' Giulia said with a squeal that still sounded more petite hummingbird than Louisa's squeals of excitement that often resembled high-pitched dog whisperer. 'I have my own boutique in Amalfi. I have loved fashion since I was a *bambina*, no, Papa?' she gushed with such passion her whole face was now aglow.

'*Si, amore*. Giulia had the best-dressed teddy bears in all of town,' her papa said with a small grin, though his face was clearly beaming with pride. Louisa couldn't quite believe her ears. She looked from this model of a woman who oozed grace, and possibly had Louisa's dream job, to Luca, who was sat with a smile on his face so big Louisa knew he was up to something. His blue eyes were dancing with flecks of tiny fairy lights. He turned from

Louisa back to his sister, with a look encouraging her to speak on.

'Oh, Louisa, you must help me, no?' Giulia said, as Matilde settled comfortably on her lap, clearly in need of a nap now after easily eating six biscuits. Louisa's brows drew together. She felt confused.

'*Scusi, ma,* I'd love to help but help with what?' she asked, again looking to Luca for some information. He simply sat with that handsome smile plastered on his ridiculously gorgeous face.

Giulia squeezed Matilde tight while at the same time kneeling up onto her heels to get closer to Louisa. Rose and their papa were nestled in their chairs, drinking hot chocolate and watching their children with utter adoration. 'Well, you see. I have been given this opportunity to do a small catwalk at next year's Milano fashion week and I have been on the lookout for a helping hand. And you are like an angel sent from heaven. Your fashion is *bellissima* – you have a good eye,' Giulia said.

Louisa looked down at her black tights and oversized silk deep purple tee and blushed. Did she really have a good eye for fashion? She had always hoped so, but it was very unique to herself. Was it Milano fashion week standard though?

Giulia continued, 'And you draw. I would like to hire you,' Giulia finished getting straight to the point, her hands now in praying position.

Louisa's mouth felt dry. She looked to Luca. His face was warm and encouraging. 'You can think about it, *amore*, if it's too much right now. There is no rush,' he noted, taking her hands in his. At that moment she had to admit the feeling of being over-whelmed was strong, but in a good way. She believed with all her might her grandpa was watching her, looking out for her at every turn, but now here with Luca and his family and how at home she felt, she knew – she really, truly knew it to be true. This was a sign and one that she was grateful for. She stood from her place on the sofa and took a seat cross-legged on the floor next to Giulia and Matilde.

'When do I start?' she asked. This was an uncharacteristically bold move for Louisa as she knew how she had reacted when Sabrina said she was moving to LA. She hadn't been all that supportive or kind about her sister's decision. Yet now with the magic of Christmas in the air and a gold thread that led the way to her dreams, she felt it was right, that she couldn't possibly miss this opportunity – even if it meant taking a huge leap of faith and leaving the comfort of home.

She had apologized to Sabrina for the way she had behaved all those years ago and more recently too. She had trodden on her sister's dreams and had often given her a hard time when she should have been applauding her for doing something so terrifying and moving halfway across the world to pursue her passion. She felt she had been forgiven.

As the bubbles of excitement danced in Louisa's stomach she realized that it was perfectly fine to chase your dreams even when the prospect of change was frightening. Look at all the wonderful things Amanda and Sabrina had achieved, and they still made time for their family. Be it via visits, phone calls or Skype, they had been there, always, she thought.

***

'It smells like heaven,' Amanda said, breathing in the aroma of the *pandoro* cake she was cutting. 'Can I just stuff my head inside the box, Zia? This smell is addictive,' she added, lifting the box closer to her nose and inhaling its sweet scent.

'Italians make the best desserts,' Zia Sofia replied with a casual shrug as she smiled lovingly at Amanda.

They had just devoured Christmas lunch and everyone was sitting in the living room watching the Italian Christmas mass while Amanda and Zia Sofia were preparing the cakes and espressos. The kitchen felt even cosier today. The often chilly room was warm and snug after the morning's festive breakfast extravaganza and recent Christmas feast preparations. The oven was finally getting a little break. No doubt it would be on again later this evening to heat up the leftovers.

Everywhere you looked there were *pandoro* boxes, golden trays with that white packaging with Pasticceria Pansa emblazoned all over it piled up, plates wrapped in foil, underneath bearing the best food in the world from *pizzaiola*, trout with mint, mashed potato, roast potatoes, stuffed peppers and risotto. Amanda was full, but her mouth already watered at the thought of a midnight feast.

'I think if I was to eat just one thing for the rest of my days it would be your starters, Zia Sofia. You make it to perfection.' Amanda was referring to the fresh plate of homemade mozzarella, prosciutto, homegrown tomatoes, artichoke hearts, salami and a boiled egg, mixed with a light drizzle of homemade olive oil. It sounded simple but the flavours and tastes that came from these pure and rich ingredients were better than anything she had ever tasted.

'But then I would happily eat buckets full of your *fiori di zucca* every day for the rest of my life if I could. Grandpa loved making those,' she continued. Her heart stung thinking about Grandpa. He would have loved today, being in Italy with the family. They hadn't experienced a Christmas in Italy in a long time. Amanda wished she'd thought about it sooner. She blinked back tears and got back to talking about the one thing she and Grandpa could talk about for hours on end: food. 'Everything was amazing, Zia. Your food inspires me.'

'You are special, my girl. Your passion will take you far,' Zia Sofia said. She kissed Amanda's cheek and plated the Mandorla Torte.

'Can I help with anything?' Dan asked, walking into the room and over to Zia Sofia. 'The food was out of this world, Sofia – thank you for having me,' he added, putting an arm around her shoulders and giving her half a hug.

227

'Ahh, *grazie, grazie*, you are a gentleman,' Zia Sofia cried, waving her arms at Dan and reaching up to grab his cheeks. 'You found a nice man, Amanda.'

'As far as best friends go, yeah, he's not bad,' Amanda said, laughing. She would find the right time to tell Dan how she felt, but right now she just wanted to enjoy Christmas Day. Having him here in Italy with her was the best present she had received and the fact that he had made the journey to be with her at a time when she had most needed it had meant everything to her. She was not about to ruin things or seem greedy. She had Dan by her side and it felt right.

'You're not too bad yourself,' Dan replied, flashing his gorgeous smile her way. As he took the tray from Zia Sofia, he leant towards Amanda. 'Are we OK?' he whispered.

'Yes, we're fine, Dan. I'm sorry, just forget everything I said please. I was tired and a lot had been going on,' Amanda replied, opening up a box of biscotti and adding them to her tray, not quite able to look him in the eye when their noses were almost touching.

'I'm sorry too. Can we talk about all this later?' he asked. He had eyelashes that would make mascara jealous, Amanda had always thought. They flickered when his eyes grew worried.

'Sure,' Amanda answered. A shiver shot down her spine and a flush rose in her cheeks at the proximity of Dan's lips.

'OK, good,' Dan said and then turned back to helping Zia Sofia carry the trays to the living room. Amanda gave them a little head-start, allowing her heart rate to go back to normal. Once she composed herself, she followed them back into the living room.

'Cake and coffee for everyone,' she said, passing out bowls of the most scrumptious *pandoro* made with Nanna's Italian custard. It was a Christmas tradition and one of her favourites. She could eat the entire cake if her sisters let her.

'Who wants to open presents?' Mum asked, kneeling down by the Christmas tree.

228

'Lou, I hope you got your sisters one of those onesies. It's quite spectacular,' Dad said to Lou, who was now back in her Olaf onesie after visiting Luca's family this morning. There was nothing like stepping in through your front door and immediately putting your PJs on.

Amanda watched their interaction. Dad was sat in the armchair near the tree, cradling a beer and, worryingly, Amanda noticed he actually seemed serious about the onesies. There wasn't a sarcastic smirk to be seen on his face. Louisa touched the tip of her nose and then pointed to Dad with a wink.

'I think that would look awesome on you, Bri,' Levi said playfully. Sabrina was curled up next to him on the rug. She looked happy, and Levi – Amanda was pleased to see – looked totally besotted. He looked at Sabrina in a way she had never seen him look at anyone in the three years she had known him.

She sat herself down next to Dan and tucked her feet underneath herself on the sofa. Once she was nice and comfy she dug into her *pandoro* and watched as Mum passed out presents. Mum looked radiant. Her peachy glow was back and the dark circles under her eyes were slowly disappearing. Amanda had thought she couldn't possibly love her mum any more than she already did, but seeing her strength shine over the past few weeks, how she put everyone's feelings and needs first, when she had just experienced the most devastating loss, well, Amanda had a new respect and admiration for her.

In that moment she vowed to look after her mum and dad the way they had, and continued to, look after their own parents. She didn't want to lie to her mum and leave her in the dark about work and what was going on with Jeff at the restaurant; furthermore, she was done putting up with Jeff and feeling sorry for herself when she was the one allowing him to treat her with such disrespect. She knew what she had to do and no doubt when she got home she wouldn't have a choice. By the sounds of Anthony's voicemails, her reputation was close to being in tatters thanks to Jeff's antics since she'd been gone.

She closed her eyes and with her last bite of the fluffy, buttery *pandoro* cake, she allowed her taste buds to take over her thoughts and her worries to melt away.

'You know, that food was better than any restaurant I've ever been to, Amanda,' Dan said quietly, leaning in to her. 'Out of all the places I've been in San Francisco, the dishes we just ate, there's no comparison. It was exceptional.' Amanda slowly opened her eyes to see Dan wink at her. She felt comforted by his words, her heart elated that Dan had loved the food that she and her family had made for him. Dan had tried her food before on many occasions, but with the produce here and the love of her aunties guiding her, the food became exquisite. It took on colours, flavours and aromas of its own.

'I'm glad you liked it, I really am. I'm so happy you're here,' she said, leaning in to hug him. The *pandoro* had settled the fuzziness in her stomach and she felt calm. No doubt the Marsala that Nanna had drenched the cake in had something to do with that. Releasing Dan from her hug she got a whiff of one of her favourite scents. He smelt of a mix of mint, green apple and lemon zest and whenever she smelt it, it wrapped her up in a comforting blanket. She could live with being best friends with Dan, she thought. He had been a pretty awesome best friend so far. As he stroked her hair, she considered herself extremely fortunate.

'You do know that the restaurant we have been talking about for the past few years can be a reality, don't you? You have all the tools,' he said, his voice calm and encouraging and forever all knowing. He knew that she knew. She was confident in her work and loved the idea of working for herself, designing her own menus, getting to know her customers more, but there was always that shred of doubt that seeped in every time she thought about it. What happened if no one came? What happened if she put her all into it and failed? She hated to admit it, but she was scared.

'I know, Dan,' she replied, patting his arm. 'Thanks.'

'Amanda, open yours,' Louisa practically yelled from across the room, where she and Luca sat by Mum near the tree. Louisa was still a big kid when it came to Christmas. She adored giving everyone gifts and she wasn't opposed to receiving them either. 'That's from Brina,' she added, kneeling up and crawling on her knees to pass the parcel to Amanda. Luca watched her, a loving awe in his eyes.

'OK, OK, oooh what is it?' Amanda asked taking the elegant gold box from Louisa. Amanda began unwrapping it carefully. Beneath the gold wrapping was a white box and inside the pristine white box lay the most stunning piece of jewellery Amanda had ever seen. 'Oh, Brina, it's so enchanting. I love it,' she said, not taking her eyes off the little diamond that sparkled, almost bewitching her as she looked at it. She held up the delicate white gold pendant and choked out a laugh. She got up and walked over to her sister, wrapping her arms around her tightly. 'I'll never take it off,' she whispered in Sabrina's ear.

'I'm glad you like it,' Sabrina said, her eyes a little watery.

'What did you get? Mine's a star,' Louisa said, holding up a necklace just as striking.

'Mine's a lemon,' Amanda replied, as she walked back to the couch to show Dan. 'I love it so much.' She sat back down, holding the precious piece in her palm. Dan gently took it from her and carefully opened the clasp. Amanda automatically turned her back to him and lifted up her wavy hair to move it out the way. Dan placed the delicate pendant around her neck, the cold white gold lemon making her shiver as it touched her skin.

'Now you know I'm always thinking about you even when I'm so far away. I hope you understand my meanings behind them and I hope you know how much I love you both,' Sabrina said as Levi wrapped his arms around her.

Amanda looked over and saw Nanna had tears in her eyes, as

did her aunties. They were a very emotional family. Of course, she knew what her sister had meant by the designs. She was always cooking with lemons, their favourite adventures growing up would involve hunting for the biggest, juiciest lemons outside in the garden, followed by an afternoon spent making the most fabulous lemon desserts with Grandpa and Nanna. 'Thank you, Sabrina, of course,' she sighed and looked over at her sister who was now helping Louisa put her necklace on.

Amanda heard Sabrina whisper, 'Louisa, you aim for the moon, even if you miss you will land amongst the stars. *Capisci*?' Louisa too teared up and squeezed Sabrina tight. Before Amanda could get too emotional she felt Dan's hand squeeze her knee as he gave her a comforting kiss on the top of her head.

They continued to open a few presents while chatting away. Amanda had refilled everyone's bowls with *pandoro* and custard and Dan was now topping up everyone's coffee. Reaching Amanda, he poured her a fresh cup and gently placed a rectangle-shaped gift on her knee.

'Merry Christmas,' he said, his eyes bright with excitement. 'Go on, open it.' He placed the coffee pot on the wooden coffee table.

'Wait,' Amanda said jumping up and racing over to the Christmas tree. She kneeled down and pulled a similar-shaped present from underneath the tree and rushed back over to Dan. She sensed that everyone was watching them, but she felt too giddy to worry about how her sisters would twist this one.

'For you,' she said, handing Dan her gift.

'Together,' Dan said taking the package from her and sitting down next to her.

Together they unwrapped their gifts. As each piece of wrapping paper fell to the floor, a butterfly began fluttering in Amanda's stomach. There was a whole cage of butterflies in her stomach by the time she had finished. She was finding it hard to form words; she just sat ogling the book that she was now holding.

She swallowed and looked up as she realized that Dan had stopped opening his gift and his eyes were watching her closely.

'But, Dan, where? How did you? This can't be.' The words tumbled out incoherently.

Dan's face immediately formed into a dazzling smile, his eyes appearing somewhat shy. 'You've had your eyes on it forever,' he said with a small shrug, before turning back to his own unwrapping. Amanda watched him as he shed the remaining paper and looked down at the gift she had bought for him.

'This is awesome, Amanda.' He paused. 'Seriously, this is unreal, you are incredible,' he continued, shaking his head and putting his book-free hand through his hair.

'It's a little battered and bruised and not exactly pristine but I thought it added character,' Amanda replied, referring to the first edition of *Tristessa* by Jack Kerouac that she had bought for him.

'That's exactly what I was thinking; it's amazing,' Dan said, leaning over to embrace her. 'I love it.'

'I'm glad you like it. I still can't quite fathom that I am now the proud owner of a first edition copy of *The Dharma Bums*. You always know exactly what to get me,' she said, pushing him away and punching him in the arm with one hand and clutching the book close to her chest with the other.

'Only the best for my best girl,' he replied, ruffling her hair playfully in lieu of a punch.

Amanda clocked Sabrina and Louisa smirking at each other from across the room. Louisa was kneeling up, looking like a meerkat, matching Sabrina's sly smile, as they both looked at Amanda and then back at each other.

Amanda simply rolled her eyes and made herself comfy again on the couch, choosing to ignore her sisters' meddling looks. Cradling her precious book, she rested her head on Dan's shoulder and let the chatter and love that filled the room take over her thoughts. She took in her surroundings. The living-room rug was littered with wrapping paper, and boxes and boxes of all sorts of Italian treats.

Amanda's family knew her all too well and seemed to be preparing her for when she got home. There were cakes from Pansa, Baci, Perugina bars, Italian herbs, cheese, sausage and *crossini*. She wasn't too sure she would be able to get through the airport with Italian sausage in her bag, but she sure would try. Grandpa always seemed to get away with it – maybe his luck would rub off on her and airport security would be kind.

She watched her family laughing, eating and chatting to one another and she felt nothing but contentment. She looked over at the painting of Padre Pio hanging on the wall and whispered 'Thank you, Grandpa. *Buona Natale.*'

Chapter 19

Grandpa's Breaded Whitebait

Ingredients:

Freshly caught whitebait
Flour
Egg (Maybe two, depending on the catch)
Breadcrumbs (Homemade is best, season to your liking ... season like
Grandpa does)
Olive oil

What to do:

Clean whitebait, and let them soak in cold water for 10 to 15 minutes,
then dry them off.

Dip the whitebait in flour, then the egg, then the breadcrumbs. Pat with
palm of your hand.

Place into frying pan with hot oil.

Cook until they turn golden brown on both sides.

Sabrina was having a lovely Christmas Day so far. In fact, she had had a lovely few days. Part of her felt guilty for allowing herself to be happy so soon after Grandpa's funeral, but she couldn't help the fact that Levi had eased the pain in her heart. She still missed Grandpa like crazy but having Levi here had made her want to focus on the good. He would ask questions and listen to her speak about her grandpa and Italy, and he grew to understand her passion for the place the more she shared her stories.

In her state of focusing on the positive, she had tried to push all thoughts of work out of her mind until she got back to California. Thinking about it now just made her stomach twist into knots and she didn't want to dampen the holidays with thoughts of Lydia and job hunting. It had been quite some time since the family had enjoyed a holiday with her aunties. If she remembered correctly they had visited for Easter once but she had been young and didn't remember too much.

Being around the table together for breakfast and for lunch had been an absolute delight and not just because of the luscious crepes or the melt-in-your-mouth whitebait and squid, but because of the immense sense of happiness she got from watching Nanna so full of life, talking, arguing, cooking and sitting with her sisters after all these years. She was savouring every bite and every moment.

***

Sabrina was sitting by the Christmas tree. After opening presents and scarfing down bowls of *pandoro*, Amanda and Zia Sofia had whipped up a fresh batch of *zeppole*, which she was happily demolishing while playing a game of Jenga with Louisa and Luca. The Italian came out in her when she played any sort of game; she wanted to win.

Unfortunately for her Luca being full-blooded Italian meant his competitive streak was hard to beat. She didn't stand a chance – the man was a Jenga master. Subsequently she resigned to losing and chose to enjoy observing Louisa and Luca in Jenga warfare while eating her weight in *zeppole*.

She took a huge bite of the fluffy Italian doughnut, chewing it slowly and allowing the flavours to dance on her tongue. Amanda made them beautifully at home but here they tasted exquisite. It had to be the most mouth-watering *zeppole* she had ever had the pleasure of tasting. Distracted by the *zeppole* she hadn't noticed Levi and Dan walk back into the living room. They had stepped out a few minutes earlier for somewhat of a private conversation.

'Bri,' Levi said looking rather serious. She immediately freaked out, stuffing the rest of the *zeppole* into her mouth and promptly choked on the powdered sugar. 'Are you OK?' Levi asked, gently bending down to tap her on the back as she coughed.

She shot to her feet, narrowly missing smacking her head on his chin and looked around anxiously for a napkin before managing to pull herself together, almost, and speak. 'Yes, I'm fine. Why are you looking at me all serious? What's wrong?' she spluttered, uncharacteristically.

'Well, Dan and I were just talking and well, I don't know whether this is the right time but with it being Christmas and all we thought it might be nice – you know like a weight off your shoulders…' He paused, taking a deep breath. Again, it wasn't like Levi to be nervous. 'Would you be interested in being our manager, please?'

Sabrina didn't register at first. Her hands were still sticky, distracting her from fully comprehending what Levi was saying. 'What do you mean? I was fired, Levi. I'm sorry but Lydia will probably not take too kindly to me asking for my job back. She's not even replying to my emails.'

'Yes, I know that, but I don't mean that. You do remember we walked? We don't report to her company any more either, remember? What I mean is, we do this together, no big company, no outside interference from people who don't get us, just our business – we build it together. You can have some time to think about it if …'

Coming up empty-handed in her search for napkins, Sabrina took a moment to lick her fingers and dust the powdered sugar off on her red and gold festive jumper, giving herself a second to let what Levi just asked sink in. She squinted her eyes and looked at Levi then at Dan, whose shoulders seemed scrunched up around his ears and whose demeanour was far from cool-hand Dan. She replayed Levi's words in her head again before a shriek erupted from her lips.

'Oh my gosh, yes, yes. I'm an idiot. Yes, I would love that. That's an awesome idea. Oh my goodness, wow, thank you so much.' She squealed throwing her arms around Levi's neck and then pouncing on Dan. 'Thank you so much, Dan, this is fantastic. Thank you for believing in me.'

'You did a great job for us, Sabrina. I don't think the whole media company was really our thing. This way we keep it in the family, focus on the music and everyone wins,' Dan said, seemingly a tad relieved himself that she had said yes. His shoulders relaxed significantly.

'That means no hanky-panky in the office, you two,' Amanda added, from her spot on the couch.

'Cover your ears, Mum and Dad,' Sabrina shouted, throwing wrapping paper at her big sister and blushing slightly. 'Dan, would you please control that one?'

Dan shrugged, putting his arm around Amanda. 'Where would the fun be in that?' he said, laughing.

'Exactly,' Amanda triumphed, looking up from her precious book.

'I promise we'll be on our best behaviour,' Levi noted, nodding at Mum and Dad and pulling Sabrina in for a hug.

Mum and Dad were laughing and Sabrina couldn't believe how giddy and light she suddenly felt.

'I've got a job, I've got a job, Nanna,' she declared to her nanna and her aunties who were watching everyone with adoration. She hugged her nanna tight, breathing in her sweet rose scent. The family had congregated around Nanna, all bar Amanda who still had her nose in her book. They stood in the middle of the room between the mounds of wrapping paper and empty bowls and espresso cups, hugging and kissing one another.

'Go get the Limoncello and Sambuca?' Nanna shouted as she kissed Levi on the cheek.

'Good idea, let's celebrate,' Dad said.

'Wait,' Louisa yelled, 'I have some news too.'

Sabrina turned to look at her baby sister, as did the rest of the family. Louisa took Luca's hand in hers. Sabrina could see Luca was standing tall, his shoulders back. He was beaming at her baby sister, a dashing smile that reached his eyes. 'Luca's sister owns a boutique in Amalfi and she has the opportunity of a lifetime next year, to put on a small show for Milan fashion week and, well, she wants me to help.' The excitement in Louisa's voice was clear as her words came tumbling out in rapid fire.

Amanda rose from the couch at an impressive speed for someone who had just scoffed half a *pandoro* cake and grabbed Louisa with umph.

'Let's not throttle our baby sister now,' Sabrina said, loosening Amanda's grip and wedging herself in between her sisters. They all looked at each other for a few moments.

'What do you guys think?' Louisa muttered, her arms squashed by her sides thanks to Amanda's grip. Sabrina saw Mum wipe away a tear, then she looked at Amanda and back to Louisa. At once the girls started jumping up and down on the spot squealing to the high heavens.

'Bloody hell, Lou, you are going to knock the socks off fashion week. Congratulations,' Amanda said, still bouncing up and down.

'This is amazing news, chickpea. You are going to blow them away,' Dad said. One by one everyone hugged Louisa and Sabrina. Dad shook Luca's hand before turning to shake Levi and Dan's, offering congratulations from before. Then he turned back to give Sabrina a big hug. 'Congratulations, sweetheart, I'm proud of you. I have a good feeling about this one.'

Sabrina wasn't a hundred per cent sure if he was referring to Levi or the fact that she was going to be her own boss and officially in control of one of the hottest bands in the world, but it didn't matter, as for once her heart had a good feeling about both.

Chapter 20

Grandpa's Hot Chocolate

Ingredients:

About 4oz bittersweet chocolate (Perugina or Lindt 70% cocoa)
2 tbsps cornstarch
1½ cup milk
½ can condensed milk
1 tbsp vanilla (Eyeball it; I'm sure Grandpa uses a dash more)
Ladyfingers

What to do:

Stir all ingredients except the ladyfingers together over medium heat until it becomes thick.

Serve nice and hot.

Probably don't need biscotti with it as it's quite sweet but as Grandpa says, 'A biscotti or two won't hurt.'

The moonlight cast a sublime glow across the sea below it. Once again a stillness descended on the Amalfi Coast. Nowhere in the world could you hear your own thoughts or feel the power of your existence like you could in Orzoro. Standing at the top of this mountain with nothing but sky and sea around her Sabrina thought of how love brought them here, of how the love she felt for her grandpa and her family felt as powerful as the view she was looking out to. Its magnitude was breathtaking and the strength of the love in her heart often took her breath away.

Staring at the creamy pizza pie in the sky, Sabrina thought of their grandpa and how she missed him so. 'Well, it's not exactly how I envisioned coming back to Italy would be after all these years,' Sabrina professed.

'I guess you truly never really know what the future holds, do you? Grandpa always told us that – and that we must live each day to its fullest, thankful for the moments and memories it provides. I think I may have lost sight of that a little bit since attempting uni. You were right, Brina, I didn't enjoy being a receptionist. I stopped believing in my dreams. Italy has given me a new life at a time I needed it most,' Louisa said.

The three of them were sat on the balcony staring out in the same direction, the moon bright and full, reflecting in the deep blue of the sea. Louisa's words comforted Sabrina. Not just her acknowledging their argument a mere few weeks ago, but in that her baby sister was listening to her advice.

'God, it's going to be tough being away from you all again. I don't even want to think about it,' Sabrina said, pulling her red zigzagged collar tighter around her neck. 'But at least it won't be too long this time,' she added airily, scooping up a plump marshmallow from her mug and popping it whole in her mouth.

'What do you mean?' Amanda asked, turning to look at her and choking on her hot chocolate.

'I'm coming home,' Sabrina said, smiling. She turned to look at her sisters. Both Amanda and Louisa's eyes glistened in the beige moonlight, their pupils dilated and twinkling under the fluorescent glow.

'Are you being serious?' Louisa said, not taking her eyes off her.

'Yes, I mean it won't be right away. I think at least two to three months while I get everything sorted with the apartment and tie up all the loose ends with the boys. There's a few gigs I want to put together for them in the US before I leave. But yes, I discussed it a little with Levi this evening and he doesn't see why I can't base myself in Manchester. Plus he knows we have quite the respectable music scene, so he thinks it will be good for the band,' Sabrina explained, playing with the second marshmallow that was swimming atop her hot chocolate.

'That's amazing news, Brina,' Amanda said. 'Are you happy to be coming home?'

Sabrina shuffled in her chair so she was no longer twisted, but instead facing Amanda and Louisa.

'Of course I am, I wouldn't have said it otherwise. California isn't really for me – all that talk of yoga and smoothies; a girl needs her fish and chips every now and again. And in light of everything that's happened, I want to be closer to you all and spend more time with Mum and Dad and Nanna,' she replied, holding her head up, determined not to cry and instead thinking of the positives to moving home now.

Grandpa had been proud of her and her job. He wasn't mad at her for being away and he would be happy that she was going home now to spend time with the family. She fought with the anger that bubbled inside her – he was supposed to be there too when she finally moved back. She tried to dispel those negative emotions. It would not do well to dwell on the past. Besides it was now that mattered – the minutes in front of her. Her grandpa would always be with her. She needed to keep living and make him proud. Italy had given her that time for pause and she knew she was making the right decision.

'About that, I'm super happy that you are moving home but I was thinking … Do you think we should suggest to Mum that Nanna stay here?' Louisa asked, twiddling her thumbs together around her mug.

'But we'd miss her. She can't stay,' Amanda said quickly, causing a silence to wash over the girls. They sat in this silence for a minute, staring out across the water. Occasionally a car could be heard on the roads miles below them, the engines wheezing up the steep paths or the horn sending out a warning to cars coming round the bends. 'I'm sorry, that was selfish of me,' Amanda continued, with a heavy sigh. 'You're right, she's been so happy with her sisters. Two and a half weeks is hardly enough time to catch up on the last twenty years. It would break my heart to separate them again now.'

'That's what I was thinking, Amanda. I know you'd miss her, but well, I thought I might stay here for a little while too. I know fashion week isn't until next year, but I feel content here and there's so much of Italy I want to see. Giulia's shop is gorgeous and she says I can work there; plus she says I can go home whenever I need to as I can sketch from home too, so it wouldn't be too much of an interruption. It would be nice to get my bearings here and get some inspiration. And that way if Nanna does want to go back to England after a few months, I can bring her back. And if she does stay, we know she'll be happy: she has me and it's not too far for you to travel,' Louisa said, with optimism in her voice, though she was looking at the floor.

'Hey, I think that's a wonderful idea for Nanna, but are you sure about staying?' Sabrina asked. Amanda took in Louisa and tried to swallow the lump in her throat. She didn't want to cry. She felt so proud of her baby sister for being brave and saying yes to such a wonderful opportunity, even when it meant completely shattering her comfort bubble. Italy wasn't too far away and besides she would need to visit more to visit Grandpa and pick up produce. She smiled and listened to Louisa.

'Yes, I've been thinking a lot and we have so much history here. I want to see it all, learn more about where Nanna and Grandpa came from. I think it will do me some good. Plus, now with this incredible opportunity I think it's the best place for me to start drawing again. Italian fashion inspires me like nothing else and Giulia is like a goddess; so really, this is the perfect place for me to be. I can work with her at the boutique and get a feel of her style, all before fashion week is upon us. It's exciting,' Louisa said, holding her head high with a clear determination in her eyes, as though if she said the words aloud and repeated them a few times she would start to believe in herself and be one hundred per cent confident in her huge decision. 'And, that way I can spend more time with Luca and see how long this holiday romance lasts,' she then added with a chuckle.

'That will be amazing, Lou – I'm so happy for you. And you do know you are capable of anything. You're insanely talented. You have to stop being so hard on yourself and letting those niggling worries get you down. Giulia is going to love having you around. I will want front row tickets to that catwalk show too,' Amanda said, a sly smile spreading across her face as she looked down at the Robin onesie she was wearing. 'I'm not sure if these onesies should grace the catwalk though. I should have known better than to make fun of your Olaf outfit,' she added, patting her fluffy red chest.

'I thought you would love them,' Louisa said poking Amanda in the ribs, with her hot-chocolate-free hand.

'I love mine – it's super cosy and perfect for sleepovers,' Sabrina said, wiggling her toes to make the bells on her elf onesie chime. She really did love it. It was doing a hell of a job keeping her toes from being frost-bitten in the Italian outdoors. 'But onesies aside, you are one hell of an artist, Lou. I'd wear anything you designed providing it's floaty and not too abstract,' she said with a wink. 'Giulia is going to see that she hit the jackpot having you on board,' Sabrina added and Amanda nodded in agreement.

'Thank you both – that means a lot. Speaking of being talented and not putting yourself down, this hot chocolate is giving me life. When are you opening up your own place?' Louisa asked, very matter-of-fact, turning the tables on Amanda.

'OK, I know, I need to start listening to my own advice, with everything it seems. I've been giving it some thought and yes I would very much love to open my own place. It seems like the right time and it would be a wonderful way of carrying on Grandpa's legacy. And from the texts and voicemails I have been getting from Anthony it seems Jeff has done a fabulous job of destroying my reputation at Rusk so I'm going to need to look for a new job anyway,' Amanda replied with a sigh, a note of defeat in her voice mixed with an air of confident determination.

'And, after spending so much time with Zia Sofia I have created a list of recipes to share on my blog and I think now is as good a time as any to really see what I can do with that too. Grandpa's recipes deserve to be shared with the world.'

'Yay. I couldn't agree more. Your blog will be amazing if you believe in it and you know your place will be the best in town. Grandpa would be so proud. You have nothing to worry about. And, Jeff, well, Jeff can suck it,' Louisa said, causing them all to double over in their chairs laughing. Through chuckles Louisa added, 'How could a snake like that possibly ruin your impeccable reputation?' Her brows crinkled with curiosity.

Amanda sat up. 'I have no idea. Something to do with food critics, false accusations and tampering with my whole routine and ordering system.' She shrugged, sipping her hot chocolate. She stared out across the shimmering water, lost in thought. The Mediterranean Sea went on for miles, a faint line in the foggy distance. Only where the wispy cloud plumes danced on the water's tip did it give pause, like maybe there was an end. Either way the sea of Amalfi made you believe that anything was possible.

***

Amanda felt a strange calm at the idea of leaving the safety net of her job. She had security there and Anthony, her boss, had been good to her over the years, but she knew in her heart that this was what she was destined to do. The thought that he, her grandpa, was guiding her was strong. She simply had to follow her instincts and let him lead the way.

'Forget about Jeff, your place will be the cream of the crop. Oh and, Amanda, you do know that when I move home the chances are the boys will be around a lot more,' Sabrina noted, gently nudging Amanda in the shin with the bells on the end of her elf shoes.

'And ...' Amanda said, rolling her eyes and pulling the robin's hood of her onesie down over her face.

'Well, it seems to me that the fates have aligned, and you and Dan can actually be together,' Sabrina replied with a casual wink.

'Uh you guys are not going to let me live this down, are you? I'm boycotting the love thing. Forget I ever said it, please. We make for tremendous friends and I'm not about to mess that up,' she whined from underneath her yellow beak. Sabrina pulled her elf hood over the ears. The wind was starting to pick up outside and the moonlight was being compromised by the grey clouds that had appeared in the sky.

'You are such a drama queen and since when do you use words like tremendous?' Louisa said, licking the whipped cream off her fingers and then wrapping them tightly around the mug for warmth. 'You should be singing from the rooftops. He's an amazing guy, seriously dreamy,' she added, nodding her head.

'What a splendid idea, Lou. I agree you should be singing about your love for the world to hear,' Sabrina teased, her voice growing louder. 'Besides, I'm one hundred per cent certain that that man loves you too,' she added. Just then a snowflake landed on the tip of her nose.

'And what makes you think that?' Amanda replied, playing

with a snowflake that landed on top of the marshmallow that was floating in her mug.

Suddenly, Sabrina and Louisa hopped up from their chairs, jingling as they did so. They both had grins sprawled across their faces to rival the cat who got the cream. They pointed towards the kitchen door and promptly ran past a nervous-looking Dan, and then into house, without answering her question.

***

Amanda shot out of her seat. 'Hey, how you doing? Do you want some hot chocolate?' Her words betrayed her, coming out high-pitched and in no way casual. She rocked back and forth between her toes and her heels. The sprinkle of snowflakes was getting heavier. She squinted to look at Dan, trying to study his facial expression to see what he was thinking. It was no use. Dan rarely gave anything away. His eyes were usually his weak spot but now they were murky and Amanda couldn't figure out if it was the nerves in her stomach that were making it so hard for her to read them. His wavy hair was slightly damp and his plump red lips were rosier than normal. A few snowflakes had settled on his long lashes, reflecting in his dark pupils.

'Can we talk?' Dan asked, his face still not giving anything away, his voice making even the marshmallows in Amanda's hot chocolate melt. He rubbed his hands together and pulled the collar of his thick grey jumper tighter around his neck. There was definitely going to be a snowstorm tonight.

'How long have you been standing there?' Amanda whispered, pushing the marshmallow around the maze of snowflakes in her mug and cringing at the thought of Dan hearing her mushy conversation with her sisters.

'Long enough,' Dan said, tilting her chin up with his hand so she was looking at him. Meeting his soulful brown eyes made her insides squirm. They were not telling her anything right now and despite the cold she could feel herself starting to sweat. This worried her.

'Look, Dan, don't you worry about me. I will be OK. I'm not going to start being clingy or anything. I don't expect you to feel the same and I'm not upset that you don't. It's probably just a phase or miscommunication.'

Dan's eyes bore into hers. He placed a finger on her lips in an effort to gently shush her and calm the words tumbling out of her mouth. For Amanda it did nothing but cause her lips to tingle at his touch, making her more flustered.

'You're calling me a phase – really, Amanda?' He tilted his head to one side and let out a gentle laugh. 'Aren't you the charmer?' The top of his jumper, atop his broad shoulders, was now covered in delicate snowflakes. Amanda's onesie was no longer keeping her from the cold. The heavy snow mixed with the heat of her body was starting to make it damp.

'You know what I mean?' she retorted, rolling her eyes and shuffling her feet in an attempt to keep her blood flowing and also to distract herself.

'It's my fault,' Dan began.

'Whoa, OK, has all that media been getting to your ego? I'm not just another girl falling at your feet. Don't think your good looks and rugged sensitivity is all that, mister, Like it's so obvious that I'd just fall for you like every other girl you meet,' she huffed and caught the marshmallow with her forefinger and thumb and popped it into her mouth, looking away from Dan and feeling irritated that she was having this conversation. This was so unlike her independent, confident self.

'You are making it incredibly difficult for me to be nice to you right now. Will you just listen?' Dan continued, with a smirk. He moved a flyaway piece of hair out of her face, sending a shiver over Amanda's body. 'As I was saying, it's my fault. And, you are right – you are not like other girls. From the moment I met you, I was yours and I never said anything. At the time, you had just come out of a bad relationship and I was in a relationship. I didn't know what to do. I knew you needed to experience the world, figure out who you were without me hovering over your every move.

'You came alive in San Francisco. You saw what you were capable of. The strong, independent woman blossomed, and I didn't want to get in the way of that. I kept telling myself it was nothing – you had a whole other life in England and I couldn't take you from your family and ask you to stay. That would have been selfish of me, especially with the band always on the move. I can't say that we wasted time, for we are the people we are today because of what we have been through. You needed that time on your own and I needed to figure myself out too.

'But, in light of recent events, I feel your grandpa is letting me know that it's time. It's time to grab hold of the things that are most important to us and make the most of every second with them.' Dan paused and closed his eyes. When he opened them again, Amanda's heart gave a jolt. 'I love you, and not just love you, I really love you, like I am in love with you, Amanda.' Dan held his breath as his eyes searched hers.

Amanda was at a loss for words. Was this a dream? She didn't know what to do. Would it be strange to kiss him? But that's what it felt like she wanted to do. Could she say it back? Would he know how much she meant it? She swallowed the marshmallow with a gulp.

'I love you too, the "I am really in love with you" one too, not just the little I love you.' She laughed and punched him in the arm, feeling her cheeks glowing pink.

Dan let out a breath and his eyes sparkled even more beautifully than Amanda had seen before. They were clear now and she could see him, truly see him once more. Before she had any more time to think about kissing him and if it would be weird or odd to kiss her best friend, Dan's gentle hands cupped her face, and he pressed his perfectly soft lips to hers.

For the first time in her life Amanda wished she wasn't holding a mug of hot chocolate. She held the mug firmly, for fear of breaking her aunties' fine pottery or ruining the moment and spilling hot liquid all over the sexy lead singer of the world's hottest rock band who was currently kissing her like she'd never been kissed before, despite the fact that she really wanted to grab hold of Dan's biceps and kiss him with all her might.

As though he had read her mind Dan released her head from his tender grip and keeping his eyes firmly on hers he took the mug out of her hands and bent down slightly to place it on the low wall. Amanda felt the absence of his touch at once but with her hands relieved of the hazardous liquid, she placed a finger to her lips and smiled, not taking her eyes of his either.

As Dan straightened back up, she had to tilt her head back to keep his gaze, with him being a head taller than her. Breaking eye contact she looked to his delicious lips, watched as they curled into a shy smile that made her knees wobble, reached out and grabbed his broad shoulders to pull him closer to her and kiss him with everything she had. She could get used to this, she thought, not wanting to pull away. She would be happy if this kiss lasted forever. That was the moment Dan chose to soften the kiss and part their lips. A little whimper escaped her. She didn't want it to end. He smiled, keeping their noses touching.

'You know, I think you were right,' he said, a little hoarsely. 'I found that someone I was looking for.' She feathered his nose with light kisses. The snow was falling heavily now. Her lips were wet from the snowflakes that had melted against the heat of his cheeks.

'Well, that makes two of us. Since meeting you, through all the good and the bad, the travel and the experiences, I've managed to find that something I've been searching for.'

Chapter 21

Grandpa's Pick and Mix

Ingredients:

Freshest, juiciest olives you can find (Italian, of course)
Breadsticks
Taralli (Must make with Grandpa one day)
Prosciutto (Always Italian, always buy fresh)
Assortment of cheeses
Salami (See Prosciutto)

What to do:

Plate ingredients on a big silver platter. Guests will not be able to resist.
There's no such thing as too much cheese.

The Amalfi Coast was alight with bright colours. The night sky
was a mix of blues, reds and golds. The sound of laughter and
people chatting the night away could be heard across the mountains. Amanda had never felt this content before. She let out a

sigh. A week ago, she had had to face the hardest thing she had ever had to go through: her grandpa's funeral. The world had felt dark and cold and the idea of celebrating Christmas, let alone ringing in a New Year without him, had seemed absurd.

But, they had done it. They had managed to have a wonderful Christmas. The warmth of her aunties' house, the cosiness of the little village, her nanna reunited with her sisters after twenty years, her mum and dad and her own sisters all together – it had been magical.

Together with her family they had celebrated, celebrated the holiday, celebrated new adventures and exciting opportunities and the man they all loved and missed terribly. High in the hills of Orzoro, life had gone on. Of course, it was not the same nor would it ever be again, but together they had found the strength to move forward. Amanda had prepared a beautiful feast alongside her zias. Nanna was happy spending the holidays with her sisters again, after all that time apart, and her best friend in the whole world had been by her side. He wasn't in San Francisco, he wasn't four thousand plus miles away, he had been there right beside her through it all.

That very same best friend currently had his arms wrapped tight around her waist and, leaning back in to him, smelling his scent, that bold scent of mint, lemon and a hint of green apple, it felt like heaven. After three years of friendship, she had thought she was going crazy having feelings for Dan, but it turned out Amanda hadn't been going insane at all and Dan felt the same; much to her relief.

She had been anxious at first. The minute 'I love you, like really love you,' had left her lips she had panicked at the thought of kissing Dan, freaked out about ruining the relationship and worried that things would be awkward, but the moment his full and perfect lips touched hers, the worries melted away. Talk about fireworks and fairy tales – it was meant to be. He was hers without a shadow of a doubt and as much as she hated to admit it, her sisters had been right all along. That had been a few days ago and with all the happiness from that Christmas evening, after having such a wonderful day, she and her family decided to extend their Italy trip a while longer to see in the New Year together.

Amanda was so happy they did, as there was a certain charm to Italy during the holidays, as well as all year round. Furthermore, neither she nor Sabrina had to rush back for work, after Sabrina was fired and Amanda had finally decided it was time to take a leap of faith and follow her heart, not just when it came to love but when it came to her passion too. She hadn't officially told anyone yet, but she had made the phone call just yesterday informing Anthony that she would not be returning to the restaurant.

Though she hated to do it over the phone, Jeff's recent antics had been the final straw. She liked her boss, Anthony, but she didn't feel she'd had his support at a time when she needed it most. So, it was done. No more dealing with Jeff and his horrible attitude and disrespect. She was in the market for some property.

'So, my best girl, apparently Manchester has quite the music scene. I think I'm going to need a sexy tour guide to show me round.' Hearing Dan's raspy voice refer to her as sexy didn't feel strange at all; instead it sent heat waves through her body and she tingled from head to toe. She leant her head back, fitting perfectly into the nook between his collarbone and the base of his neck and remained there for a good minute watching as another wave of fireworks soared into the sky, exploding with a bang of green and silver.

'Is that so?' She smiled, turning in to him, her fluffy slipper socks slipping a little on the tiles as she wrapped her arms around his neck. 'Hmm, OK, under one condition.' She bit her lip, a flutter of butterflies escaping in her stomach. She was about to tell her plans to the world, because Dan was just that, he was her world.

'Ooh you have a proposition for me?' he said, squeezing her

tighter, his grey hoodie feeling snuggly. She played with the draw-strings as she took in his features. Amanda could understand his heartthrob status now and wasn't quite sure how she hadn't seen it before. His brown eyes were mesmerizing, and his Cupid's bow was enough to make any girl jealous. She laughed out loud at his statement, rolling her head back, opening herself up to the little kisses he began smothering her neck with. She liked his kisses. She smiled brightly, thinking to herself that this side to their relationship simply fit.

'Not that kind of proposition,' she said, pulling away, slightly breathless. She ran a finger along his jawline and bit her lip again. 'I'll show you around Manchester, if, while doing so, you help me look for the perfect spot for my restaurant or possibly café – I haven't quite decided yet, but I have a bunch of ideas in my head. Ooh and you might need to be a blogger boyfriend for a bit too. You can help me with the food shots, not boob shots.'

She laughed as excitement rose in her voice as she thought of dessert menus and the perfect lunch to feed her customers. Whatever she decided, she knew it was going to be homey, where everyone was welcome, and everyone was fed and looked after. As for her blog, she felt a sense of happiness in having a place to write and teach Grandpa's recipes to the world.

Dan's eyes lit up with pride. With his hands around her waist he picked Amanda up off the ground and twirled her round. 'Yes,' he exclaimed. 'You know it, baby girl, I'm so proud of you. Of course I will help you look for a place – not sure I can promise to not get distracted with your second request though.' He put her down, his eyes full of desire, scanning her figure from head to toe, then grabbed her face and planted a firm and happy kiss on her lips.

'It feels so good to be right hey, Lou?' Sabrina's voice snapped Amanda back into the real world. Dan let go of her face slowly and placed an arm around her neck in a protective stance. Amanda wiped at her tingling wet lips and smoothed a hand through her hair, slightly flustered realizing they weren't the only two on the balcony.

'It sure does, Brina,' Louisa responded, clinking her glass of champagne against Sabrina's and wiggling her eyebrows in Amanda's direction.

'There has to be a limit to the number of weeks you can go around bragging about this,' Amanda said, pointing a finger from herself to Dan as he walked by her side. She walked over to the small table that they had placed on the balcony for the evening's drinks and treats and surveyed its contents, checking she had remembered to bring everything up.

'Ooh I don't know about that. I'm pretty sure I won't ever get tired of saying "I told you so",' Sabrina replied, popping a *taralli* into her mouth.

Amanda picked up a glass of bubbly and passed it to Dan. When she looked at him there was no stopping the butterflies running wild in her belly. The fairy lights that decorated the balcony gave his brown hair a highlighted golden hue and his skin looked tanned even in the winter. He was truly handsome.

'You know, now that we're together and you're part of the family, you have to stick up for yourself with these two,' she said, nodding her head in the direction of where her sisters were sitting by the table and sending a mock stern look Dan's way. 'Call it brotherly love if you will, but you have to give as good as you get otherwise they will just keep terrorizing you.' She picked up an olive and piece of fresh mozzarella between her finger and thumb and slowly placed it in her mouth savouring the milky flavour of the soft mozzarella and the sharp hit of vinegar that delighted her taste buds from the olive.

'It doesn't seem to be me they are terrorizing, my love,' Dan said. He had one hand in the pocket of his hoodie, the other holding his champagne glass, and he was studying her, taking in the way she enjoyed her food. When she looked to him, he smiled so cheekily Amanda knew she would be lost to him forever. Out of the corner of her eye, Amanda noticed her sisters clinking glasses once more and helping themselves to the delicious spread she had so lovingly prepared. She would never live this down, she thought, ever.

'Have we got enough champagne?' Levi's booming voice came through the door before he did. He walked onto the balcony with Nanna, Mum, Dad and all the aunties following behind. Luca was the last to make it up the steps, bringing with him a tray that made Amanda's stomach rumble. Louisa had certainly found herself a keeper. Amanda was going to need a gym membership if she spent any more time around Luca and his out-of-this-world pastries.

Grandpa would be proud Louisa had found herself a man who could cook. Her breath caught at the thought. She moved away from the table and her sisters' judging glares. Between herself and Luca, her grandpa's passion for food would certainly live on – she was going to make sure of it. Just then she got another idea, she would possibly be able to import desserts from Luca's bakery and have specials on the menu every now and again and maybe even vice versa. They could work together providing business for each other.

Grandpa would have thought the idea brilliant, working as one big family, helping others. Furthermore, she wouldn't mind learning one or two of Luca's secret family recipes. Despite the fact that she would always be biased and hold her own family's recipes in high esteem above all else, being able to whip up a batch of Luca's cinnamon cookies whenever she felt like it couldn't do any harm.

'Are you OK, hon?' her mum asked, walking up to her and taking her hand. Amanda rested her head on her mum's shoulder and breathed in the comforting scent of peonies and freesias, the notes of her mum's favourite perfume. The scent had healing properties, she was sure of it. Whenever she felt overwhelmed, sad, lonely or had been away and missed home, she would get out her small bottle of the fragrance and spray a dash on her wrists. It always made her feel comforted and at home.

'I think so, Mum, just missing him a lot and thinking of ideas. Are you OK?' she asked, watching the wine swirl around in her glass.

'I know, sweetheart, I miss him too and yes, yes I'm OK. He's up there looking after us all. I can feel it,' Mum said, in a confident whisper. Mum looked beautiful this evening. She always did, but tonight they had all opted for comfort with no need to get glam and attend some extravagant New Year's party and Mum had on her gorgeous red cashmere jumper, slightly oversized, that the girls had saved up for and bought her a few Christmases ago. It fit her to perfection and brought out the rosy pink flush in her porcelain cheeks.

'I think he would be laughing at this crazy bunch we've got here,' Amanda replied, tilting her head in the direction of her growing family and putting an arm round her mum.

'Without a doubt, sweetheart – you girls made him so proud. He loved you all with all he had. Promise me you won't forget that?' Mum said, tucking a loose wave back behind Amanda's ear.

Amanda stood upright and wiped her eyes on Dan's cardigan, which she had borrowed and was most likely not going to give back. It was way too silky soft and smelt like Dan; then she squeezed her mum's arms tight. 'I promise. He will forever be in my heart and mind, Mum, that I guarantee.'

'Good and I'm looking forward to hearing these ideas, you know …' Mum started.

'Would you ladies like a cake?' interrupted Luca, with an apologetic bow of his head. He really was the most gorgeous specimen. His blue eyes were like honest to goodness sapphires.

'Dan, you need to start taking cooking classes from this guy right here. He just asked me if I wanted cake, homemade cake, be still my beating heart,' Amanda shouted across the balcony, making her mum laugh and Luca blush.

Dan wandered over and placed a hand on the small of Amanda's back. Yes, Luca was ridiculously good-looking and beautifully old-fashioned and a complete and utter gentleman, and though she wouldn't have thought it possible for someone to rival Luca's beauty, Dan had him beat with his long hair, muscular frame and delicious pout. Dan released the butterflies in Amanda like no one ever had before and no one else ever would. His knockout good looks and rugged sexiness were an added bonus.

These two men should not be allowed in the same vicinity as each other, she thought, and Levi too. Thinking about it, the whole band were a dangerous bunch. There really should be a law against that many drop-dead gorgeous musicians forming a band; the world didn't stand a chance. Taking a sip of bubbly and of course, a bite of the crisp, flaky, melt-in-your-mouth *sfogliatelle* she now had in her hand, she leant in to Dan's solid chest and let him wrap his hands around her waist. This was slowly becoming her favourite place to be, wrapped in his embrace. She closed her eyes allowing the bubbles to fizz on her tongue, and the citrusy scent of the *sfogliatelle* to fill her nose.

***

Amanda could feel Dan behind her. He was swaying slightly to the music that was playing through the open bedroom door. Mum had put on one of Grandpa's favourite CDs to make it feel like a proper New Year's Eve party. Amanda opened her eyes and blinked. They were fuzzy from the champagne daydream she had momentarily been in. Then she tilted her head and turned round to look at Dan.

Being so close to him sent a shiver down her spine. She didn't think she would ever get tired of being able to wrap her arms around him whenever she wanted. 'I love you,' she whispered in Dan's ear.

A mischievous grin appeared on his face. He kissed her lightly on the nose. 'I love you too,' he said, his voice sounding raspier than usual, his eyes boring into hers as he placed his hands on both her cheeks and leant down, kissing her hard and heavy.

Amanda kissed him back, rising on her tiptoes so she could give just as good as she was getting. As Dan's tongue teased hers she wondered why it had taken her so long to realize what she had in front of her. She pulled away from him, breathless, 'All this time,' she said, hitting him in the chest and staring him down.

Dan smirked and shrugged his shoulders. 'All this time,' he said. She couldn't resist him. She pulled him by his shirt collar, so she could reach him better, and kissed him again with all the passion she had inside her. A part of her thought she had better start listening to her sisters more often – all this time and she had been missing out on his touch.

'Would you two please get a room!' Sabrina shouted from the other side of the balcony. Amanda stopped what she was doing, but before she could answer her sister back, Levi lifted Sabrina up in the air and showered her with kisses.

'It seems Levi got his wish.' She laughed, taking a break from kissing and resting her head on Dan's chest. 'He's dating my sister after all,' she said, recalling a conversation she and Levi had had back in San Francisco many moons ago. Levi being the boyish charmer and flirt that he was, had inquired as to whether Amanda had a sister and joked that Amanda should set them up. Looking at them now, Amanda wondered why she ever doubted him.

'Is Luca the only one here with manners?' Louisa tutted, looking from Amanda and Dan, to Sabrina and Levi who were still snogging. 'Sorry, Dad,' she added. Amanda turned to look at her baby sister. At that moment Luca picked Louisa up and twirled her around, planting a hard kiss on her lips. Amanda tilted her head back and let out a roar of laughter.

'*Mamma mia*,' Nanna exclaimed clapping her hands together as a golden flash of fireworks erupted in the sky and the church bells rang out in the distance, signalling it was the start of a New Year.

Acknowledgements

May I suggest that you grab a cup of tea or coffee, as I feel like my list of thank you's is going to be a pretty long one.

I want to start by saying a huge thank you to HQ Digital for being such an incredible team to work with and for giving me this amazing opportunity. My editor Hannah Smith, you are amazing. Thank you for believing in me, for your endless support, for making sense of my rambles, and for having been a beacon of light during a difficult time in my life. I have loved every minute of working with you on this book.

A massive thank you to Victoria Oundjian for your guidance, support and kindness at the very, very beginning of my books journey. I couldn't have done it without you and I am beyond grateful.

Rebecca Raisin and Holly Martin, thank you for being there for me, answering my questions, giving me advice and looking out for me. I am incredibly grateful for all you taught me and for your love and support.

To all my incredible author friends, you inspire me daily and I love you all so much. It has been a joy to get to know so many of you through the wonders of social media. You have all been a blessing in my life and I thank you for welcoming me, and my sister Kelly, into your world with open arms.

Thank you from the bottom of my heart to you, the reader, and to every single person who tweets, comments and spreads the word about my book. You are all wonderful and it means everything to me.

To my family, The Knotts, The Osterfelds, The Sharpes, and my wonderful friends all around the world, thank you for dealing with my days of hibernation, me talking about writing, writing, editing and writing, nonstop and for all your love and encouragement. You are all awesome and inspiring and I love you all tons.

Mum and Dad, I love you more than words can ever express. Even though that never stops me from trying, but I will try and keep this one short and sweet. Thank you for your endless supply of love and support. You go above and beyond in all that you do, and I am eternally grateful.

My Nonni and my Grandparents, you all have helped shape me into who I am today and inspire me in all I do. Your love is truly a gift. Thank you!

Kelly, Chris and Jen, the sibling love is real. You all mean the world to me. I may be the big sister, but I learn from each of you every single day. I am so lucky that you all are mine! That goes without saying to my awesome brother and sister-in-laws too. I love you all!

Last but not least, to my husband Chris, inspired by our love and our story, I put pen to paper. Thank you for believing in me and encouraging me every step of the way, not just in my writing but with everything I set my heart on. You are amazing, and I love you.

Dear Reader,

I just wanted to say the biggest of thank-yous to you. It's still kind of crazy to me that you are reading this book, my book, a book written by me, so it truly means the world that you picked it up and gave it a chance. Know that I appreciate you and think that you are awesome.

I very much hope that you enjoy the journey of Amanda, Sabrina and Louisa. These girls have been with me for the past few years now and they are a huge part of me. I'm incredibly excited that I now get to share them with you. My own journey of writing this book has been one of learning, growth, heartache and happiness. It's a little piece of my heart that I am passing on to you.

Please know that whatever your dream may be, you are more than capable of achieving it. Always believe in yourself and no matter what life throws at you, hold your head high and give 110%. You are amazing and can do anything you set your mind to!

Thank you again for reading my first book.

All my love and hugs,

Lucy xx

Dear Reader,

Thank you so much for taking the time to read this book – we hope you enjoyed it! If you did, we'd be so appreciative if you left a review.

Here at HQ Digital we are dedicated to publishing fiction that will keep you turning the pages into the early hours. We publish a variety of genres, from heartwarming romance, to thrilling crime and sweeping historical fiction.

To find out more about our books, enter competitions and discover exclusive content, please join our community of readers by following us at:

🐦 *@HQDigitalUK*

📘 *facebook.com/HQDigitalUK*

Are you a budding writer? We're also looking for authors to join the HQ Digital family! Please submit your manuscript to:

HQDigital@harpercollins.co.uk.

Hope to hear from you soon!